KT-177-311
ACC. No: 05126643

Praise for C.L. Taylor:

'Claustrophobic and compelling.'
Karin Slaughter

'Smart, packing a punch to the heart, and dark in all the right places.'
Sarah Pinborough

'Terrifying ... this brilliant book stayed with me long after I finished the last page.'
Cass Green

'Highly original – kept me utterly enthralled.'
Liz Nugent

'Twisted, unbearably tense, and a shock ending.'
C.J. Tudor

'*The Missing* has a delicious sense of foreboding from the first page, luring us into the heart of a family with terrible secrets and making us wait, with pounding hearts for the final, agonizing twist. Loved it.'
Fiona Barton

'Fans of C.L. Taylor are in for a treat.'
Clare Mackintosh

'Black Narcissus for the Facebook generation, a clever exploration of how petty jealousies and misunderstandings can unravel even the tightest of friendships. Claustrophobic, tense and thrilling, a thrill-ride of a novel that keeps you guessing.'
Elizabeth Haynes

'A gripping and disturbing psychological thriller.'
Lucy Clarke

'As with all her books, C.L. Taylor delivers real pace, and it's a story that keeps calling the reader back – so much so that I read it from cover to cover in one day.'
Rachel Abbott

'A dark and gripping read that engrossed me from start to finish.'
Mel Sherratt

'Pacy, well-written, and anxiety-inducing.'
Lisa Hall

'A compulsive read.'
Emma Kavanagh

'Kept me guessing till the end.'
Sun

'Haunting and heart-stoppingly creepy, *The Lie* is a gripping rollercoaster of suspense.'
Sunday Express

'A rollercoaster with multiple twists.'
Daily Mail

'5/5 stars – Spine-chilling!'
Woman Magazine

'An excellent psychological thriller.'
Heat Magazine

'Packed with twists and turns, this brilliantly tense thriller will get your blood pumping.'
Fabulous Magazine

'Fast-paced, tense and atmospheric, a guaranteed bestseller.'
Mark Edwards

'A real page-turner … creepy, horrifying and twisty. You have no idea which characters you can trust, and the result is intriguing, scary and extremely gripping.'
Julie Cohen

'A compelling, addictive and wonderfully written tale. Can't recommend it enough.'
Louise Douglas

See what bloggers are saying about C.L. Taylor . . .

'My eyes were simply glued to the page, I couldn't tear them away!'
The Bookworm's Fantasy

'An intriguing and stirring tale, overflowing with family drama.'
Lovereading.co.uk

'Astoundingly written, *The Missing* pulls you in from the very first page and doesn't let you go until the final full stop.'
Bibliophile Book Club

'Imaginative, compelling and shocking – *The Fear* is a highly engrossing read.'
The Book Review Café

'*The Fear* is a dark tale of revenge and just when you think you know where the story's going, the author takes you by surprise!'
Portobello Book Blog

'[*The Missing*] inspired such a mixture of emotions in me and made me realise how truly talented you have to be to even attempt a psychological suspense of this calibre.'
My Chestnut Reading Tree

'Tense and gripping with a dark, ominous feeling that seeps through the very clever writing ... all praise to C.L. Taylor.'
Anne Cater, Random Things Through My Letterbox

'C.L. Taylor has done it again, with another compelling masterpiece.'
Rachel's Random Reads

'In a crowded landscape of so-called domestic noir thrillers, most of which rely on clever twists and big reveals, [*The Missing*] stands out for its subtle and thoughtful analysis of the fallout from a loss in the family.'
Crime Fiction Lover

'When I had finished, I felt like someone had ripped my heart out and wrung it out like a dish cloth.'
By the Letter Book Reviews

'*The Fear* is a gripping, fast-paced read.'
The Book Whisperer

'*The Missing* has such a big, juicy storyline and is a dream read if you like books that will keep you guessing and take on plenty of twists and turns.'
Bookaholic Confessions

'Incredibly thrilling and utterly unpredictable! A must-read!'
Aggie's Books

'A gripping story.'
Bibliomaniac

'It's the first time I have cried whilst reading. The last chapter [of *The Missing*] was heart-breaking and uplifting at the same time.'
The Coffee and Kindle

'Another hit from C.L. Taylor ... so cleverly written and so absorbing that I completely forgot about everything else while reading it. Unmissable.'
Alba in Book Land

C.L. Taylor is a *Sunday Times* bestselling author. Her psychological thrillers have sold over a million copies in the UK alone, been translated into over twenty languages, and optioned for television. C.L. Taylor lives in Bristol with her partner and son.

By the same author:

The Accident
The Lie
The Missing
The Escape
The Fear

For Young Adults:

The Treatment

C.L. TAYLOR

Sleep

avon.

Published by AVON
A division of HarperCollins*Publishers*
1 London Bridge Street,
London SE1 9GF

www.harpercollins.co.uk

A Hardback Original 2019

1

A catalogue record for this book is
available from the British Library

HB ISBN: 978-0-00-830131-6
TPB ISBN: 978-0-00-822103-4

Typeset in Sabon LT Std 11.25/14.5 pt by Palimpsest Book Production Limited,
Falkirk, Stirlingshire

Printed and bound in Great Britain by CPI Group (UK) Ltd, Croydon CR0 4YY

This book is produced from independently certified FSC™ paper
to ensure responsible forest management.

For more information visit: www.harpercollins.co.uk/green

In memory of my beautiful friend, Heidi Moore.

To die, to sleep –
No more; and by a sleep to say we end
The heartache and the thousand natural shocks
That flesh is heir to – ’tis a consummation
Devoutly to be wished.

Hamlet, Act III, Scene I,
William Shakespeare

Chapter 1

If you're reading this then I am no longer alive. Someone has been stalking me for the last three months and, if I am dead, it wasn't an accident. Tell the police to speak to my ex-boyfriend Alex Carter about what happened in London. That's where all this started.

The following people came to Rum for a walking tour, arriving on Saturday 2nd June. I am pretty sure one of them killed me.

- *Joe Armstrong*
- *Christine Cuttle*
- *Fiona Gardiner*
- *Trevor Morgan*
- *Malcolm Ward*
- *Melanie Ward*
- *Katie Ward*

Their bookings and contact details can be found on the laptop in reception and in the medical files in the right-hand drawer of the desk. I have written down everything that's happened since they arrived (and before) on the attached pieces of paper.

I hope you're not reading this. I hope it's screwed up in the bottom of a bin and that I've managed to escape. I don't know what else to say. Please tell my parents that I love them, and Alex that I hope he's okay and that he shouldn't feel bad about the way things turned out. I wish I'd never come here. ~~*I wish I had never agreed to*~~ *I wish a lot of things. Mostly that I could turn back time.*

Anna Willis
Acting Manager, Bay View Hotel, Isle of Rum

P.S. I am so sorry about what happened to David. Please tell his family that he was a wonderful man, full of heart and dry wit, and I was very fond of him. Please reassure them that his passing was very quick and he didn't suffer.

Part One

Chapter 2

Anna

THREE MONTHS EARLIER

Sunday 25th February

The mood in the car couldn't be more different than it was on Friday. On the way to the Brecon Beacons I couldn't hear the radio above the chatter and laughter. The team groaned when I told them we'd be spending a weekend in February on a team-building retreat, but most of them rallied once they got in the car. Now, on the way back to London, they're subdued – physically and mentally exhausted and, more than likely, hungover. Mohammed, sitting beside me in the passenger seat, is snoring. Peter, who amused the table with his impression of Michael Mackintosh over dinner last night, now has his head against the window and his coat pulled up over his shoulders. Beside him, Freddy Laing has his headphones jammed over his ears, his eyes shut and his arms crossed over his chest. I doubt he remembers what he said about me last night. I know he was drunk, they all were, but it doesn't excuse the things he said when he thought I'd gone to bed.

'I can't believe she's going for the marketing director job. She's got no chance.'

Freddy's voice drifted across the hotel lobby to the desk where I was waiting impatiently for the receptionist to replace my wiped room card. I knew immediately that he was talking about me. Helen Mackesy, director of marketing, had been poached, leaving a vacancy. And it had my name on it. Unfortunately, Phil Acres, sales promotion manager, had been making noises about going for it too.

'She's really out of touch with digital marketing,' Freddy said. 'She's been in the job for so long she can't even find the pulse, never mind put her finger on it.'

There was a low laugh. Mohammed, most probably. I knew it wouldn't be Peter. He was forty, eight years older than me, and kept himself to himself. Mo and Freddy were closer in age, mid-twenties, and sat together at work. They spent more of their time chatting than working but I never told them to be quiet. They were professionals, not children. As long as they got their work done and didn't disrupt the others I let it go.

There was a pause in the conversation, then Freddy laughed uproariously.

'MySpace advertising. Fucking love it. Yeah, she's probably been telling Tim that blogs are the next big thing in social media marketing. GeoCities blogs!'

More cold, cruel, mocking laughter. My stomach tightened. I'd *worked* to get where I was. I'd been desperate to go to university to study design after my A-levels but we couldn't afford it. Mum had been working two jobs and I owed it to her to start helping out financially. After what felt like a million interviews, and two years working in a hotel bar, I was finally offered a job as a marketing assistant for a computer software firm. My boss, Vicky, was brilliant. She took me under her wing and taught me everything she knew. That was twelve years ago and digital marketing was still in its infancy but I loved it. I still do.

'Miss Willis,' the receptionist called as I marched across the lobby, the blood pounding in my ears. 'Miss Willis, your room card.'

There was a yelp of surprise, the squeal of trainers on tiles and more laughter. By the time I reached the lounge, Freddy and Mo were gone.

Mo snorts in his sleep, snapping me back to the icy, glistening road beyond the windscreen. The drizzle that clung to our hair and faces as we got into the car a little after 8 a.m. is now icy hail. The wipers speed back and forth, squeaking each time they sweep left. The sky is inky black and all I can see is a blurry refraction of the orange-red tail-lights of the car in front. We've finally hit the M25. Not long now until we're back in London. I'll drop the boys at a tube station, then go home. But I'm not sure I want to.

Squeak. Swish. Squeak. Swish.

The wipers move in time with my pulse. I've had too much coffee and my heart jumps in my chest whenever I remember what Freddy said last night. After he fled the lobby I searched the ground floor of the hotel for him, fuelled by anger and indignation, then gave up and went to my room to ring Alex, my boyfriend.

He didn't pick up on the first ring. Or the second. He isn't a fan of phone calls at the best of times but I wanted to hear a friendly voice. I needed someone to tell me that I wasn't a bad person or shit at my job and everything was going to be okay. I texted him instead.

I've had a really shit night. We don't have to chat long. I just want to hear your voice.

A text pinged back a couple of seconds later.

Sorry, in bed. We can talk tomorrow.

The curt tone of his message sliced through what was left of my self-confidence. We'd drifted apart. I'd sensed it for a while but I was too scared to bring it up because I didn't have the energy to fix what was broken or the head space to deal with a break-up. I poured myself into my work instead. Sometimes I'd stay late because I couldn't bear the thought of going home and sitting on the sofa with Alex, each of us curled into the armrests, ignoring the space between us but feeling the weight of it, as though it were as large and real as another person.

Maybe I shouldn't go for the marketing director job. Maybe I should give up work, leave Alex and move to the countryside. I could go freelance, buy a small cottage and a dog, take long walks and fill my lungs with fresh air. There are days at work when I feel I can't breathe, and not just because of the pollution. The air's thinner at the top of the ladder and I find myself clinging to it, terrified I might fall. Freddy would love it if I did.

Squeak. Swish. Squeak. Swish.

Get. Home. Get. Home.

The hail is falling heavily now, bouncing off the windscreen and rolling off the bonnet. Someone snorts in their sleep, making me jolt, before they fall silent again. I've been driving behind the car in front for a couple of miles now and we're both keeping to a steady seventy miles an hour. It's too dangerous to overtake and besides, there's something comforting about following their red fog lights at a safe distance.

Squeak. Swish. Squeak. Swish.

Get. Home. Get. Home.

I hear a loud, exaggerated yawn. It's Freddy, stretching his arms above his head and shifting in his seat. 'Anna? Can we stop at the services? I need the loo.'

'We're nearly in London.'

'Can you turn the heating down?' he adds as I glance from the rear-view mirror to the road. 'I'm sweating like a pig.'

'I can't. The heater on the windscreen's not working and it keeps fogging up.'

'I'm going to open a window then.'

'Freddy, don't!'

Anger surges through me as he twists in his seat and reaches for the button.

'Freddy, LEAVE IT!'

It happens in the blink of an eye. One moment there is a car in front of me, red tail-lights a warm, comforting glow, the next the car is gone, there's a blur of lights and the blare of a horn – frantic and desperate – and then I'm thrown to the left as the car tips to the side and all I can hear is crunching metal, breaking glass, screaming, and then nothing at all.

Chapter 3

TWELVE HOURS AFTER THE ACCIDENT

There's someone in the room. My eyes are closed but I know I'm not alone. I can feel the weight of their gaze, the pinprick crawl of my skin. What are they waiting for? For me to open my eyes? I want to ignore them and go back to sleep but I can't ignore the churning in my belly and the tightness of my skin. They want to hurt me. Malevolence binds me to the bed like a blanket. I need to wake up. I need to get up and run.

But I can't move. There's a weight on my chest, pinning me to the bed.

'Anna? Anna, can you hear me?'

A voice drifts into my consciousness, then out again.

'Yes!' But my voice is only in my head. I can't move my lips. I can't get the sound to reverberate in my throat. The only part of me I can move is my eyes.

Someone's walking towards me, their cold blue eyes fixed on mine. There's no rise and fall of a nose and mouth, just a smooth stretch of skin, pulled tight.

'Don't be scared.'

They draw closer – staccato movements, like a film on freeze-frame – move, stop, move, stop. Closer and closer. I screw my eyes tightly shut. This isn't real. It's a dream. I need to wake up.

'That's right, Anna. Close your eyes and go back to sleep. Don't fight it. Let the pain and guilt and hurt go.'

I'm dreaming. I have to be. But it's too vivid. I saw blue curtains hanging on a white frame around my bed, a white blanket and the mound of my feet.

No! No! Stop!

I scream, but the sound of my voice doesn't leave my head. I can't move. I can only blink frantically – a silent SOS – as I'm grabbed by the wrist. They're going to hurt me and there's nothing I can do to stop them.

'Open your eyes, Anna. I know you can hear me. Anna, open your eyes!'

Alex?

He is beside me, his face pinched with worry, his eyes ringed with shadows, stubble circling his lips and stretching along his jawbone.

'Anna?'

There's a needle in the back of my hand. Alex catches it with his thumb as he rubs soft circles onto my skin. A sharp pain travels up the length of my arm.

Stop. The word doesn't travel from my mind to my lips. Why can't I speak? A wave of panic courses through me.

'Rest, rest.' Alex touches a hand to my shoulder, pressing me back into the bed.

Alex? Where am I?

There's a blue curtain, hanging from a rail surrounding the bed, and a white blanket, pulled tight, pinning me to the sheet. At the end of the bed is the mound of my feet. Am I still in the dream? But it's not a faceless stranger wrapping their fingers around my wrist, it's Alex. I focus on my hand, resting limply on his, and tense the muscles in my forearm. My fingers contract and then I feel it, the softness of his skin under my fingertips. I'm not dreaming, I'm awake.

'It's okay,' Alex says, mistaking the relief in my eyes for fear. He gingerly perches on the bed, avoiding my legs. 'Don't try to speak. You've been in an accident. You're in the Royal Free Hospital in Hampstead. You had some internal bleeding and you've been operated on. They had . . .' he touches his throat, '. . . they had to give you some help breathing, they said your throat might hurt for a few days, but you're going to be okay. It's a fucking miracle that you . . .' He swallows and looks away.

Survived?

The memory returns like a juggernaut, smashing into my consciousness. I close my eyes to try block it out but it doesn't disappear. I was in the car. I was driving and it was hailing and the windscreen wipers were going back and forth and back and—

I snatch my hands up and over my head, cradling my face with my arms as the truck slams into the side of the car. The seat belt digs into my collarbone and chest as I am thrown forward, then I am turning and spinning and twisting and my head smashes against the steering wheel, the seat rest, the window and my arms are wheeling around, my hands reaching for something, anything to anchor myself, to brace myself for impact, but there's nothing. Nothing. Everyone is screaming and all I can do is pray.

'Anna, please.'

I am vaguely aware of someone pulling on my arms, gripping my elbows, trying to move them away from my face.

'Anna, stop it. Please. Please, stop screaming.'

'Anna? Anna, it's Becca, your nurse.'

Someone touches my fingers, tightly twisted in my hair. I hold on tighter. I can't let go. I won't.

'Is it my fault?' Alex's voice buzzes in and out of my consciousness. 'I shouldn't have mentioned the accident. Fuck. Is she going to stop? This is really . . . I can't . . . I don't know . . .'

'It's okay. It's all right. She's disorientated. One of the other nurses said she reacted violently when she came round in post-op.' Someone pulls on my arms again. I can smell coffee. 'Anna, sweetheart. Are you in pain? Can you open your eyes for me, please?'

'Why is she screaming? Isn't there something you can . . .'

'Can you press the alarm button?'

'Alarm? Why? What's . . .'

'I just need a doctor to see her. Can you just press . . .'

'Is she going to be okay? She looked at me. She tried to speak. I thought—'

'Anna. Anna, can you open your eyes? My name's Becca Porter. I'm your nurse. You're in hospital. Are you in any pain?'

'Sorry, excuse me. Would you mind waiting outside the curtains for a minute. I'm Dr Nowak. Thanks, great. So, who do we have here?'

'Anna Willis. Road traffic accident. Spleen laceration. She came round after post-op, her vitals were fine. She's been asleep for the last hour or so. I heard screaming a few minutes ago and—'

'Okay. Anna, I'm just going to have a look at your tummy, all right? Does it hurt when I press here?'

No. It doesn't hurt there. It hurts here, in here, inside my head.

I know the nurses are about somewhere – I can hear the soft squeak of shoes on lino, a low cough and a murmur of voices – but I can't see anyone. I've been staring around the ward for what feels like forever. Most of the other patients are asleep, reading silently or watching films on iPads. Everyone apart from the young woman opposite, who's also awake and restless. She's younger than me, late twenties tops, with a long, narrow face and dark hair tied up in a messy bun on the top of her head. The first time our eyes met we both smiled and gave a polite nod before letting our gaze drift away again, but we keep meeting each other's eyes and it's getting embarrassing. My throat's still too sore to speak much above a whisper and I'd have to raise my voice to hold a conversation with her. I feel like I should apologise though. She was probably here last night when I screamed the place down. She must have been terrified. I imagine they all were. I didn't even realise what had happened until the nurse, Becca, woke me up to check my blood pressure and asked how I was feeling. They'd rushed me away for a scan after they'd sedated me, worried that something had gone wrong with the operation and I was bleeding again. I can't remember much about it, just a white ceiling, dotted with lights, speeding past as they pushed me down a corridor and then the low hum of the MRI machine. Apparently Alex stayed at the hospital until after the scan, then, reassured that I wasn't in any danger, he did as the nurse suggested and went home for a sleep.

I thanked Becca for looking after me and I apologised for the screams I could only vaguely remember making. She kept a pleasant smile fixed to her face the whole time but when I asked where my colleagues were, her smile faltered.

'I'm not sure,' she said. 'I know the lorry driver was taken to another hospital but I don't know about your friends. I can find out for you though.'

I didn't see her again. The next time my blood pressure was checked it was a different nurse. Becca's shift had ended, she said. She wouldn't be in until tomorrow. I asked her the same question, if she knew what had happened to the others in the car. She genuinely didn't seem to know but said she'd find out. When I saw her the next morning she said she was sorry, she hadn't had time but the doctor would be along soon and she was sure he could answer my questions. I started to panic then. Where were Freddy, Peter and Mo? Had they been taken to a different ward? Unless they hadn't been as badly injured as me. They might have walked away unscathed, a quick visit to hospital to be checked over and then sent straight home. But . . . my tender stomach tightened as I remembered what Alex had said about my recovery being a 'miracle'.

The sound of wheels squeaking on lino makes me turn my head. A nurse has appeared in the doorway, pushing a trolley.

'Excuse me. Nurse.' I raise my hand and wave but she doesn't so much as glance my way, my voice is so quiet. I watch despairingly as she turns left and walks further down the ward.

'EXCUSE ME! NURSE!' The woman in the bed opposite shouts so loudly that all heads turn in her direction, including the nurse's. She waggles her hand in my direction as the nurse approaches, still pushing the trolley. 'The woman over there was trying to get your attention.'

I smile gratefully and attempt to sit up as the nurse comes over, but I feel as though my stomach muscles have been slashed and the most I can manage is a vague craning of my neck.

'Everything okay?' Up close I can see that it's Becca, the nurse who was so kind to me yesterday.

'Please,' I beg. 'I'm going mad here. I need to know what's happened to my team . . . the . . . the people who were in the car with me. I need to know they're all right.'

Her eyes cloud as she gazes at me. A shutter's come down; she doesn't want me to see what she's feeling. She glances down at the watch hanging on her uniform.

'Your partner will be here in about half an hour. Maybe it would be best if he were—'

'Please,' I beg. 'Please just tell me. It's bad news, isn't it? You can tell me. I can take it.'

She looks at me as though she's not entirely sure that I can, then she sighs and takes a shallow breath.

'One of your colleagues is in a pretty bad way,' she says softly. 'He's broken his back in several places.'

I press a hand to my mouth but it doesn't mask my gasp.

'But he's stable,' Becca adds. 'He should pull through.'

'Who is it?'

She grimaces, like she's already regretting talking to me. Or perhaps it's confidential information.

'Please. Please tell me who it is.'

'It's Mohammed Khan.'

'And the others? Peter Cross? Freddy Laing?'

As she lowers her gaze, my eyes fill with tears. No. No. Please. Please don't let them . . . please . . .

She takes my hand and squeezes it tightly. 'I'm so sorry, Anna. We did everything we could.'

Chapter 4

Mohammed

Mohammed's brain feels dull and woolly, as though it's not pain-relieving meds that are flowing through his veins and capillaries but a thick, dark fog. He likes the fog because, as well as anaesthetising the ache in his limbs, it has stupefied his brain. Whenever he tries to latch on to an emotion – anger, regret, fear – it twirls away on a cloud of smoke. As a teenager, wrestling with his hormones and the pressure of exams, Mohammed had looked longingly at his dog, Sonic, curled up on the floor by his desk, and wished he could swap places. What would it be like, he wondered, to be a dog; to find joy in base behaviours – food, play, affection – and not overload your brain thinking about the future, death, the nature of an infinite universe, global warming, war and disease. It didn't take much to make a dog happy – running around outside, catching a ball, a scratch behind the ears. What made him happy? Hanging out with his mates, staying up late, watching films, his PlayStation. Dogs lived in the moment but he didn't. He was studying for exams, the outcome of which would shape his future.

He feels a bit like Sonic now, lying around, not thinking, just waiting, although what he's waiting for he isn't entirely sure. Movement in the corner of his eye makes him turn his head. He doesn't recognise the short, suited, middle-aged man standing in the doorway of the ward but he watches him, vaguely registering the way his eyebrows knit together in frustration, as he scans the supine bodies in their metal beds. He's obviously a visitor, looking for his loved one. The consultants look much more assured when they enter the ward. Two new emotions appear in the fog of Mohammed's thoughts but, instead of disappearing, they twist together, travel down to his chest and curl around his heart. Disappointment and regret.

He turns his head away from the door and closes his eyes, half listening to the slap, clack of leather-soled shoes on the ward floor, so different from the soft pad of the nurses' shoes. The sound grows louder and louder, then there's a soft cough.

'Mohammed?'

He opens his eyes. The short, suited, middle-aged man is standing at the end of his bed, hands in his pockets and an anxious but determined look on his face. There's something about his prominent nose, strong jaw and deep-set eyes that looks vaguely familiar but he's too tired to work out why.

Instead he says, 'Yes, I'm Mohammed. Who are you?'

'Mind if I . . .' The man gestures at the chair beside the bed and, with no reason to say no, Mohammed nods for him to sit down.

'Steve,' the man says, pulling at the thick material of his suit trousers as he takes a seat. He's thickset – muscle rather than fat, Mohammed thinks bitterly as he instinctively glances at the shape of his own legs beneath the tightly tucked hospital bedding. 'Steve Laing, Freddy's dad.'

Mohammed looks back at him, eyes widening in surprise. For a second or two he is lost in confusion. He was told that Freddy had died in the crash. Why would Steve Laing be in the hospital? Unless . . . he feels a flicker of hope in his heart . . . unless Freddy isn't really dead. Could they have made a mistake? Could he have? Maybe he was too out of it to take in what the nurse told him. Maybe . . .

His hope evaporates, leaving an empty chasm in his chest. There was no mistake. He cried when he heard. He cried for a very long time. Not just for Freddy and Peter but for himself too.

'I brought you some magazines,' Steve Laing says, reaching into his bag and plonking a pile of film and music magazines onto Mo's bedside table along with a bar of Galaxy, a packet of Skittles and some jelly babies, 'and some chocolates and stuff.'

'Thanks.'

They stare at each other, just long enough for it to become awkward, then Steve looks down at his lap and runs his palms back and forth on his knees.

'It's good to see you looking so . . .' He shakes his head sharply and looks back up at Mo. 'Nah, I'm sorry, mate. I could give you that sugar-coated shit about you looking well and all that but that's not who I am. I tell it like it is and I imagine you've had quite enough of people tiptoeing around you and telling you to think positive and all that.' He pauses, but not long enough for Mo to reply. 'The truth is that what happened to you, what happened to Peter and my Freddy, was a fucking travesty. A tragedy. It never should have happened, Mo. Never should have fucking . . .' He turns his head sharply as tears well in his eyes.

'I'm sorry,' Mo says, his throat tightening. 'About Freddy. He was a really good bloke.'

'Too right.' Steve Laing drags the back of his hand over his eyes and looks back at him, lips pursed.

'I . . .' The words dry up on Mohammed's tongue. He wants to tell Freddy's dad how he tries not to think about his son because, each time he imagines Freddy's death and the fact that he's gone forever, he feels completely disconnected from his body, spinning a thousand miles above the earth, untethered, fearful and out of control. He wants to tell him that but he won't. Because that's not the sort of thing you say, especially not to someone you only just met.

Instead he says, 'I can't even begin to imagine how hard this must be for you.'

Steve nods sharply and the pain in his eyes seems to lessen. They're back on safe ground, social niceties and surface pleasantries.

'The thing is, Mo, the reason I'm here is to ask you what happened. Not details,' he adds quickly, sensing Mo's mounting discomfort. 'I don't want you to talk me through the crash. No, mate, that would be cruel and I'm not a cruel person. You lived through that once, no need to do it again. Unless . . .' He tails off.

Mo's heart thunders in his chest. 'Unless what?'

'Unless you were a witness at the court case but, from speaking to your parents, I'm not sure you'll be out of here in time.' He pulls a face. 'Sorry, mate. I'm not trying to be insensitive.'

'You spoke to my parents?'

'Yeah, your big boss . . . Tim something . . . put me in touch with them. That's not a problem, is it?'

'No, of course not.'

Another pause widens between the two men, then Steve clears his throat.

'I'm trying to get a picture, Mo, of what happened that day. I know the police are doing their own investigation but this is for me, for my own peace of mind.'

'Of course.'

'Let's start with Anna Willis. What's your take on her?'

Mohammed closes his eyes, just for a split second, then opens them again. 'What do you want to know about her?'

Steve raises his eyebrows. 'Whatever you've got.'

Chapter 5

Anna

THREE WEEKS AFTER THE ACCIDENT

Wednesday 14th March

In the last half an hour the churchyard has transformed from a quiet, peaceful oasis in the heart of West Sussex to a thoroughfare for grief. I must have watched seventy, maybe a hundred mourners, all dressed in black with bowed heads and downturned eyes and matching mouths, walk the gravel path from the gate to the open door of the church. My stomach rumbles angrily and I press a clenched fist to my abdomen to silence it. I forgot to eat breakfast, again.

I didn't eat for two days after the nurse told me that two of my team were dead. How could I spoon cereal into my mouth and slurp down tea like nothing had happened? How could I laugh and chat with the nurses when Peter and Freddy were lying in the mortuary? Instead I cried. I cried and I cried and I turned my head away from everyone who came to visit me, screwing up my eyes to block out faces creased with concern that I didn't deserve. Only when Dr Nowak told me that if I didn't eat something they'd fit me with a feeding tube did I finally agree to try half a slice of toast.

'Anna.' Alex touches my shoulder. 'I think we should go in now. It's due to start.'

It took me fifteen minutes to get out of the flat and into the car, and now we're parked up I don't want to get out again. Everything about driving terrifies me now: the motion, the proximity of other cars, swerving around roundabouts. I only made it home from the hospital because I kept my eyes tightly shut the whole way while Alex played my favourite album on loop. When we finally drew up outside our flat the tips of my fingers were red and numb from gripping the seat belt so tightly. Now, I press my cheek against the passenger side window. It's cool beneath my burning cheek but it does nothing to calm my churning, aching guts.

'I can't go in there, Alex. What do I . . . what do I say to his parents?'

'What people normally say – I'm so sorry for your loss, et cetera, et cetera, or nothing at all. You rang them last week, Anna. You don't have to go through all that again.'

It took me two days to work up the courage to ring Maureen and Arnold Cross. I was Peter's boss. It was only right that I rang them. But I was also the person who drove the car that rolled off the verge of the M25 and killed him. If I'd have been concentrating properly, if I'd have checked my side mirrors instead of glaring at Freddy in the rear-view mirror, I would have seen the half-ton truck drift towards us from the middle lane. I could have taken corrective action, moved us out of its path. And Peter would still be alive. If I'd let Freddy open the window, if I hadn't let my irritation about what he'd said the night before distract me, then the lives of three people, and everyone who loved them, wouldn't be destroyed.

A family friend answered the Cross family's landline. He repeated my name loudly, as though announcing it to the room. There was a pause, then a woman said softly, 'I don't want to talk to her.' When an elderly man added, 'I will,' I felt faint with fear. Peter's dad. I couldn't speak for several seconds after he said hello, my throat was so tight. *I'm sorry*, that's what I said, over and over. *I'm so, so sorry. I can never forgive myself.* There was a pause, a silence that seemed to stretch forever and I braced myself for his fury. It was what I deserved. Instead he said simply, 'We miss him,' and silent tears rolled down my cheeks. 'We both do,' he added. 'Every time the phone rings we think it's him, checking if Maureen's sciatica is any better or asking me for gardening advice. Sometimes we . . .' His voice quivered and he coughed, then sniffed loudly. 'They say the lorry driver who ploughed into you fell asleep at the wheel. No alcohol or drugs. A micro-sleep, they reckon, less than thirty seconds long. Tell me Peter didn't suffer,' he begged. 'Just tell me that.'

'Anna.' Alex nudges me gently. 'Did you hear what I just said?'

'No, sorry. I was—'

'They don't blame you for what happened, Anna. No one does.'

'Freddy's dad does.'

'He was angry. His son has just died. Sorry,' he apologises quickly as I turn sharply. 'I know, I know.'

I couldn't face another call straight after I'd spoken to Peter's dad, so I waited until the next day to call Steve Laing. My hand still shook as I picked up the phone, but I didn't feel the blind panic I'd felt the day before. I knew what was coming – pain, sadness, grief and disbelief – and I determined to be more of a comfort this time around. I'd tell him how popular Freddy had been on the team, talk about his achievements and take my time answering any questions Steve Laing might want to ask me.

Only he was nothing like Arnold Cross. When I introduced myself, he exploded down the phone at me. How dare I ring him while he was grieving? It was down to my negligence that his son was dead – mine and the company I worked for. Did I have children? Did I have any idea of the hell he was going through, his child dying before him? I tried to apologise but he shouted over me. Had I ever driven a car in such treacherous conditions before? Did I have any points on my licence? Had I ever been caught speeding or made a claim on my insurance? All I could do was stare in horror at the white patch of wall in front of me as he ranted and raged and took all his anger and grief out on me.

I didn't ring Mo or his parents. When I was still in hospital I asked a nurse if I could use a wheelchair to go and see him, but she told me he didn't want any visitors. When I asked again a couple of days later I was told that Mo didn't want to see me and it would probably be for the best if I didn't ask again.

'The CPS aren't pressing charges against you,' Alex says now. 'It's the lorry driver they're gunning for.'

'But maybe Steve Laing was right. I hadn't driven on the motorway when it was that icy before and—'

'We're going home.' Alex starts the engine. 'Coming here was a mistake.'

'No!' I rest my hand on the steering wheel. 'I need to do this.'

It's standing room only and we're crushed up against strangers in the back of the church. Alex is pressed against my right shoulder and a tall man with a bald head keeps bumping my left. The people at the front of the church are bundled up tightly in their hats, coats and scarves despite the orange glow of Calor gas heaters dotted at the end of the pews. Tim, my boss, is sitting in a pew near the back, but it's the woman in the row at the very front that I can't take my eyes off. I can only see the back of her grey hair but, from the way it's resting on the shoulder of the man beside her, it can only be Peter's mother. A fresh wave of guilt tears through me. If it weren't for me, none of us would be here now and Peter would be . . .

A shadow falls across my face and all the air is knocked from my lungs. The coffin, lifted high on the shoulders of six grim-faced men, appears in the entrance to the church. The gentle murmuring of the congregation stops suddenly, as though someone has sharply twisted the volume control to the left, and Alex tightens his grip on my hand, pulling me after him as he takes a step back to make way. I want to look at him, at my shoes, anywhere but at the shiny wooden box that moves past me, but I keep my chin tipped up and my gaze steady. I need to face the reality of the devastation I caused. I owe Peter that. But my bravery doesn't last long. The moment the coffin turns into the aisle I collapse against Alex.

'I need to get out,' I whisper between sobs. 'I need some air.'

'I'll come with you.'

'No.' I touch him on the arm. 'I won't be long. I just need to be alone for a few minutes.'

I feel the weight of his gaze as I slide past him and move through the mourners but he lets me go.

Out in the fresh March air I pull off the hat, coat and scarf that make me feel suffocated and I inhale deeply, sucking cold air into my lungs, pushing out the damp, sorrowful scent of the church. My stomach clenches violently, bile touching the back of my tongue and, for one horrifying moment, I think I'm going to be sick. I fight the sensation, breathing shallowly and staring at the cloudless grey sky until it passes, then I start to walk. I drift from gravestone to gravestone, reading the inscriptions, looking at the dates, noting the flowers – or lack of them. As a distraction it only partially works. I feel lost in a fog of sadness and regret whenever I pass someone who died young. There's one grave that particularly upsets me. A man and a woman are listed on one stone, John and Elizabeth Oakes. He died aged fifty-nine in 1876. She died twenty years later aged seventy-six. Their children are listed below them – Albert, Emily, Charlotte, Edward, Martha and Thomas. Six children and not one of them made it past their fifth birthday. The grave is old and uncared for; moss clings to the children's names and the angel that sits atop the stone is chipped, her face worn away with age. I scan the cold, hard ground around the grave, looking for daisies or dandelions that I can bunch together with blades of grass. A clump of bowed snowdrops at the base of a tree catches my eye.

I crouch down beside the flowers and pinch one of the stems between my index finger and thumb, then pause, mid-snap. Someone's watching. I can feel their gaze resting on me, like a weight across my shoulder blades. I turn sharply, expecting to see a photographer behind a gravestone, or a journalist dressed in black with a faux-sad expression. The local press have been hounding me for an interview since I left hospital.

But whoever was watching me isn't interested in a chat. I catch a glimpse of a black coat or jacket disappearing around the side of the church and then they're gone. I abandon the clump of bright snowdrops – the idea of plucking them so they can wither and die on a gravestone suddenly feels wrong – and walk back towards the church. As I approach the leaf-strewn porch, the door opens and Alex slides out to the piped opening chords of 'All Things Bright and Beautiful'.

'Okay?' His eyes search my face.

'Not really, no.'

'Do you want to go back in?'

I glance towards the side of the church, where the figure in black disappeared. There's no one there now. Just row after row of grey gravestones, some aged, some new and – my breath catches in my throat as I notice it for the first time – a large hole in the ground, with green, sack-like material surrounding it. Peter's plot. Alex turns his head, following my line of sight, and his hands twitch at his side. For one second I think he's going to reach for me. Instead he shoves his hands into his pockets and shivers.

'It's cold out here. Shall we go?' He inclines his head in the direction of the car.

I take one last, long look at the plot then nod silently, but Alex is already halfway down the path.

My boyfriend is behind the wheel, hunched over his phone as I reach for the passenger door handle. It's splattered with mud; the whole side of the car is. I'll offer to pay for a valet when we get back to London. It's the least I can . . .

It's so small I almost didn't notice it.

SLEEP

Written just above the front wheel arch, like someone's wet their finger and carved the word into the mud.

'Alex.' He looks up from his phone as I tap on the window, surprise then irritation registering on his face. I beckon him with one hand and point towards the wheel arch with the other. 'Something weird.'

He sighs silently and opens his door.

'What?' he says as he steps out.

'Someone's written something on the car.'

'What!' His irritation turns to fury in an instant.

'It's not damaged. It's just weird. Look.'

He joins me and looks where I'm pointing.

'SLEEP?' He's nonplussed.

'Don't you think it's weird?'

'A bit.'

'What do you think it means?'

He shrugs. 'That some teenager was bored? It's more original than *clean me*, anyway.'

'But it's not funny. It's not witty. It's not . . . anything.' I glance back towards the church – I just had the strongest sensation that we were being watched – but the churchyard is still deserted.

'Exactly. It's nothing to worry about.' Alex wanders back to his side of the car and pulls on the door handle. He smiles as our eyes meet over the top of the car. 'I won't be losing sleep about it, anyway.' He laughs. 'Losing *sleep*. Get it?'

'Yeah.' I close my eyes tightly and think about 'SLEEP' and what it could mean, all the way home.

Chapter 6

Anna

EIGHT WEEKS AFTER THE ACCIDENT

Thursday 26th April

I feel like a balloon on a string, floating above the pavement. Alex's hand is wrapped tightly around mine but I can't feel the pressure of his fingers on my skin. I can't feel anything. Not the pavement under my feet, not the wind on my cheeks, not even my laboured breath in my throat. Tony, my stepdad, is walking ahead of us, his white hair waving this way and that as the wind lifts and shakes it. His black suit is too tight across his shoulders and every now and then he tugs at the hem. When he isn't pulling at his clothes he's glancing back at me, over his shoulder.

'All right?' he mouths.

I nod, even though it feels like he's looking straight through me, talking to someone further down the street. I barely recognised the woman who stared back at me from the mirror this morning as she pulled on the white blouse, grey suit and black heels that had been laid out on the bed for her. I knew it was me in the mirror but it was like looking at a photograph of myself as a child. I could see the similarity in the eyes, the lips and the stance but there was a disconnection. Me, and not me, all at the same time. I barely slept last night. While Alex snored softly beside me, curled up and hugging a pillow, I lay on my back and stared at the dark ceiling. When I did fall asleep, sometime after three, it wasn't for long. I woke suddenly at five, gasping, shrieking and clawing at the duvet. I'd had my hospital dream again, the one about the faceless person staring at me.

'It's going to be okay, sweetheart,' Mum says now, trotting along beside me, her cheeks flushed red, the thin skin around her eyes creased with worry. When we got out of the car she took my right hand and Alex took my left. I felt like a child, about to be swung into the air but with fear in my belly rather than glee. At some point Mum must have let me go because now her hands are clenched into fists at her sides.

'Anna.' Mum's gloved hand brushes the arm of my coat. 'This isn't about you, love. You're not the one on trial. You're a witness. Just tell the court what happened.'

Just the court: the judge, the jury, the lorry driver, the public, the press, and the family and friends of my colleagues. I need to stand up in front of all those people and relive what happened eight weeks ago. If I didn't feel so numb, I'd be terrified.

'Anna!'

'Over here!'

'Anna!'

'Mr Laing!'

'Mr Khan!'

The noise overwhelms me before the bodies do. Everywhere I look there are people, necks craned, arms reaching in the air – some with microphones, others with cameras – and they're all shouting. My stepdad wraps an arm around my shoulders and pulls me close.

'Give her some space!' He raises an arm and swipes at a camera that's just been shoved in my face. 'Out of the way! Just get out of the bloody way, you imbeciles.'

As Tony angles me out of the crowd I search desperately for Mum and Alex but they're still trapped in the throng of people by the courthouse entrance.

'Anna! Anna!' A blonde woman in her early forties in a pink blouse and a puffy black gilet presses up against me and holds a digital Dictaphone just under my chin. 'Are you satisfied with the verdict? A two-year sentence and two of your colleagues are dead?'

I stare at her, too shocked to speak, but she registers the turn of my head as interest and continues to question me.

'Will you go back to work at Tornado Media? Was that your boyfriend you were with?'

'You're having trouble sleeping, aren't you?' a different voice asks.

I twist round to see who asked the question but there's a sea of people following us down the steps – dozens of men in suits, photographers in jeans and anoraks, a dark-haired woman in a bright red jacket, an older lady with permed white hair, my mother – pink-cheeked and worried – and, on the other side of the group from her, the thin, anxious shape of my boyfriend.

The blonde to my right nudges me. 'Anna, do you feel responsible in any way?'

'What?' Somehow, in the roar, Tony heard her question. Someone behind me bumps against me as my stepdad stops sharply. 'You bloody what?'

It's like a film, freeze-framed, the way the crowd around us suddenly falls silent and stops moving.

The blonde smiles tightly at Tony. 'Mr Willis, is it?'

'Mr Fielding actually, who's asking?'

'Anabelle Chance, *Evening Standard*. I was just asking your daughter if she felt in any way responsible for what happened.'

The skin on my stepdad's neck flushes red above the white collar of his shirt. 'Are you bloody kidding me?' He stares around at the crowd. 'Can she actually say that?'

'It was just a question, Mr Fielding. Anna' – she tries to hand me a business card – 'if you'd ever like to chat then give me a—'

He knocks her hand away. 'You're treading a very fine line. Now, get out of our way, before I make you.'

Mum and Alex wrap around us like a protective shield, Alex beside me, Mum next to Tony, as we hurry away from the noise and chaos of the courtroom.

'Have you got a tissue, love?' Mum asks as we reach the car. 'You've got mascara all down your face.'

I touch a hand to my cheeks, surprised to find that they're wet.

'Yes, I've . . .' I reach a hand into my suit pocket and feel the soft squish of a packet of Kleenex. But there's something else beside them, something hard with sharp corners, something I don't remember putting into my pocket when I got ready this morning. It's a postcard. The background is blue with white words forming the shape of a dagger. The words turn red as they near the point of the blade and a single drop of blood drips onto the title: *The Tragedy of Macbeth*.

'What's that?' Mum asks as I flip the card over.

I shake my head. 'I don't know.'

There are two words written on the back, in large, looping letters:

For Anna

I look from Mum, to Dad and then to Alex. 'Did one of you put this in my pocket?'

When they all shake their heads, I flip it back over and read the quote:

Methought I heard a voice cry 'Sleep no more! Macbeth does murder sleep' – the innocent sleep, Sleep that knits up the ravelled sleave of care, The death of each day's life, sore labour's bath, Balm of hurt minds, great nature's second course, Chief nourisher in life's feast.

I know this quote from studying *Macbeth* at A-level. It's Macbeth talking to Lady Macbeth about the frightening things that have happened since he murdered King Duncan.

'Anna?' Alex says. 'Are you okay? You've gone very pale.'

I glance back towards the courthouse and the throng of faceless people milling around.

'Someone put this in my pocket.'

'It wasn't that bloody journalist, was it?' Tony says. 'Because I'll get on the phone to her editor if I need to. I won't have her harassing you like this.'

'Let me see that.' Alex leans over my shoulder and peers at the card. 'Is that a quote from Shakespeare?'

'It's Macbeth telling Lady Macbeth about a voice he heard telling him he'll never sleep again.'

'Oh, that's horrible.' Mum runs her hands up and down her arms. 'Who'd give you something like that?'

'Here, give me that.' Tony takes the card from my fingers, rips it into tiny pieces and then drops them into a drain. 'There. Gone. Don't give it a second thought, love.'

No one mentions it all the way home but the words rest in my brain like a weight.

Chapter 7

Steve

Saturday 28th April

Steve Laing bows his head and crosses himself as he crouches beside his son's grave. He's not a Catholic but it feels like the right thing to do. It shows respect. He touches a hand to the grave marker, tracing a finger over the cold imprint of his son's name, and his chest burns with grief and rage. He still can't quite believe it, that his son's body is buried deep in the ground, six feet below him. It doesn't feel real. How can it be? Freddy was young, he was strong, he went to the gym three times a week and played squash every Saturday. He'd had chickenpox as a kid. Broken his arm when he fell off the slide. But he wasn't one of those kids in the park with snot dribbling over his top lip. He was healthy, hardly had a day off school. The only time Steve had had to take him to A&E was when he got so pissed at a house party for a mate's fifteenth birthday that he ran into a glass door and knocked himself out. When he came round he claimed he'd had his drink spiked. Steve could see in the twitch of his lips that he was lying but he admired his gumption. Freddy could be a gobby little shit, always trying to talk himself out of trouble. He was loud too. He filled the house with his booming voice and his clumsy-arsed ways. Steve had lost track of the number of times he'd shouted at him to 'keep the bloody noise down' when he crashed into the house late at night, clattering around in the dishwasher or bashing every pot and pan together as he tried to make himself a snack after a drinking session with his mates. But he was never angry with him, not really. Freddy was all he had after Juliet had died. Fucking cancer, stealing the kid's mum away from him five days before his eleventh birthday. If cancer were a person he'd have beaten the shit out of it and smashed its face to a pulp.

The house is quiet now. So bloody quiet it makes him want to turn on every stereo and sound system in the place and scream at the top of his voice. That's the worst thing about death, the silence it leaves behind. But not in Steve's head, there's no peace there. Some days he feels as though he's going mad, all those thoughts, buzzing around like wasps. He kept them quiet for a bit – planning the funeral and preparing for the trial – but they started up again afterwards, louder and angrier than ever. It's the powerlessness he can't cope with. He couldn't save Freddy. He couldn't grab hold of the surgeon's knife, plunge his hand into his son's chest and massage his heart back to life. He couldn't speed up the police investigation. He couldn't talk to the CPS and, other than a prepared statement, he couldn't speak to the judge or jury. His son had been taken from him and he couldn't do a fucking thing about it. 'Trust us,' the police told him. 'Let us do our job.' But they hadn't, had they? Not really. Not them, not the CPS and not the fucking judge.

He traces a finger over his son's birth and death dates. Twenty-four. Just twenty-four. At the funeral the vicar had said something about an 'everlasting sleep' that had really riled him. Death wasn't like sleep. It wasn't relaxing. You didn't dream and you couldn't be woken up. A dark cloud of despair had descended when the last of the mourners left Freddy's grave. For most of them it would be the only time they'd visit it. They'd miss him, of course they would, but they'd get back on with their lives, whereas Steve felt his had been indefinitely paused.

It was his mate Jim who'd thrown him a lifeline. 'If you feel that justice hasn't been done, mate, then maybe you need to mete it out yourself. If you know where she is I can send someone after her. She won't even see them coming. If that's what you want.'

Steve wasn't sure if it was. He prided himself on being a gentleman. He'd never once lifted his hand to a woman. But it was different if a woman was a murderer, wasn't it? He'd have had no qualms about hurting Myra Hindley or Rose West. And that's what this woman was, wasn't it? A murderer. She'd taken the lives of two young people and crippled another. She hadn't looked him in the eye at the trial. Hadn't even acknowledged he was there. But she will. She'll know who Steve Laing is, and she'll remember his son. He'll make sure of that.

Chapter 8

Anna

Wednesday 2nd May

Our flat is a very different place at four o'clock in the morning. Unusually for London, the air is cool and still, the bedroom wrapped in shadows, the darkness punctuated only by the glow of streetlamps slipping through the gap in the curtains. Alex is asleep, curled up on his side, hugging the duvet. He came back from work yesterday evening to find me wrapped in a blanket on the sofa, staring dully at the TV. He stood in the doorway, watching me, waiting for an acknowledgement.

'Hi,' I said, then let my gaze return to the TV. A single glance was enough to assess his mood: rigid posture, tight jaw, cold eyes. He was angling for a fight. Again.

'What this?' He picked up the empty mug from the side table.

'A mug.'

'And this?' He picked up a plate.

I looked at him. 'What are you doing?'

'What are *you* doing?'

He stalked out of the living room, mug and plate in hand. I heard them crash into the sink then the sound of the fridge door opening and closing and a curt *fucking hell.*

'Anna.' He was back in the doorway again. 'There's no food in the house. You said you'd go to the supermarket.'

'I did.'

'And?'

'Someone followed me.'

'Not again.' He rested his head against the white glossed wood of the door frame. 'Anna. You *need* to let this go. Steve Laing is not out to get you. The person who was responsible – the lorry driver, *not* you – has been charged and sent to prison. The coroner's court case has been dismissed. It's finished. Over.'

He didn't understand. How could he? I hadn't got any proof that someone had been following me. I hadn't confronted them or taken their photo. I didn't even know what they looked like, but I'd felt them watching me. I'd been fine leaving the house. I'd made it all the way to Tesco without feeling a horrible prickling sensation from the base of my skull to midway down my spine. The sun was shining and I was in a good mood because I'd just binge-watched three episodes of *Catastrophe*. Steve Laing hadn't crossed my mind once and then it happened, the absolute certainty that someone was standing behind me, watching me as I bent down to take a loaf off the shelf. When I turned around there were five other people in the aisle – a man in a suit, an older woman, a woman about my age and another woman, slightly older than me with a toddler in a buggy. The child stared me out, his blue eyes wide and anxious. His mother looked down at him, at me, and then wheeled the buggy around and disappeared back down the aisle. Irritated with myself for overreacting, I headed straight to the tills with my basket. It wasn't until I got home that I realised I'd forgotten half the things Alex had asked me to buy.

'Did you ring Tim today?' He crossed his arms over his chest.

'Yeah.'

'And?'

'I gave my notice.'

He raised his eyes to the ceiling. 'I'm struggling to pay the bills as it is. If this is a permanent situation then . . .' He sighed heavily. 'I really don't think I can deal with this, Anna. I knew you'd be a bit . . . upset . . . for a while but I can't live like this. If you're not thrashing around in bed because you can't sleep you're sitting around in jogging bottoms watching reruns of *Friends*. Have you even had a shower today?'

In another life, the life I lived before my world was shattered, I would have bit back at Alex and told him that maybe he should be a bit more sympathetic. Instead I looked at him and said, 'It's not working, is it? Between us?'

'It's . . .' He looked down at the grubby beige carpet and shook his head. 'No, it's not.'

I'd imagined this conversation in my head a hundred times since the accident, but actually having it was surreal. I'd expected to burst into tears or feel a jagged pain in my chest. Instead I felt detached, as though I were watching the break-up scene happen to two other people. We'd been drifting apart for a long time, way before the accident, but you'd have to be a cruel kind of bastard to leave someone when they needed you most. We didn't dislike each other, we hadn't had blazing rows or shagged someone else or been cruel, but we were living separate lives. We weren't even sharing the same bed any more, not really. There might be an hour or two – between my insomnia and Alex getting up for work – when we lay on the same sheet but we rarely touched. I couldn't remember the last time he'd kissed me goodbye or hello. And the most telling thing was, I didn't really mind.

'What do you want to do?' I asked. 'Do you want to keep the flat?'

He looked shocked. He'd come back from work expecting a fight. He might have secretly wanted this but he hadn't expected us to have this conversation now.

'I'm happy for you to have it,' I said. 'I'll go back to Reading and live with Mum and Tony for a bit.'

He looked up and met my gaze but I couldn't read the expression in his eyes. 'You've been thinking about this for a while, haven't you? Us splitting up?'

'Haven't you?'

The air between us was suddenly very still, heavy with sadness.

'Are you moving out today?' He glanced at the open bedroom door and the room beyond it, looking for suitcases or signs that I'd already started getting my things together.

I looked at the kitchen clock. It was after seven. 'I don't know. It's probably too late.'

'Good.'

'Good?'

'I'm glad you're staying tonight. I'm not sure I could cope with you just upping and leaving. I feel a bit . . .'

'Shocked?'

'Yeah.'

'I know what you mean.' I paused, suddenly unsure whether I'd misread the situation. 'You do want this, don't you, Alex?'

'Yeah, yeah, I do. It's just . . . weird. I feel . . .' He faltered. 'I feel like I need to give you a hug or something.'

'Okay, sure.' I said yes only because saying no would have been harder.

I shifted the blanket and book on my lap to one side and tried to get up from the sofa as Alex crossed the room. We met in the middle, an awkward hug with him reaching down to me and me reaching up, a huge space between our bodies. It was like embracing a stranger.

'I'm sorry,' he said as he pulled away. 'I feel like I've let you down.'

'You haven't let anyone down. I'm not the person I was. I don't think you are either. We've both changed. No one's to blame.'

He looked at me steadily and said nothing. He didn't have to.

We had beans on toast for dinner, the plates resting on our laps as we sat on the sofa and pretended to watch a film. It was better than the alternative, sitting across the kitchen table from each other, shovelling food silently into our mouths as we tried to think of something to say. We went to bed at the same time and automatically reached for our books. It felt as though we were in a bizarre sketch show, the couple who'd just split up but were acting as though nothing had happened.

'Have you made plans, beyond living with your parents, I mean?' Alex laid down his book but kept his gaze, and his body, facing forwards. A wave of sadness passed over me. It was real. We were splitting up. We no longer fitted together like pieces of a puzzle. Time had changed us. We'd become warped and incompatible.

'I was thinking about moving to Scotland.'

'*Scotland*?'

'Yeah. One of the islands maybe. I . . .' I discarded my book, twisted onto my side and pulled the duvet up over my shoulders. Looking at Alex's side profile, I had a flashback to the first time I'd seen him – his long nose, strong brow and slightly recessive chin.

He looked at me curiously. 'Since when have you wanted to live in Scotland?'

'I've wanted to get out of London for a while, you know that. I told you when we first met.'

'You said you wanted to move to the Cotswolds or Norfolk, not Scotland.'

'There was a programme the other day, on the TV. I was only half watching it but I got sucked in. The Scottish Isles . . . they looked so beautiful and wild and remote.'

'And cold. And rainy. And miserable.'

I shook my head. 'No, not miserable.'

'You won't know anyone.'

'Good. I don't like people.'

He laughed. 'And I don't imagine they have a thriving marketing industry.'

'I don't want to be in marketing any more.'

'So what will you do? Become a fisherwoman?'

'I thought I might work in a tea shop or a restaurant or something. Or I could clean maybe, be a cleaner.'

'Clean?' One of his eyebrows twitched in disbelief.

'Why not? I don't want to do what I did, Alex. I don't want the pressure or the . . . the responsibility.'

He looked grave for a second as my words sank in.

'This is some weird kind of grief thing, isn't it? Making reckless decisions. I read about it online.'

'No, it's not. I've given it a lot of thought.'

'But . . .' He looked at me steadily. 'You're the messiest person I've ever met. Who the hell's going to employ you as a cleaner?'

We both laughed then.

'I just want you to be happy,' Alex said as he twisted round to turn off his bedside lamp.

'I want you to be happy too.'

He didn't reply. Instead he pulled the duvet up over his shoulders and buried his head in his pillow, shifting and shuffling as he made himself comfortable. I studied the shape of his head and the curve of his shoulder as his breathing grew slower and deeper. Then, when I was sure he was asleep, I slipped out of bed.

I lean back in my chair and stretch my arms above my head. 5.04 a.m. I rarely fall asleep before four. I've tried hypnosis apps, lavender, Night Nurse and Calms but nothing works.

I've just spent the last couple of hours searching for jobs in the Scottish Isles. There were more than I expected, particularly in Orkney, but where I want to live, the isle I fell in love with when I watched the BBC documentary, was Rum. The thirty-one residents are outnumbered by the animal life – deer, eagles and ponies – that run wild on the rough, rugged terrain. But there's only one job available – 'General Help' at the Bay View Hotel. Duties including reception work, cleaning and website updating. The salary's pitifully small and the hours are relentless. I'd barely get time to rest, never mind think. It's just what I want.

As Alex said, I'm hardly qualified to be a cleaner but I worked in a hotel bar for a couple of years after school and I can do the website stuff standing on my head. I peer into the laptop screen, reread my application again, checking for typos or errors, then grab the mouse and click 'Send'.

I stifle a yawn as I close the laptop and stand up. The sun is coming up now and a sliver of bright light slips into the room where the curtains don't meet in the middle. Below a blanket of grey cloud the sky is streaked orange and red and I can just make out the arc of a white sun peeping between the buildings opposite and—

Movement in the corner of my eye makes me turn my head. Someone just ducked down behind a car at the end of the road, on the opposite side of the street. I steady my hand on the glass and squint into the distance. There's a piece of paper fluttering under the windscreen wiper of my car.

'Alex?' I whisper his name then cross the bedroom and step into the hall, pulling the door closed behind me. I turn on the hallway light, pull on my coat, slip my feet into my shoes and grab my keys. Less than two minutes later I'm down the communal stairs and opening the front door. I pause in the doorway and glance along the street. There's no one else here, just me and a large tabby cat that stares indifferently at me from a low wall, several houses down. I put the door on the latch and dart out of the house. It only takes twelve frantic strides to get me from the front door to the car. I snatch the piece of white paper from beneath the windscreen wiper then speed back into the house. I shut the door behind me, release the latch and unfold the paper. There are three words printed in the centre.

YOU WILL SLEEP.

In Memoriam

In Memoriam

Emily and Eva Gapper

Emily Gapper, devoted wife and mother. Passed away on 13.2.2015 to be with our darling daughter, Eva Gapper. Knowing that the two of you are together is my only comfort. Forever in my thoughts, my beautiful girls. Love and miss you always . . .

I have always prided myself on my ability to read people; to interpret their body language, intonation and micro-expressions. It's not so much a gift as a survival technique, an arsenal in my armour that was fashioned in my childhood – a necessity when faced with a mother as emotionally stunted as mine.

Take you, for example, Anna Willis, sitting in the window, lit by the glow of your laptop, then sprinting along the pavement with your oversized cardigan wrapped around your body and belted by your arm gripping your waist. I might have been too far away this time to study your face but I've been nearer. I've been close enough to study your pale skin, wide unblinking pupils, the sweat prickling at your hairline, your repetitive throat-clearing and the way you twist your hands. Your anxiety and your pain shine like a beacon but only to your nearest and dearest, sweet Anna. And, of course, to me.

I was going to retire. I was going to leave this life behind me and take up new pursuits. But he wants you gone and I couldn't say no. I have never been able to say no to him.

I thought I'd want to hurry your passing, Anna, to get it over and done with quickly, but this will be the last time I ever do this, my final flourish, so to speak, and I want it to be perfect. When the time is right I will help you sleep.

Chapter 9

Anna

Alex walks into the kitchen, dressed in his suit and smelling of shampoo and aftershave. He holds out a hand. 'Show me that note.'

I tried to wake him after I ran back up the stairs with the piece of paper I found under the windscreen wiper but he swatted me away and told me to go back to sleep. I tried again when his alarm went off at six thirty but he peered at it through bleary eyes, shook his head and said he needed the loo. I trailed him to the bathroom, note in hand, then retreated to the kitchen when I heard the shower start.

'Someone put it on my car,' I tell him again.

Alex takes one look at the note, flips it over to look at the blank other side then crumples it up and throws it in the bin. 'Sounds supportive to me. Maybe someone else on the street has noticed that you stay up all hours of the night.'

'But they've underlined "will". It makes it sound threatening.'

'Maybe it's the journalist that's been hassling you for an interview. *Give me an interview and you'll sleep better*, that sort of thing. Was there a business card with it?'

'No, nothing.' I pause. 'I think it's Steve Laing.'

Alex frowns. He doesn't recognise the name.

'Freddy's dad. Remember what he said after the trial, that justice had only partially been done? I really think it's him, Alex. First "sleep" written in the dirt, then the postcard, now this.' I reach into the bin and pull out the crumpled ball of paper. 'Maybe he thinks I fell asleep at the wheel too? Or that I feel too guilty to sleep.'

Alex reaches under the kitchen table for his shoes and eases his feet into them. 'Anna, put the note back in the bin.'

'But it's evidence.'

'Of what?'

'That someone's . . .' I tail off. What was it evidence of exactly? That someone had noticed I was still awake at 5 a.m. and had left a sympathetic note on my car? It wasn't illegal to write in the dirt on someone's car either. If it were, hundreds of 'clean me' pranksters would be in jail for defacing grubby vans.

'Has anything else happened that you haven't told me about?' Alex stands up and pulls on his coat. 'Any weird phone calls or emails?'

'No, just, you know, the feeling that someone's been watching me.'

My boyfriend, ex-boyfriend, clamps his top teeth over his bottom lip and gazes down at me, his brow creasing as his eyes search mine. 'The trial was covered in the paper, wasn't it?'

'Yeah.'

'And they mentioned our address? The street, anyway.'

'Yeah.'

'Probably a member of the public then. Some weirdo who's

become obsessed with the case. Or not,' he adds as he registers my startled expression. 'It could be something to do with Steve Laing, like you say. Either way, you need to stop worrying about it. Whoever it is isn't going to bother you at your parents' house.'

It's a reassuring thought but I'm fooling myself if I think I'll be out of the flat today. I've got too much stuff. There are pots and pans, dishes and cutlery in the kitchen. Books, clothes, DVDs and music in the bedroom. Ornaments, photo frames and pictures in the living room. Then there's all the furniture that belongs to me. It's going to take me days to get everything packed up.

'Alex.' I reach out to touch him on the arm but my hand falls away before I make contact. We aren't together any more. Lingering touches are no longer appropriate.

'Yeah?'

I want to ask him not to go to work. To stay in the flat with me and watch a film and get drunk or play a board game and listen to music. I know if I stay in the flat alone I'll flinch at every noise, peer out of the window, pace and worry and google real-life stories about stalkers. But I can't ask Alex not to go to work. Not least because he doesn't have to protect or comfort me any more. I have to let him get on with his life.

'Can I leave my furniture here?' I ask instead. 'Until I'm settled? And some boxes of stuff?'

He shrugs. 'I guess, until I get a new place anyway.'

'Thank you. I'll arrange for a man with a van to pick them up. I'll leave the car outside too. I'll probably sell it. Unless you want it.'

'You're getting rid of your car?'

'Yeah.' I'm surprised at his reaction. He's seen how difficult it is for me just to get into the passenger seat. There's no way I can face driving again. Not for a long time. 'I'll get a train to Mum and Tony's later, once I'm packed up.'

That's assuming they'll be okay with me staying. Ever since they've retired they've had a succession of long-lost relatives and old friends to visit. I might have to kip on the sofa.

'Wow.' Alex looks stunned, as though the reality of what we're doing has finally sunk in. 'You're not going to be here when I get back, are you?'

'No.' I look up at the ceiling and blink back tears.

'Jesus.' He looks me up and down, his gaze resting on my lips, the top button of my pyjamas and the chipped nail varnish on my toes. 'I guess this is goodbye then.'

I nod, suddenly unable to speak.

'One more hug before I go?' He doesn't wait for me to respond. Instead he pulls me into his arms, squeezes me tightly then lets me go. The embrace barely lasts five seconds.

'Take care of yourself, Anna,' he says as he walks out of the kitchen and into the hallway. He opens the door to the flat and steps outside without looking back. I have never felt more alone.

Part Two

Chapter 10

Anna

Saturday 2nd June

Day 1 of the storm

'Anna. Anna?'

I turn and smile. Even after a week I'm still not used to the way David says my name. I feel as though I've been rechristened. Back in London I was Anna – An-na – emphasis on the first 'n' and the last 'a'. Now I'm Ah-nah. My name sounds softer and warmer when David says it in his soft Scottish burr. For the first couple of days on the island my shoulders remained up by my ears, tight, knotted and wary. But I can feel them loosening; the tension that curled me into myself is fading away. I'm softening, just like my name.

'Yes, David.'

'Do you have the list of guest names?'

'Yeah.' I swipe a piece of paper from the printer under the desk and hand it to him.

I had my reservations about David when he interviewed me on the phone. He was direct, gruff and pompous, continuously referring to me as 'young lady' (even though I'm thirty-two years old) and repeatedly asked me if I was prepared to work hard and not moan. I pictured him as a tall man, broad shouldered, bearded, ex-military. When the ferry docked on Rum and I walked down the ramp and onto the quayside I passed the small, round, pink-cheeked man in a yellow waterproof jacket and bowled straight up to the bearded man in a flat cap, standing beside a large black Labrador.

'Anna?' I felt a tap on my shoulder and turned sharply.

'David?'

'Yes.' He held out a hand. 'How was your journey?'

He had told me on the phone that visitors weren't allowed to bring cars to Rum, and I'd boarded the small boat with a dozen or so people who were also on foot. Half of them had bicycles. The rest wore bulging rucksacks on their backs. I was the only one dragging a suitcase behind me. I carried it up to deck three and took a seat next to the window. After a couple of minutes the ferry pulled away from Mallaig, the sea as grey as the sky. After about forty minutes we passed Eigg, to our left, rising out of the sea like the dark nose of a whale. If Eigg was a whale then Rum was a dragon's back, curving out of the water. I thought I was prepared to see it for the first time – I'd watched and rewatched the Small Isles programme on iPlayer after David confirmed on the phone that he'd give me a three-month trial – but my breath still caught in my throat and my stomach tightened with anticipation. I left the lounge and stepped onto the deck, smiling as the wind slapped my cheeks then lifted my hair and wrapped it around my face. With the sky and the sea stretching for miles I felt as though I was being transported to another world, not a tiny community on the west coast of Scotland. I felt vital and energised, alive and free.

I didn't tell David any of that. Instead I said, 'Rum's a long way from Reading. It took forever. But the ferry ride took my breath away.'

He smiled broadly, his eyes almost disappearing in the rise of his cheeks as he read the expression on my face. 'Still gets me too, even after all these years. That everything?' He gestured towards my suitcase and I nodded.

'Okay.' He picked it up. 'This,' he raised a hand in the direction of the dozen or so buildings surrounding us, 'is what we call "the village", by the way. We're on the other side of the island – Harris.'

I climbed into his white Land Rover and for the first time in months I didn't close my eyes after I fastened my seat belt. I still clung to the hand rest as the car climbed the hills, juddered over the stony roads and swung around tight corners but I drank in the view: the hills as grey as an elephant's hide, the grass, the gorse, the sky stretching forever, the sea and the—

'Ponies! Look!'

David laughed. 'Yeah, there's a few. Deer too.'

By the time we arrived at the Bay View Hotel, nestled into the side of a hill and separated from the rest of the island by a shallow river that we had to drive through, I felt drunk with happiness.

'That's the mausoleum, isn't it?' I said, pointing at the grey-brown sandstone building that stood incongruously in a field of green. With its pitched roof and imposing pillars, housing three granite tombs, it looked as though it had been dropped from the sky or whisked through time from ancient Greece.

'That's right.' David nodded. 'It's Sir George Bullough's family mausoleum. He's buried there along with his son and wife.'

I suppressed a shiver, remembering the last time I'd been in a graveyard.

'And who lives there?' I pointed at a small cottage on the edge of the river; the hotel's other neighbour.

'Gordon Brodie. He guides the walks. He's also the caretaker at the primary school. Part time.' He laughed. 'There's only four children.'

'Four children in the whole school?'

'Five next year when Susi McFarlane's little one turns four. There's only thirty-one of us living here, remember.'

'Can they not go to school on the mainland?'

'The secondary school children do but there's only three ferries a week at this time of year. Most of them can only come back every other weekend. They stay with relatives and what not.'

I stared at the darkening sky. 'What if there's a storm?'

'Then there's no ferries for a while.' He shrugged. 'We make do.'

Now, David scans the list of names on the printout in his hand, nostrils flaring as he runs a bitten-down fingernail down the page.

'We've got seven. That'll mean two trips in the Land Rover.'

He reaches behind the desk and slides the keys off their hook on the wall. He presses them into my hand. 'There you go then.'

'No.' I dangle them from my thumb and forefinger like I'm holding a dirty nappy or a wet tea towel. 'I can't.'

'What do you mean you can't? You told me on the phone that you can drive.'

'I can but I . . . I was in an accident a few months ago and I ended up in hospital. I haven't been behind the wheel since.'

'Well, you'll need to soon.' He snatches the keys back, shaking his head as he sidesteps from behind the reception desk. 'Because I won't always be available to fetch and carry the guests. I did warn you that you'd have to pull your weight— Oooh.' He presses a hand to the wall, steadying himself.

'David, are you okay?'

He waves me away. 'Just a . . .' He presses a clenched fist to his chest. 'Just a bit of indigestion. Oh God, I thought I was going to be sick there.'

A bead of sweat rolls down his temple then gets lost in his stubble.

'David, are you sure you're okay? I could call someone.' I touch a hand to the phone, prepared to ring the Small Isles medical practice on Eigg. There's no doctor on Rum. One visits once a fortnight, on a Thursday, but today is Saturday. There's a team of first responders though. The nearest is in Kinloch, which is a fifteen-minute drive away, on the other side of the island.

'No, no.' He straightens up, still rubbing at his chest. 'I'm fine. Double-check the rooms are in order while I'm away. Oh, and check on the bread. It'll need to come out of the oven in twenty minutes. Don't just stand there looking vacant, girl. There are jobs to be done.'

Cold air blasts across the lobby as David opens the front door and disappears outside. Dark clouds, heavy with rain, scuttle past the window as trees whip back and forth in the wind. According to the weather forecast this morning we're due a storm soon. That won't go down well with the guests who came here to walk, cycle, fish and deer-stalk but we should still be able to get them to Kinloch Castle and the craft shops. And if the weather's really bad there's a TV in each of the bedrooms and books and magazines in the lounge. And the hotel is well stocked with booze and firewood. I jump as my mobile phone scuttles across the desk, then snatch it up. It's a text from Alex:

I've been thinking about you. I hope you're well and happy and that the fresh island air is helping you sleep.

Chapter 11

Alex

Alex grips the bunch of flowers a little tighter as the doors to the Royal Free Hospital slide open and a cloud of warm, bleach-scented air hits him full in the face. It's a beautiful summer day and his shirt is sticking to his back. He wants to take off his jacket, get some air to his skin, but he's worried about the sweat patches under his arms. He glances at his watch: 2.55 p.m. He didn't want to risk being late, so got here early and spent the last hour sitting in KFC around the corner, sipping a Coke. He'd rather have had a coffee but he was worried about bad breath.

He takes a seat in the waiting area near M&S and rummages around in his pocket for the packet of mints he bought on his way here. He pops one into his mouth then props the flowers between his knees and wipes his palms on his jeans. He knows he's being ridiculous, sweating and worrying like a thirteen-year-old on a first date, but he can't slow his hammering heart or shake the sick feeling in his stomach. He's never done anything like this before, never got so worked up about someone he barely knows. But Becca likes him, she must, or she wouldn't have replied to his Facebook messages, never mind agree to a date. His stomach clenches as his phone vibrates in his pocket. Is she cancelling? Is she, as he sits in the hospital foyer and waits for her to finish her shift, secretly sneaking out of a back entrance so she doesn't have to see him?

He looks at the screen and heaves a sigh of relief. It's just Anna.

Are you trying to be funny?

He frowns, confused, and rereads the message he sent her earlier. It was a nice message, wasn't it? Asking how she was doing.

He looks around to check Becca's not on her way over to him (it wouldn't be done to be caught texting an ex), then taps out a reply.

No. What do you mean?

She replies immediately.

The comment about sleep.

He cringes. Oh, that. If he's honest he's barely given those messages a second thought since she left. He's thought about her, obviously; you don't spend nearly two years with someone and then forget all about them the moment they walk out of the door, but he's enjoyed having the bed to himself and waking up without her lashing out in her sleep, or else staring at him, wide-eyed and frantic from across the room. He did feel guilty though, logging on to Facebook when he returned home to piles of boxes and a flat stripped of Anna's things. Her side of the bed was barely cold and there he was, searching for the nurse who'd cared for her. The attraction was there from the first time they'd laid eyes on each other – an invisible spark that made him catch his breath. He was sure she'd felt it too, from the way her cheeks had coloured and she'd glanced away, at Anna's unconscious form. He tried telling himself that he was misreading her friendliness, that looking after relatives was as much a part of her job as caring for her patients, but Becca genuinely seemed to enjoy their little chats while Anna slept and she checked her vitals. He was terrified when Anna came to and started screaming. Her eyes were glassy and empty, as though she were looking straight through him. And the noise, he'd never heard anything like it. He could have hugged Becca for the professional way she'd taken charge of the situation. He hadn't, of course. Not only would it have been wholly inappropriate, but Anna's return to consciousness also made him feel utterly ashamed of himself. What kind of despicable shitbag was he, perving over the nurse while his girlfriend recovered from a horrific accident? If he was being kind to himself he'd explain it away as a coping mechanism, a way of climbing out of the pit of fear he'd fallen into after her stepdad had rung him, his voice cracking as he broke the news about the accident.

But Anna hadn't died. She'd survived the crash and the operation, and when the surgeon told them both that, other than a scar across her mid-section, there would be no lasting damage, he raised his eyes to the white ward ceiling and said thank you to a God he didn't believe in. He knew it was his duty to look after her when they got home, he owed her that much after two years together, but he could barely drag himself out of bed in the morning after being kept up by Anna half the night, thrashing around fighting night terrors. He felt trapped and unhappy whenever he returned home. It wasn't her fault, he knew that, but he couldn't stop the resentment from rising, threatening to burst the banks of his patience like a river after a storm.

He hadn't expected her to end things. He thought she'd keep plugging away at their relationship, as she always had. But no, she'd had enough too. He was so grateful she'd had the courage to speak up that he'd hugged her, so shocked that he asked her to stay one more night in case there was anything left to be said. There wasn't, other than a strained conversation about a note she'd found on the car. As he'd walked to the tube afterwards he couldn't help but feel relieved that Anna was no longer his responsibility. And guilty for feeling that way.

'Alex?' Someone touches him on the shoulder, making him jump.

He almost doesn't recognise the woman smiling down at him, in her red mac with her long brown hair swept across her forehead and resting on her shoulders. Brown eyeliner is smudged in the corner of her eyes and her lips shine cherry red.

'Becca?' He stands, hastily, and presses an awkward kiss into her cheek. 'You look lovely. I almost didn't recognise you.'

'Thanks a lot.' She laughs and takes the flowers he pushes into the space between their bodies. 'These smell lovely,' she says as she dips her face to the bouquet of white lilies and roses. She looks up at him, her nose still buried in the blooms, and he thinks how lovely her eyes are, how smiley, the most startling cornflower blue.

His stomach tightens as she looks away from him, her blue eyes flitting over the diners who surround them, folded over magazines, coffees and mobile phones, all lost in their own little worlds.

'What is it?' he asks as a frown creases Becca's smooth brow.

'Nothing.' She straightens and shakes her head lightly.

'Are you sure? You looked like you were looking for someone.'

She reaches round for her hair, gathers it in her hand and swings it over her shoulder. She's nervous, Alex thinks with a pang of surprise, as she continues to twist her hair and gaze wonderingly at him. The urge to put an arm around her shoulder and pull her close is almost more than he can bear.

'I was just . . .' She shifts her weight from one leg to the other. 'Things are definitely over between you and Anna, aren't they? She's not suddenly going to jump out at us and call me a boyfriend stealer?'

He laughs, amused by her paranoia. 'No, of course not. Like I told you by text, things were over between us long before her accident.'

'Good.' She slips her arm through his and taps her head against his shoulder. 'Then I've got you all to myself.'

Chapter 12

Anna

Alex hasn't replied to my last text and now I'm regretting snapping at him. He was only wondering how I'm doing but the mention of sleep was like a jab in my chest. I thought, by coming here, that I'd leave what happened behind. But grief can't be cast off like a jacket. It becomes part of you, an invisible film welded to your skin. Some days you feel it, some days you don't, but it's always there.

'Come in, come in, come in.' My boss shepherds five guests into the centre of the lobby, two men, two women and a teenage girl, their coats and bags dappled with rain. He squeezes past them to reach the reception desk and stands next to me.

'Welcome to the Bay View Hotel, the best hotel on Rum,' he says, his hands spread wide in greeting. Several of the guests smile. One, a thin, midde-aged woman wearing a red cagoule and a matching bobble hat, forces a laugh. The Bay View Hotel is the *only* hotel on Rum.

'Anna here will check you all in,' David continues, 'and I'll carry your suitcases and bags up to your rooms.' He turns to the man standing nearest to him – tall, average build, dark hair, wearing a pale blue fleece, dark trousers and walking boots – and reaches for one of the straps of his rucksack. The man lurches backwards as though stung, knocking into the woman in red who's standing directly behind him.

'Sorry, sorry.' His eyes dart wildly behind his frameless glasses as he searches for somewhere, anywhere, he can stand in the small lobby without touching another person. 'I've just . . . I've just . . . I've got important stuff in here and I . . . I—'

'No problem.' David raises a hand in apology, his lips pulled tightly over his teeth in a half grin, half grimace. 'If you don't want me to take your bags that's no problem at all.'

'You can take mine.' The woman in the red cagoule squeezes through the crowd then reverses up against David so her rucksack is almost pressed against him. 'It's killing my shoulders.'

The balding older man who was standing next to her raises his left hand in protest, a gold wedding ring glinting on his finger. 'I told you I'd carry it for you, Mel, but you did insist . . .'

The woman ignores him and gives David the nod to help her remove her rucksack. He glances over at the husband and nods tightly.

'Actually, ladies and gents, I've got to get back to the dock to collect the other guests. If you'd like me to take your bags to your room, just deposit them here and I'll bring them up to you when I get back. Anna will show you where you need to go. When you're settled in do come down to the lounge where there's a complimentary tot of whisky waiting for you. When the other guests arrive I'll explain the itinerary for the week.'

He raises his hands in the air as he sidles out of the hotel, sidestepping like a crab. I see a flash of relief on his face when he reaches the front door.

With David gone the guests turn hesitantly in my direction. First to reach the table are the couple. The woman takes charge, nudging herself in front of the man so she can spread her hands wide on the desk.

'Melanie and Malcolm Ward. And . . . Katie.' She takes off her bobble hat then glances at the small, sallow-skinned teen who looks like she'd rather be anywhere else. 'Also Ward,' she adds.

Unlike the girl in her oversized parka and pink Converse, Melanie and Malcolm are kitted out like serious hikers in branded waterproof jackets with walking poles, well-used walking boots and bulging rucksacks. Malcolm's clutching a map in a plastic slip. Melanie has mousey-brown hair tied back in a ponytail and a fringe that finishes just above her remarkably thick eyebrows and red-rimmed glasses. She looks lithe and strong, as though she could leap up Rum Cuillin without drawing a breath. Her husband is older: mid to late fifties. His grey hair is receding, showing a large expanse of forehead, speckled with liver spots. His brows have thinned so much at the edges that they appear to end mid-pupil, making him look as though he's permanently frowning.

I enter their details into the laptop, then reach round to the hooks and hand Melanie a bunch of keys. 'There you go, you're in rooms 7 and 8. They're at the front of the hotel. If you walk up the stairs to the first floor, the rooms are directly opposite you as you come—'

'At the front?' Melanie glances at Malcolm, who sighs heavily.

'Yes.' I force a smile but it has no effect on the pained expression on Mrs Ward's face.

'So no view of the sea?'

'No, I'm sorry. We allocate the rooms according to the list

the walking tour company sends us and I'm afraid . . .' I shrug. 'W was at the end of—'

'Seriously?' Malcolm Ward says. 'That's how rooms are allocated? In this day and age? I spent my entire childhood being last for everything because my surname is at the end of the alphabet.'

I glance at Katie, who looks like she's wishing the ground would open up and swallow her.

'It took us the best part of two days to get here,' Melanie says. 'We've come all the way from London. Malcolm was ever so excited about having a sea view. Weren't you, Malcolm?'

He nods. 'Gloria at the Hikers' Friend practically guaranteed it.'

'But you'll have an amazing view of the mountains.' I glance at the closed front door, willing David to walk through. When I first arrived he told me, in no uncertain terms, that he was the face of the hotel and he would be the primary point of call for the guests. *I tend to their every need*, he said, then added quickly, *Well, almost.*

Melanie leans into the desk, her pupils small and black behind her glasses. 'Can't you change it?'

'I can't really. All the rooms have been allocated. We are a very small hotel and we can only accommodate eight—'

'I'll swap.' A woman in her mid to late sixties, with white hair cut short at the sides and as curly as a sheep on the top, steps around Melanie. 'If I've got a sea-view room.'

I search her face as she smiles warmly up at me.

'That's very kind of you.' I return her smile. 'What's your name, please?'

'Christine Cuttle.'

'Like the fish?' Malcolm comments.

'Yes.' Christine smiles tightly. She's probably heard that a thousand times.

'Thank you, Mrs Cuttle,' I say. 'I'll just check the—'

'Christine, please.'

'Okay.' I glance down at my screen. 'You're in luck,' I tell Melanie. 'Christine is down to take Room 1, which has a sea view.'

Melanie squeaks with joy and shares a look with her husband. She pauses and glances back at Katie. Her smile slips. 'You won't be next to us any more.'

Katie shrugs. If anything she looks slightly relieved.

'She's only across the corridor,' I say. 'It's a small hotel, all the rooms are very close together.'

Melanie's pinched expression slackens. 'Do you mind, Katie? This is your break as much as ours.'

Again the young girl shrugs. 'I don't care about views.'

'And you're quite sure,' Melanie says to Christine. 'About swapping with us? You really don't have to, you know.'

Oh yes you do, her face and her tightly curled hands say. *You do now you've offered.*

'I'm more than happy,' Christine says. 'I could never grow tired of looking at that landscape. It's so beautiful here.' She returns her gaze to me. 'You're very lucky to live here.'

'Yes,' I nod. 'I am.'

Having dispatched Christine, Melanie and Malcolm to their rooms I beckon the final guest, standing stiffly near the door, to approach reception. He avoids eye contact as he walks towards me, then draws to a halt about a foot from the desk. A loud crack of thunder breaks the silence, making both of us jump. Two seconds later lightning tears through the dark sky beyond the window, and the rain, which has been falling lightly for the last hour or so, suddenly buckets down.

I laugh. 'Welcome to Rum!'

The guest keeps his gaze fixed on the shiny expanse of desk

that separates us. He's younger than the others, I'd guess late thirties. His dark hair is thick and curly but it's receding either side of his widow's peak. Though he's of average build his face is strangely fleshy, all cheeks and chin, with a long, wide nose. His eyes blink rapidly beneath the sheen of his wireless glasses.

'Trevor Morgan.' He holds out a hand and I raise mine to shake it.

'No.' He slaps his palm against the desk. 'The key.'

'Oh.' I glance at the laptop, then twist round to the key rack. 'You're in Room 2, at the back of the hotel. If you go—'

'I'll find it, thank you.' As he takes the key from my outstretched hand his eyes meet mine. He couldn't have looked at me for more than a second, but the uncomfortable tightening in my chest lasts long after he slips silently up the stairs.

Fifteen minutes later, the front door opens and David strides in with a man and a woman around my age, both wearing rucksacks. The man's tall, with a long hipster beard and dark hair, shaved around the sides and long and swept back on the top. The woman's about five foot five with blonde wavy hair, a sturdy physique and a scowl on her face. Her expression couldn't be more different from the man's. He positively beams at me as he crosses the lobby, his heavy boots reverberating on the polished wooden floor.

'Joe Armstrong.' He holds out a hand. 'You must be Anna. David told us all about you.'

I shake his hand and return his smile. 'Has he now?'

'All good!' David calls as he hangs his coat on a hook. 'Well . . . mostly.'

'Fiona Gardiner.' The blonde woman squeezes herself between Joe and the wall.

'Nice to meet you.' I offer her my hand and she shakes it firmly.

'Okay . . . um . . .' I tap at the keyboard. The system is showing that they've been allocated separate rooms. 'Mr Armstrong, it says here that you're in Room 6, which has a view of the mountains. Ms Gardiner, you're in Room 3, with a view of the sea.' I look back up at the guests. 'You're welcome to choose which of those rooms you'd like. I can cancel the second room. You won't be charged twice, there's obviously been some kind of mistake in the booking.'

'I'm sorry?' Joe Armstrong looks at me blankly. 'I'm not sure I understand.'

Fiona gives me an equally confused look and I feel the colour rise in my cheeks. David, heading into the dining room, chuckles as he opens the door. He knows exactly what I've done.

'I thought you were a couple,' I explain. 'I'm sorry. It's just when you walked in together I assumed—'

'Oh, God, no!' Joe laughs heartily then catches the hurt look on Fiona's face and quickly corrects himself. 'Not that . . . Fiona's lovely. I'm sure you'd make a wonderful girlfriend but . . .' He runs a hand over his hair. 'We're not a couple. We don't know each other. We only got chatting on the dock.'

'It's my fault, sorry.' I shoot Fiona an apologetic look. 'I'm new. I haven't worked on reception before.'

'Right.' The edges of her lips rise but it's more of a grimace than a smile. She holds out her hand. 'If I could just have my key?'

'Of course.' I hand her the key to Room 3 and Joe the key to Room 6.

'Can I take that for you?' Joe says as Fiona adjusts her rucksack.

'No, thank you,' she says tightly. 'I'm quite capable of carrying it myself.'

I turn back to the laptop as they plod their way up the stairs, Fiona leading and Joe following behind. As their footsteps reverberate on the guest corridor above my head, David pops his head out of the dining room door.

'Sorry,' he says with a laugh. 'I could have corrected you but where would the fun be in that?' His eyes flick towards the top of the staircase. 'We've got a few interesting personalities this week. I think they're going to keep us on our toes.'

Chapter 13

Steve

Steve turns up the collar of his coat, mentally cursing his lack of umbrella and phone as he passes yet another South London street that doesn't contain a pub called the White Hart. Still, no Google Maps and no GPS is infinitely preferable to the alternative, a stretch inside for murder. So far, other than the burner phone in his desk drawer and one very short phone call, there's no evidence linking him to Jim Thompson, and he intends to keep it that way.

'Where the fuck is – ah!' He stops at the entrance to a small, characterless back street, hurries down it and pushes at the door of the White Hart.

He raises his eyebrows as he walks in. Yet another old boozer that's been transformed into a gastropub with colonial-style ceiling fans, stripped floors, an oak bar and a selection of craft ales. Fucking hipsters, he thinks as he walks up to the bar and orders a pint of Heineken. They like to pretend they're knitting their own houses, serving food on dustbin lids and turning their backs on technology but they're capitalist bastards at heart, just like the rest of us.

He takes a sip of his pint and casually glances around, looking for Jim. It's been a while since he last saw him but he immediately recognises the balding bloke in the thick glasses sitting on his own in the corner, a newspaper spread on the table in front of him. They were unlikely cell mates, back in the day (a *long* way back in the day), Steve in for fraud and Jim in for GBH, but they shared the same scathing sense of humour, a similar background and the same moral code.

'All right?' He sets his beer down on Jim's table and pulls out a chair.

Jim doesn't immediately answer. Instead he carefully folds his newspaper, tucks it into his bag, then sits back and gives Steve a long look.

To his immense irritation Steve's pulse quickens and his heart thuds in his chest. He's got no reason to be scared of Jim. Well, he does, Jim's track record more than speaks for itself, but they're . . . acquaintances, if not exactly friends. And Jim did offer to help.

'All right, dickhead!' Jim says suddenly. Steve ducks, but not quickly enough to avoid Jim's outstretched arm, and his temple throbs from where Jim slaps it.

He shakes his head and smiles convivially, his pulse slowing. 'I think we both know who the dickhead is.'

'Anyway,' Jim reaches for his pint, 'I would ask how you are but I don't think we need to go there, do we?'

Steve shakes his head.

'For what it's worth, I'm sorry. Sounds like Freddy was a good kid. God knows you couldn't shut up about him.'

'Yeah.' Steve keeps his eyes fixed on the other man's face, his small brown eyes like marbles behind his thick-rimmed glasses.

He doesn't want to think about being in prison and getting pictures and letters from six-year-old Freddy asking when he was coming home. Biggest regret of his life that was, missing so much of his son's childhood.

'So.' Jim runs his thumbnail down the side of his nose and scratches it vigorously. 'Nice as it is to see you, Steve, this can't happen again. Us going for a beer I mean.' His eyes flit from Steve's to the barman, wiping down the optics.

Calm on the outside, nervy on the inside, Steve thinks as he takes a sip of his beer. I'm not the only one who doesn't want to go back inside again.

He sets his beer back down, rests his elbows on the table and leans towards his ex-cell mate. 'It's been a while,' he says, 'since we spoke and I just want to check everything's in place. That it's actually going to happen.'

It's the silence he can't stand. The trial was less than six weeks ago and, after the initial furore from the press and the calls and visits from friends and relatives, it's as though it never happened. Like Freddy never died. Everyone's just getting on with their lives like nothing's amiss. But something is very much amiss and Steve seems to be the only one who's noticed it.

'Like I told you,' Jim says, lowering his voice, 'I've got someone in place up north.'

'And . . .' Steve feels a knot form in his stomach. He just wants it over with, quickly, so justice is done, so he can tell his boy he did him right. So he can sleep.

'They're biding their time, building up trust. No point storming in and fucking it up. If they can make it look like an accident, or suicide, they will. Easier all round that way.'

Steve's chest is so tight he can barely get the words out. 'And if they can't?'

Jim shrugs and sits back in his chair. 'What do you care? You want her dead. She'll be dead.'

Chapter 14

Anna

Sunday 3rd June

Day 2 of the storm

Last night I didn't fall asleep until after two. As soon as I shut my eyes Freddy, Peter and Mo's faces emerged from the darkness behind my eyelids, slack-jawed and hollow-eyed. *How can you sleep, Anna, after what you did?* When I opened my eyes their faces remained, swimming through the gloom of my room. *You did this, Anna, you destroyed our lives.* I turned over and pulled the duvet over my head but that made me feel like I was suffocating. I couldn't breathe. *Neither can we, Anna,* said the voices in my head. *Neither can we.*

I'd only been asleep for what felt like five minutes when there was a knock at my door. It was five thirty, David announced. Time to get up. I dragged myself out of bed and stood under the shower, eyes closed as the warm water smoothed my hair to my scalp and ran over my body. Afterwards, wrapped in a towel, I stood at my bedroom window and stared out at the roll of the hills and the huge expanse of sky that seemed to stretch into infinity. Even with rain hammering at the glass and the sky as black as slate it was breathtaking. I'd felt so small and trapped in London, like a mouse in a maze, speeding through tight, crowded streets, zipping underground on the tube, popping back up into the maze. Every day I took the same route to work, back and forth, back and forth, never finding the escape route because I never thought to look for it. Until the crash.

'Excuse me.' Now, a deep rumbling voice from the doorway makes me jolt in my chair.

'You must be Gordon.' I stand up as a giant of a man, with a woolly beard, a waterproof coat that hangs halfway down his thick thighs and a bright blue beanie pulled low over his face, drips his way across the lobby to the reception desk.

'And you must be Anna.' He winks as he shakes my hand. 'Makes a nice change from David's ugly face giein' me the boak of a morning.'

'I thought I heard your dulcet tones, Gordon.' David pokes his head round the dining room door. Compared to Gordon's thick Scottish accent he sounds almost plummy. 'The guests are just finishing up breakfast and they'll be right with you.' He closes the door then opens it again. 'And there's nothing wrong with my face.'

Gordon laughs then crosses his arms over his thick chest and gives me a nod. 'You're not coming with us? The rain's eased up a bit.'

I shake my head. 'I'd love to but I need to clean the rooms, change the linen and prep for lunch.'

'Change the linen and prep for lunch!' He does a terrible impression of an English accent then laughs again. 'I can see why David employed you. You add a bit of class to the aul' place.'

'Really? And there was me thinking he employed me because no one else wanted the job!'

'Well, he cannae speak highly enough of you.'

I feel a swell of pride at the compliment and touch the back of my hand to my cheek. 'No school caretaking for you this week?'

'Naw. It's half term. Though if this weather gets worse again,' he glances back at the narrow window by the front door, 'I might have to go to the school to check on the roof.'

As I open my mouth to ask him another question the door to the dining room opens and Katie appears. She stops in her tracks at the sight of Gordon, then is jolted into the lobby as Melanie gives her a gentle shove.

'You can't just stop walking halfway through a door, Katie. You nearly tripped me up!'

She nods at Gordon and says a cheery hello as she nudges Katie to go up the stairs. Malcolm, following directly behind her, strides over to us.

'I take it you're the guide,' he says, holding out a hand.

'You tek it right.' Gordon wraps Malcolm's hand in his huge paw. 'Gordon Brodie.'

'Malcolm Ward. I don't suppose I could ask you a few questions about the route we'll be taking today, could I? It's just we have a fourteen-year-old with us and . . .'

As he drifts away from reception with Gordon smiling bemusedly down at him, Fiona, Christine and Joe file out of the dining room. They all nod and smile at me then traipse up the stairs. Five minutes later they all troop down again, day packs in their hands and thick jumpers pulled over their clothes. David pops his head round the door as they all put on their hiking boots and waterproof jackets.

He does a head count, then looks over at me and frowns. 'We're missing one.'

'Trevor Morgan. He headed out about half an hour ago.'

Gordon, still flanked by Malcolm, raises his eyebrows. 'Alone?'

I nod.

'Well, I hope he knows what he's doing. It's pretty treacherous out there if you don't know the lay of the land, especially in this weather.'

Malcolm snorts through his nose. 'We're not afraid of a bit of mud and rain, are we, girls?'

Melanie smiles and shakes her head. Katie, the sleeves of her jumper poking through the cuffs of her parka and covering her hands, doesn't look quite so sure.

'Come on then.' Gordon opens the front door and a blast of cold air whooshes into the lobby, making me shiver.

As the guests file out, closing the door behind them, David rests a hand on the door frame and grins at me.

'How are you doing? Desperate to get the next ferry out of here yet?'

'God, no!'

He laughs. 'You might change your mind once you've seen the state of their rooms!' He inclines his head back towards the dining room. 'Let's grab a quick coffee and I'll show you what's where.'

David told me that it wouldn't take me more than twenty minutes tops to strip and change the linen and clean a room but I spent nearly twice that doing the first one – Joe Armstrong's – because my perfectionist streak kicked in and I wanted everything to look just right. But it did feel weird, fitting the spare master key into his bedroom door and letting myself into his private space. I felt like a burglar, standing alone in front of his crumpled, unmade bed, his rucksack resting against a wall, his dirty clothes flung over a chair and his possessions scattered on the bedside table, desk and bathroom shelf. The feeling wore off though and, after I'd stripped and remade the bed, I didn't have any compunction about lifting the books, earplugs and bottle of water on his bedside table and wiping underneath. In the en suite I snatched up his washbag, not looking to check whether it was closed or not, and swore under my breath as something fell out and clattered to the floor. It was a small white box with 'Accu-Check Mobile' written across the top. *Test cassettes only for Accu-Check Mobile blood glucose meter* it said on the bottom of the packaging. I tucked it back into the washbag, desperately hoping I hadn't broken anything and that Joe had spares in his rucksack. There were first aiders on the other side of the island but if any of the guests had serious medical issues we'd have to radio to the mainland for help. I'd tell Joe about my clumsiness, I decided as I finished his room, just as soon as he got back from his hike.

I cleaned Christine Cuttle's room next (very neat, nothing on any of the surfaces apart from a large bottle of Bowmore whisky) then, as I opened the door to Melanie and Malcolm's room, a wave of exhaustion crashed over me and I had to sit down. I hadn't had more than two or three hours' sleep and, after frenetically cleaning two rooms, my energy levels were running on empty. All I wanted to do was drag myself up to my room, lie down on the bed and go to sleep but there was no way I could do that. Not when I was still trying to make a good impression on David. Sighing, I launched myself up and out of the chair, splashed water on my face in the en suite then popped a Pro Plus into my mouth.

That was twenty minutes ago and I've still got two rooms left to service. I swerve past Trevor Morgan's – David told me he'd requested that I skip his room today – and unlock the door to Katie's bedroom. By the time I walk out of Fiona's room my back aches, my head hurts and I'm dripping with sweat. I check my watch – 12.30 p.m. David's been prepping lunch while I've been cleaning but there's no time for me to grab a quick shower; the guests will be back soon. Instead I stuff the mop, bucket and cleaning products back in the storage room at the end of the corridor and run up to my room for a quick sink wash and to change my shirt. As I hurry back down the stairs to reception, the front door opens and a very wet and windswept Christine walks in, closely followed by Melanie, her cheeks flushed pink. I shiver as cold air blasts through the small space.

'Good walk?' I ask as they peel off their coats and hiking boots and deposit them on the hooks and racks.

'Exhausting,' Christine blows, untying her shoelaces.

'Slippy,' Malcolm adds as he squeezes past her, the calves of his trousers spattered with mud.

His bald head shines with sweat under the ceiling spotlight as he whips off his hat. Katie trails into the lobby behind him, the picture of teenage misery. 'I know!' she snaps when Melanie tells her she needs to change her shoes.

Joe and Fiona are the last two to walk through the door, the former shouting a cheery 'See you tomorrow, mate!' to Gordon, who raises a hand from the doorstep then pulls the door closed.

While Joe looks exhilarated, Fiona seems irritable and worried. As the others peel off their wet clothing and stomp up the stairs to grab a shower and get changed she stands with her back to the door, still in her coat and boots, frowning down at her mobile phone.

'Who's ready for lunch?' David says, suddenly appearing in the doorway to the dining room like the shopkeeper in *Mr Benn*. A warm, yeasty smell wafts out of the room behind him, filling the lobby. 'We've got soup, freshly baked bread, jacket potatoes, cheese, ham, quiche, salad.'

There are nods of approval and murmurs of appreciation

from the guests ascending the stairs. As Joe passes the reception desk, I raise a hand to get his attention. As I do so, Fiona calls out David's name and crosses the lobby, waving her phone at him.

'Yep.' Joe flashes me a wide smile and passes a hand over his beard, still wet from the rain.

'I cleaned your room earlier,' I start, 'and I'm afraid there was a bit of an—'

'I was told by the booking agent that there's mobile reception on Rum,' Fiona says to David. He has his back to me but I can tell from the hunch of his shoulders that he doesn't like her tone of voice.

'I dropped something,' I say, looking back at Joe, who's patiently waiting for me to continue, 'as I was cleaning your bathroom.'

'I'm waiting to hear from someone—' Fiona senses me watching. It's a split-second glance but it's enough to make her lower her voice so I can no longer hear.

'Sorry.' I look back at Joe.

He shakes his head. 'She didn't stop whining about the fact she couldn't get a signal for most of the hike. Why she bothered to bring her phone with her I have no idea. She spent more time looking at it than she did at the view.'

'There was some signal this morning.' I reach into my back pocket for my own phone then tuck it away again when I see the 'Emergency Calls Only' message. 'But not now it seems.'

'Probably the weather,' Joe says. 'It didn't stop raining the whole time we were out there. I feel like I'm half fish now.'

I laugh. 'Sorry, I'm keeping you from getting changed, I'll get to the point. I dropped something of yours on the bathroom floor by mistake, a blood-sugar testing kit or something. It fell out of your washbag. I was worried it might be broken.'

'Was it the device or the cassettes?'

'The . . .' I rack my brain to remember what I read on the box but tiredness has clouded my brain. 'The cassettes, I think.'

'They'll be fine.' His frown fades and he smiles. 'No need to worry.'

'Oh, good.'

He moves to climb the stairs then pauses and looks back at me. His eyes linger on mine and there's something in the intensity of his gaze that makes my stomach twist in a way it hasn't since I first laid eyes on Alex at a crowded house party. The room stills. Fiona and David's voices fade away and the wind stops howling. I couldn't look away, even if I wanted to.

'I guess I'll see you in a bit,' Joe says, breaking the spell.

For a second I don't know where I am or what we're talking about.

'For lunch.' He gestures at the window. 'Although if this weather gets any worse we might be seeing more of each other than we thought.' He laughs and puts on a voice like a film voice-over artist. 'And when the storm struck there was no escape . . .'

I had hoped that the exhaustion all the guests felt after their walk earlier would continue on to the evening and they'd all retreat to their rooms again. But no, after dinner, everyone apart from Trevor and Katie decided to retire to the lounge to have a few drinks. As it was David's evening off that meant I had to stay on reception, fulfilling drinks orders, answering queries and dealing with issues until well after eleven. At a little after midnight, after tidying the lounge, locking up and checking everything was in order, I dragged myself up the two flights of stairs to bed. Somehow I pulled off my clothes, changed into my pyjamas, washed my face and cleaned my teeth. Then, with the tiny bit of energy I had left, I dropped onto my bed, pulled the duvet up around my shoulders and closed my eyes.

That was nearly two hours ago.

I don't understand how my brain can go from 'I'm about to black out with tiredness' to 'I did lock the front door, didn't I?' and 'I must remember to tell David about Fiona's lamp that isn't working' to 'Have I been misreading the situation or is Joe interested in me?' And then it's one long dark swirl into 'How can you even think about flirting with Joe when Freddy and Peter are dead?'

Guilt is such a furtive emotion. It lurks in the shadows of the mind, waiting for the chance to steal the limelight from happiness, contentment and peace, growing ever more powerful until it pushes them completely offstage. During the day I'm too busy to think about anything other than what needs to be done. My feelings about the crash curl up and sleep while the sun is up but, as soon the world around me slows and quietens, they yawn and stretch then bound around my brain, clamouring to be heard.

Sighing, I get out of bed. There's no point even pretending to sleep. I may as well go downstairs and do some of the jobs I had planned for tomorrow.

As I pull on my dressing gown there is a flash of lightning, visible through the gaps in the curtains. Thunder has been rumbling for hours and the rain that's been falling steadily all day is now hurling itself out of the sky. I cross the room and open my door, stepping lightly. I don't want to wake David. He looked shattered at dinner time and it wouldn't do for us both to be exhausted tomorrow. I pad quietly down the stairs, pausing in the stairwell by the guest corridor to listen. There's the faint rumble of snoring but no other noise. I continue down the stairs to reception, running my hand lightly over the polished wooden banister as I move further away from the orange glow of the emergency lighting and the hotel grows darker. I keep my gaze fixed forwards, blinking into the gloom. Once I'm at the bottom of the stairs there's a light switch near the door that leads into the lounge and—

I freeze as a beam of light swings across the lobby, from left to right and back again, then disappears.

'Hello?' My voice is little more than a whisper.

There's no reply but I hear the low creak of drawers being opened and closed. Someone is sitting in my seat behind reception, rummaging through the drawers of the desk, using a mobile phone torch as a light.

'Hello?'

I cover my eyes with my arm as the light swings in my direction.

'Oh God, Anna. You scared me!'

'Could you . . .' I wave my free hand around. 'I can't see a thing.'

'Sorry, yes, of course.'

There's a click of a light switch being pressed and I lower my arm to see Fiona standing at the bottom of the stairs, her blonde hair spread over her shoulders, her face make-up free.

'What's going on?'

'Sorry.' She shoots me an apologetic look. 'I woke up with the most terrible period pain and I didn't pack any painkillers. I didn't want to wake anyone so I came down here. I thought there might be a first aid kit or something in reception.'

'There is, but there aren't any painkillers in it.' Nothing's out of place on the desk. If she looked in the green first aid kit in the bottom drawer she's already put it away.

'Yeah.' She laughs softly. 'I know that now.'

'You should have woken me. In fact,' I gesture up the stairs, 'I can get you some now if you want.'

'Do you mind?' She presses a hand to her belly. 'I'd really appreciate it.'

'No problem at all.'

She doesn't say a word until we reach the stairwell to the guest corridor, then she clears her throat and says, 'You and Joe seem to be getting on well.'

Her random comment throws me for a second.

'All the guests are lovely,' I say vaguely.

Fiona's breath catches in her throat, as though she's got something to add, but she doesn't say another word until we reach my room and I hand her two ibuprofen.

'Thanks,' she says without meeting my eyes, then turns on her heel and goes.

In Memoriam

In Memoriam

In loving memory of Mavis Mascull,
1943–2014.

Reunited with her dearest Edward
'Ted' Mascull.
Sweet is her memory, dear is her name, deep in our
hearts she will always remain.

It's curious how deceptive appearances can be and yet we still label people based on what we see, hear and assume. What is it they say? It only takes seven seconds to make a first impression. We'd like to think we don't judge others but we do. Of course we do. Everyone does. It makes life less confusing to fit people into neatly labelled boxes.

So let's see. What boxes can we slot the inhabitants of the Bay View Hotel into?

– the owner
– the receptionist

– the couple
– the teenager
– the hipster
– the single girl
– the pensioner
– the loner

Did you spot your label in there, Anna? Of course you did! You're the receptionist. Congratulations. You're playing your role to a tee – sitting behind the desk, tapping away busily at the laptop, smiling at the guests as they mill around the lobby. You're courteous, well turned out and eager to help. It's astonishing really, how well you pretend to be something you're not.

Have you considered that everyone else might be doing the same thing too?

Chapter 15

Anna

Monday 4th June

Day 3 of the storm

There's a collective moan from the guests when David walks into the dining room and announces that, due to the weather, today's hike has been cancelled.

Malcolm pushes his fried breakfast away from him and moves to stand up. 'Is Gordon still out there?' He inclines his head towards the lobby. 'I'd like a word if so.'

David shakes his head. 'Afraid not. He's had to drive over to the school. Lightning struck it in the night and he needs to check for damage.'

I raise my eyebrows but I can't say I'm surprised. The view of the storm from my bedroom window last night was absolutely breathtaking. Lightning ripped through the black sky like scissors tearing through cloth and each boom of thunder made my heart jump in my chest.

'We'll go out anyway,' Malcolm says now. 'Trevor's already headed out.'

Melanie, who's trying and failing to convince Katie to eat her last piece of toast, looks up at her husband. 'There's no way I'm taking Katie out in that. She'd get blown off a cliff.'

'So we leave her behind. As long as she's got her phone she's happy.'

Katie rolls her eyes and mutters something under her breath. I can only assume from the look on her face that it's about the mobile phone signal. It still hasn't reappeared, although the Wi-Fi's still going strong.

'I'm not leaving her here on her own,' Melanie says. 'She's fourteen.'

Malcolm shrugs. 'Fair enough. I'll go on my own if you—'

'Normally,' David interjects, 'I'd suggest a trip to the castle or the craft shops but I had a call earlier to say they'll be closed today because of the weather.'

Christine sits back in her chair, sighing heavily as she crosses her arms over her chest. 'So we're stuck in the hotel.'

'There's a selection of board games in the lounge.' I can hear the forced cheeriness in David's voice. 'And playing cards, chess, backgammon. We have a selection of DVDs you can borrow if you'd like to watch a film in your room. And of course there are plenty of books.'

'Someone told me a tree came down last night and took out one of the sheds.' Joe, who's spent most of the conversation staring out of the window, turns to look at David. 'I've done a bit of general labouring. I'm happy to help.'

'Aye.' David nods. 'We took a fair bit of damage in the night, especially in the garden. A few roof tiles have come loose too.

You're very welcome to help but do be careful. I'm not sure my insurance covers storm damage to guests.'

Joe glances at me. 'Maybe Anna can show me what needs doing.'

'But I've got to—'

'No, no,' David says, laying a heavy hand on my shoulder. 'You show Mr Armstrong the garden. I'll do the dishwasher. You can do the rooms when you come back.'

As he turns to go back into the kitchen a small smile plucks at his lips.

As we step out of the front door I turn to say something to Joe but it's so windy I can barely breathe, never mind speak. Instead I gesture for him to follow me. As we reach the corner I pause and point across the grounds and the rolling fields to the cliff top and the sea beyond it. It looks like a series of rolling mountains, granite grey, with foam cutting through like white quartz veins.

'It's amazing!' Joe shouts, holding a hand over his eyes to shield his face from the sleeting rain. 'I've never seen anything like it!'

'Makes you feel alive, doesn't it?'

He shakes his head in awe. 'And you get to live here!'

He's right of course. I am ridiculously lucky to live here. Even on a day like this when I can barely take one step in front of the other without being shoved by the wind against the hard brick of the hotel.

'The power of the sea,' Joe breathes, utterly transfixed. 'It's beautiful and terrifying, all at the same time.'

I subtly watch him as he continues to stare out to sea. He looks like some kind of Hipster Action Hero with his tight black jeans, his hands in his pockets, the hood of his khaki coat up over his head and his damp beard poking out. All he needs is a craft ale in one hand and the image would be complete. It's not a look I've ever found particularly attractive but there's something about Joe that I like. He's not pretentious for one. I've overheard him talking to several of the other guests and he's always friendly and interested in both them and their lives. Then there's the fact that, beneath his bushy brows, he's got ridiculously sexy eyes.

Joe glances as me, as though sensing me watching, and I look away, embarrassed at being caught.

'Why'd you leave?' he asks.

'Sorry?'

'London, that's where you're from, isn't it?'

'Um . . . I'm actually from Reading but I lived in London for five years.'

He waits for me to continue. There's an intensity behind his gaze that makes me feel, not uncomfortable exactly, but as though he's looking into me, rather than at me.

'I . . . um . . . I was in a car accident. It made me re-evaluate what I want from life.'

He raises his eyebrows, not in surprise but recognition as though I just said something he can relate to.

'You?' I venture.

He shrugs. 'I just fancied some fresh air.'

That makes us both laugh and I gesture for him to follow me to the back of the hotel.

'Over there!' I shout, pointing across the garden where a willow is lying across what used to be the gardening shed. The brick walls have survived but there's not much left of the roof.

I turn to check if Joe's seen it too, but as I twist to look at him he lunges at me, arms outstretched, and shoves me hard. There's a loud cracking sound, like a plate being thrown at the ground, and all the air is knocked from my lungs as I fall onto the wet grass and Joe lands on top of me. I lie still, too stunned to speak, then he rolls away and stares up at the sky, arms spread wide.

'Jesus Christ,' he breathes as he twists onto his side to look at me. 'Are you okay?'

I stare at him in shock. 'What the fuck? Why would you—'

I'm silenced by his outstretched arm. He's pointing at the path that runs around the house. It's strewn with the sharp shards of broken roof tiles, dozens and dozens of them.

'They came down like a guillotine!' he says. 'Just slid straight off the roof. I wouldn't have spotted them if I'd been standing right next to you. We'd have both been brained.'

'Thank you.' I scramble to my feet, my jeans, hands and the side of my face caked in mud. 'You . . . God . . . you probably just saved my life.'

He shrugs good-naturedly. 'You'd have done the same for me. You still up for going to check out that tree or do you want to go back inside?'

There wasn't anything we could do about the tree or the shed. The tree was too wet and heavy to lift and Joe figured we'd only cause more damage to the brickwork if we tried to drag it off. There was no way of getting into the shed to save the lawnmower, strimmer, hedge trimmer and other electrical equipment from the rain, so we abandoned it and went back to the house. While Joe went to tell David the bad news I headed up to my room to shower. I was just about to come back down the staff stairs when I heard voices from the stairwell next to the guest corridor. Malcolm and Melanie Ward were having a conversation just below me. I paused, out of sight, not wanting to interrupt.

'She's completely shut down,' I heard Melanie say.

'It's understandable. She's been through a lot.'

'I've tried to talk to her about it but she changes the subject each time I mention her dad.'

Dad? I'd assumed Malcolm was Katie's father.

'She misses him. Just give her time.'

'Yes, but . . .' Melanie fell silent as I shifted my weight from one leg to the other and the floorboard creaked in protest.

Malcolm cleared his throat. 'Let's go and see where she is.'

I waited at the top of the stairs until their footsteps receded, then went down to the guest floor and headed for the cleaning cupboard at the end of the corridor. Whatever was going on with Melanie, Malcolm and Katie, I told myself as I pulled out the mop and bucket, it wasn't my concern. 'It's none of my business,' I reminded myself as I unlocked the couple's room and stared around the small space at their things.

The lobby is empty as I drag the black sacks of rubbish down the stairs but I can hear the guests chatting and laughing in the lounge and smell the warm, hearty scent of David's steak and ale stew drifting through the hotel. With all the rooms apart from Trevor's cleaned and changed, I hang the spare master key on the rack behind reception then haul the rubbish out of the front door and round to the back of the hotel where the bins are kept. I give the back wall a wide berth, keeping my eyes fixed on the roof. It's scary, thinking what could have happened if Joe hadn't pushed me out of the way.

I stifle a yawn as I throw the black sacks into the bin. I need to get more sleep. David hasn't picked up on my tiredness yet but it's only a matter of time. I'm going to start making mistakes if I'm not careful. Already today, when I was servicing the rooms, I couldn't remember if I'd changed Fiona's bed or not. It wasn't until I pulled back the duvet and saw how tightly the sheet had been tucked in that I realised I had.

I'll get a coffee, then have a power nap after lunch, I tell myself as I walk back to the front of the hotel. But the moment I open the door David, standing by the reception desk with Trevor Morgan, calls my name.

'Could I have a quick word, Anna?'

'Sure.' My stomach tightens as I approach the desk. David's not smiling. Neither is Trevor. I gesture at my sopping wet coat. 'I'll just get out of my wet things.'

'You serviced the rooms this morning, didn't you?' David says as I peel off my coat and hang it on the peg then slip my feet out of my boots and pull on my work shoes.

'Yes. I finished the last one about . . .' I glance at my watch. 'Twenty minutes ago. Is there a problem?'

'You went into my room,' Trevor says. 'And I told David that I didn't want it cleaned.' His hair is slicked back and his fleece is a darker shade of blue on the shoulders, as though the rain soaked through his coat. I didn't hear him come back from his walk. He must have returned while I was round the back, doing the bins.

I look from Trevor, his small, beady eyes dark and intense behind his glasses, to David. He flashes his eyebrows at me; a gesture of sympathy rather than surprise. He thinks Trevor's making a fuss about nothing.

'I didn't clean your room,' I say. 'I didn't even go in.'

'Then who folded up my towels?'

'I'm sorry?'

'Someone came into my room and folded up the towels I left hanging over the shower rail.'

'I don't know how that happened but it wasn't me. As I said, I didn't go into your room.'

David shrugs his shoulders as though to say it wasn't him either.

'You took something of mine.' Trevor holds a hand out towards me. 'I'd like it back.'

'Everything okay out here?' Christine Cuttle pokes her head out of the lounge, her expression pure nosiness. 'I heard raised voices and wondered if—'

'Everything's fine, Christine. Thank you.' David gestures for her to go back inside.

No one says a word until the lounge door clicks closed. Then I look back at Trevor.

'What's been taken from your room?'

'Something of mine. From my bedside table.'

'What was it?'

'You know what it was.'

'I really don't.' I look at David again, horrified that I've been accused of stealing. 'I swear to God, I haven't been in your room or taken anything.'

'As I said to you earlier, Mr Morgan,' David says, his tone decidedly more calm and measured than mine, 'perhaps whatever you've lost has slipped down the side of the bed. If you could tell us what it is that's gone missing maybe we could help you look.'

Trevor glares at him, his eyes dark, angry slits in his thick, doughy face. 'I don't want anyone in my room. Not you, not her, not anyone. What I want is for my belongings to be returned.'

I feel sick with worry. Stealing from guests is a sackable offence and I'm on a three-month probation. If David takes Trevor seriously I could be on the next ferry home.

'I told you,' I start. 'I haven't been in your—'

David stops me with a sharp wave of his hand. When he touches his fingers to his lips I swallow down my protest and stare at the floor.

'I'm sorry some of your belongings have gone missing, Mr Morgan,' David says steadily, 'but I have no reason to believe Anna ignored my request not to enter your room. I also don't believe that she took your belongings. Anna's new but I trust her and if she says she didn't take your things then I take her at her word.'

All the tension in my chest vanishes and I breathe out steadily. He believes me. *Thank God*. I glance up at Trevor. He's staring down at David, his eyes steely and cold. David doesn't look away. Instead he forces a smile and says, 'If there's anything else I can help you with, do please let me know. Otherwise I'll see you in the dining room for lunch. It'll be served in half an hour.'

Trevor continues to stare at him for a few more beats, then he turns on his heel and stomps up the stairs.

'Anna,' David says as Trevor's footsteps fade away, and it's all I can do not to throw my arms around him and kiss him on his rough, red cheek.

Instead I say, 'I genuinely didn't go into his room.'

'I know.' He beckons me closer and lowers his voice. 'But I think someone else might have done.'

Chapter 16

Mohammed

Mohammed stares at the ceiling and counts the number of tiles as the doctor talks to his parents. It's the same speech Dr Newman delivered to him a couple of days earlier. The words wash over him: T6 incomplete injury, damage to the thoracic nerves in the back, a total hospital stay of three to nine months, hard to say exactly how long, possibly up to two years until full potential is reached, suspected paraplegia, a form of paralysis in which function is substantially impeded from the waist down.

He hears his mother's small gasp of pain and the low rumble of his father's voice as he throws question after question at the doctor. A single tear dribbles from the corner of Mohammed's eye.

'It's okay, darling.' His mother bends over him and, using the sleeve of her cardigan, gently dabs at his face.

He feels like a child again. No, not a child. A child would be able to run away and hide. He feels like an amoeba or a living corpse. A brain trapped in a body that won't respond no matter how much he screams at it to do his bidding.

The hands are the worst. Not his, theirs, the nurses', the doctors', his parents'. He was never that keen on being touched before the accident; he shied away from hugs and cringed at arm squeezes, handshakes and backslaps. Now, he's forever being touched or wiped or moved or stroked and he can't do anything about it. He has to lie there and take it because, apparently, he's supposed to be grateful that he's alive. Grateful? Another tear escapes and winds its way into his hairline. He's going to be in a wheelchair for the rest of his life. He's never going to walk or run or cycle or ski ever again.

'Please don't cry, Mo.' His mother wipes the tear away, then moves her hand to his hair. She strokes and strokes and strokes it as though he's a dog but he doesn't object because he knows the simple action is comforting her, at least.

'Where's Gran?' he asks.

His grandmother was the first of his family to see him after the accident, the first face to peer into his that didn't belong to a nurse, doctor or police officer. Her face gave him more comfort than the powerful drugs that had been pumped into his veins and plunged into his muscles. His grandmother was the rock he could cling to. She was the exact opposite to his mother – solid rather than neurotic, stable rather than emotional, and reliable rather than flighty. He'd never seen his gran cry, not once. Not when Granddad had died, not when she'd battled illness and certainly not that day, when her eyes searched his and she asked him how he felt. He knew he could tell his grandmother the truth and she wouldn't judge him and she wouldn't flinch.

'I'm angry,' he told her. 'I'm so angry I could scream.'

'That's normal,' she said. 'That's okay.'

'Is it?' he bit back. 'Do you know what I told the doctor

when he said that Freddy was dead? I said I was envious. That I wished I was dead too.'

'Do you still feel that way?' His grandmother's cool, steady eyes searched his.

'No.'

Her face softened just the tiniest bit and her hands, gathered tightly in her lap, unknotted.

'Your gran couldn't be here today,' his mother says now. 'But she sends her love. So does Tim. He said to take all the time you need. He did tell me that Anna's not going back . . .' His mother presses a hand to her mouth, smothering the second half of her sentence. She's said something she shouldn't.

'Please,' Mo says. 'I told you not to talk about her.'

Why did everyone want him to talk about Anna all the time? It's like she's haunting him. No, *taunting* him. She was the only one to walk away from the accident unscathed. Literally, *walk away*.

Logically he knows that the crash wasn't her fault, that there was no way she could have known a lorry would career across the motorway and smash into the car she was driving, but he doesn't want to see the sorrow in her eyes as she walks up to his bedside and tells him how very sorry she is. And he doesn't want her sympathy. He doesn't want anyone's sympathy. He wants to close his eyes and wake up at home, in his bed, back in his normal life. But sleep is more torturous than consciousness. Sleep is hope. Cruel, cruel hope. He's lost count of the number of dreams he's had where a doctor tells him they've made a mistake, there's nothing wrong with his spine and he's free to go home. So now he fights sleep, not because he can't cope with the dreams but because it hurts too much to wake up.

Chapter 17

Anna

Tuesday 5th June

Day 4 of the storm

'Any sign of the key?' I ask David as we carry armfuls of plates, bowls and cutlery from the kitchen into the dining room. It's breakfast time, the guests' fourth day on Rum, and lightning is slashing through the dark sky beyond the windowpanes. When I opened the front door earlier the wind nearly sucked me straight out of the hotel. Anyone who was hoping to go hiking today is going to be sorely disappointed.

'Nope.' David shakes his head. 'You did go through all your pockets, didn't you?'

'I told you, I put it back on the board.'

Yesterday lunchtime, after Trevor had stomped back up the stairs to his room, David asked me where the spare master key was. He jangled his keyring at me, the one he wears on a chain that clips to his trouser loops. It holds all the master keys for the hotel. The spares, including the one I'd used to open all the guest bedrooms, are kept behind reception.

'It's on the . . .' I pointed at the board. There was no key on the top left hook.

'But I'm sure I . . .' I darted behind the desk and checked the carpet, the desk and the drawers. 'I definitely put it back, David. I hung it up before I took the rubbish out.'

'You didn't accidentally drop it into the bins?'

'No, I'm sure I didn't.'

But I wasn't completely sure. If I'd forgotten whether I'd changed Fiona's bed maybe I'd forgotten where I'd put the master key too. Lack of sleep hadn't just robbed my body of energy, now it was playing tricks with my brain. As David watched I checked the pockets of my work trousers and my coat. He waited patiently at reception while I checked both the cleaning cupboard and the linen cupboard and didn't once criticise or pass comment when I pulled on my outdoor gear and headed out to the bins. When I returned, empty-handed and smelling faintly of rotten food, he shrugged.

'I'm sure it'll turn up.'

'But what if one of the guests took it and let themselves into Trevor's room?' I said, keeping my voice low as Joe popped out of the lounge, nodding at us as he crossed the lobby and opened the toilet door.

For the first time that day David looked genuinely stressed. 'Then they can let themselves into every room in this hotel.'

He's still worried now, I can tell by the hunch of his shoulders and the tight, pained expression that crosses his face whenever he thinks I'm not watching. I swiftly change the subject.

'Did you know,' I place the plates and bowls I've been carrying on the sideboard, 'that the storm would be this bad?'

He gives me a sideways glance as he does the same. 'Of course I knew. You can't live on Rum and not check the weather regularly. But business is business. If I cancelled a booking every time there was a storm I'd have to sell up and get out within a year. It'll pass by the time they're due to get their ferry back and if they're lucky they might get a day or two of hiking, if they don't mind a bit of mud.'

'You know the Wi-Fi's down, don't you?'

He sighs. 'Aye. The guest with the wife . . . the bald bloke . . . what's his name?'

'Malcolm Ward?'

'That's the one. He came down to reception just before breakfast to tell me. His wife was watching a programme on iPlayer when it suddenly stopped streaming.' He shrugs. 'You just wait for the carnage when they all realise they've got no way of contacting their families.'

'But we've still got the landline, right?'

'For now.'

'Doesn't it worry you? The thought of being cut off from the world like that?'

'Isn't that why people come to Rum? For the most part? To get away from all that crap. Isn't that why you're here?'

'Pretty much, yeah,' I lie.

'There you go then. Anyway, Gordon down in the cottage has a satellite phone if we get really stuck. Not that I've heard from him today.' He reaches into the sideboard and takes out the plastic containers full of cornflakes, Rice Krispies and muesli, raising his eyebrows as he places them on the top. 'Did you fill these up already?'

'Yes, last night.' I don't mention that it was at one o'clock in the morning because I couldn't sleep.

'Well done.' He gives me an approving nod then gestures towards the kitchen with his thumb. 'Don't rest on your laurels, girl, there's bread that needs to come out of the oven.'

The first guest appears in the doorway of the dining room at 7 a.m. on the dot. I'm not surprised that it's Trevor. He doesn't say a word to me or David; instead he weaves his way through the tables and takes a seat nearest the window.

'You take his order,' David says, smoothing his apron over his belly. 'I'll get to the kitchen.' He laughs. 'Where I belong.'

Ignoring the strange, strained silence his disappearance leaves behind, I reach into my pinny for my notebook and pen and approach Trevor.

'Good morning.'

He doesn't look up.

'What can I get you?'

'Sausages, bacon and a fried egg. No beans, no tomatoes, no black pudding, no toast.'

'Okay.' I write it down. 'And what can I get you to drink?'

'Coffee.'

Would it hurt you to say please? I *nearly* say it but catch myself just in time.

'Great. I'll bring it over in a second.'

As I turn, all the other guests, apart from Katie, appear in the doorway to the dining room. Joe heads for the table he sat at yesterday while Christine, Malcolm, Melanie and Fiona chat animatedly. I wait for a gap in the conversation, then ask if they'd like individual tables or to sit together. Melanie glances back into the lobby.

'Or would you like to wait for Katie?' I add.

She shakes her head. 'She said she wanted a lie-in today. She might not be down until ten.'

I smile but inwardly I cringe. David won't be pleased when I tell him. He'll have to keep the kitchen open for another few hours, just for one person. He's been making noises all morning about checking the generator in the basement, just in case we lose power.

'No worries. So, table for four then or . . .'

Christine looks at the other three, who nod in approval. 'Table for four.'

'I don't think this storm is going to lift,' Fiona says as they follow me across the room. 'Before Google went down the Met Office report said it's only going to get worse.'

'Seriously?' Malcolm says. 'I'm not sure how many more rounds of Gin Rummy I can play without going stark raving mental.'

'It is a disappointment,' Christine says as she sits down and tucks in her chair. 'I was really hoping to go to the castle today. Anna, I don't suppose you or David could take a few of us to the castle in the Land Rover?'

'I'll ask him for you.'

When I walk back into the kitchen David is wiping the edges of a plate with a dishcloth; two sausages, three rashers of bacon and an egg sit awkwardly in the middle.

'There you go.' He hands it to me then wipes the back of his hand across his damp brow.

'Are you okay?'

He shakes his head. 'It's boiling in here. I think the heating might be screwed. Have any of the guests complained?'

A single bead of sweat rolls down the side of his face. It's warm in the kitchen, it always is, but it's no warmer than normal. And the dining room's actually a little cold.

'David, I think maybe you should get yourself a glass of water and have a sit-down for a bit. I can take over here.'

'No, no.' He waves me away. 'You need to look after the guests. I'm fine. Probably got a cold coming or something. Hope it's not the bloody flu.'

*

David appears in the doorway to the kitchen as I head towards him with Trevor's empty plate. Our first breakfast guest left the dining room about ten minutes ago. When the other guests called 'good morning' as he crossed the dining room, he nodded and raised a hand but said nothing.

'David,' I say. 'Would you like me to—'

'Hang on.' He holds up a hand, lips moving as he does a quick head count. 'We're missing one.'

'Katie Ward. Her mum said she's having a lie-in. She should be down for ten o'clock.'

David glances at his watch and groans. It's only seven thirty-five.

'I'm happy to make her breakfast when she comes down,' I say. 'I can do a fry-up no problem.'

'Okay, but I'll have to show you how to use the dishwasher.' He pushes at the swing door, then pauses and grips the door frame instead. His brow and upper lip are glistening with sweat.

'David? Are you all right?'

He presses a hand to his chest and stares at me with wide, frightened eyes. 'I can't . . .'

'Sit down.' I grab a chair from the nearest table and drag it along the carpet but, before I can reach him, he crumples to the floor.

'David? DAVID!' I drop to my knees, vaguely aware of the guests rushing across the room towards us, and reach for David's wrist. His eyes are closed and his chest is still. 'Call an ambulance!'

I hear a shout, footsteps pounding the wooden floor in the lobby, and then I'm surrounded by people pressing against me, all talking at once.

'What happened?'

'Did he faint?'

'Is it a heart attack?'

'Is he breathing?'

'Please!' I find my voice. 'Please be quiet.' I slide my fingers back and forth over David's wrist. I can't find a pulse but I don't know if that's because my own heartbeat is pounding in my ears, I'm doing it incorrectly . . . or there isn't one.

Behind me the guests are arguing about who's the most experienced at giving CPR.

'The landline's not working,' Joe says, appearing by David's head, out of breath with panic etched across his face. 'I tried pressing nine but there's no dialling tone. And my mobile hasn't got a signal. We need to find Gordon.'

'I can't leave David.'

'Anna, it's okay,' Malcolm says. 'We've got this.'

He hauls me off the ground and onto my feet as Christine leans over David's lifeless body and pulls on one of his shoulders so he slumps onto his back. 'Some space!' she shouts as she interlocks her fingers. 'Please, everyone, give me some space!'

I stare at the scene before me as though in a dream. It doesn't feel real.

'Anna?' Joe shakes me by the shoulder and peers into my face. 'Anna, we need to find Gordon. We need to get David an ambulance. NOW.'

As he drags me across the dining room all I can hear is the rhythmic sound of Christine pumping David's chest.

Chapter 18

Trevor

The ground squelches under the thick soles of Trevor Morgan's hiking boots, spraying his trousers with mud with every step. He shivers beneath his thick Gore-Tex jacket and looks back at the Bay View Hotel. He'd only just set off on his morning walk and was crossing the driveway when he saw the commotion in the dining room out of the corner of his eye. He paused by the window, watching as the guests jostled around the kitchen door. It wasn't until they moved away that he noticed the hotel owner lying on the floor with the older lady kneeling beside him, her hands clenched over his chest, her white head bobbing up and down.

He continued to watch as the dining room door was pulled closed from the lobby and Christine – he vaguely remembered her telling him her name – stopped pounding the hotel owner's body and instead took his hand in one of hers. Trevor couldn't see her face but he saw her lean over him and tenderly stroke the hair from his brow. Trevor turned sharply away, hands shaking as he pressed them over his eyes. When he looked back the woman had shifted her weight and was stroking her hand from the hotel owner's forehead to the bridge of his nose. She was closing his eyes.

The man was dead then.

Trevor had looked death in the face dozens of times. Mostly men, but he'd watched women die too. He'd cried the first time it had happened, drank himself into a stupor to numb the pain, barely slept for days. The second time was easier, but only marginally. The last time he'd seen a man die he'd barely blinked.

But he did when Christine whipped round, sensing him watching. Her eyes fixed on his and he hurried away.

He'd just turned left at the edge of the hotel and was heading towards the cliff top when he heard footsteps crunching on gravel and two figures, one male and one female, hightailed it down the drive. He continued to watch them until they were too small to see clearly, then raised his binoculars. They seemed to be heading towards the small cottage at the foot of the hill. He'd already checked it out the day before. Unoccupied. The owner hadn't returned. If the running couple thought there was any chance of an ambulance, or a hearse, crossing the flooded road they were very much mistaken. The Bay View Hotel was completely isolated from the rest of the world, something that made him very happy indeed.

Chapter 19

Anna

'Gordon?' I pound the door of the cottage with both fists as Joe runs to the nearest window, cups his hands around his face and peers inside. The rain has dissolved the feeling of shock and disbelief at seeing David collapse in the dining room. Now all I feel is cold-blooded terror.

'Hello? Is there anybody in there?'

Joe disappears around the side of the cottage, then reappears next to me seconds later. His dark hair lies flat on his forehead and rain drips off his nose and clings to the wiry strands of his beard. We couldn't have run for more than ten minutes but the rain has soaked through my jacket, jumper and T-shirt and is plucking at my skin with icy fingers.

Joe says something but the wind whisks his voice away and I shake my head.

'There's no one in there,' he shouts, thumping the door with a fist. 'All the lights are off. And there's no car.' He extends an arm towards the small rectangle of gravel, striped with dark tyre marks, to the side of the cottage. 'He can't have come back from the school yesterday.'

'Try your phone again,' I shout back.

He shakes his head. 'No signal.'

'Shit.' I thump both fists on the door then rest my head on the wet wood. I don't know what to do. I tried to get the land-line behind reception to work but the phone lines must have gone down in the storm. Everyone tried their mobiles – Malcolm even ran upstairs to wake Katie to try hers – but no one had any reception. With no internet our only option is to get hold of Gordon's satellite phone but he's not here. God knows when he'll be back.

'We'll have to put David in the Land Rover and try to drive across to the village.'

Joe touches me on the shoulder. 'What?' he shouts in my ear.

'Drive.' I mime holding a steering wheel.

He shakes his head. 'The river's flooded. I can see it from here.' He points away from the cottage, in the direction of the valley between the mountains. Even from this distance I can see there's a fast-flowing river where a shallow stream used to be.

'We have to try. Come on.' I gesture for him to run back to the hotel with me but I don't make it more than a couple of hundred metres before a stitch gnaws at my side and I have to stop. Joe waits by my side as I double over, sucking in cold air, then touches a hand to my back.

'We'll get pneumonia if we stay out here much longer.'

As I straighten up I see Melanie running towards us with what looks like a sheet of green tarpaulin held over her hair.

'Is David okay?' I shout as she gets nearer. 'Did Christine manage to . . .'

My words fall away as she shakes her head.

*

No one says a word as I walk into the lounge, dripping water with every step, but Christine, Katie, Malcolm and Fiona all look up.

'Is it true?' Even as the words leave my mouth I can see from the tired, worn expression on Christine's face that it is.

'Cardiac arrest,' Malcolm says. 'The poor bugger didn't stand a chance.'

'Malcolm!' Melanie goes over to him and slaps him on the forearm. 'Have some respect.'

I ignore them both. 'Where is he?'

Katie stifles a sob. Fiona, sitting nearest to her, flinches but doesn't reach out a consoling hand. Christine eases herself out of her chair and crosses the lounge.

'He's still in the dining room,' she says softly. 'I've covered him with a sheet. Did you manage . . .' She glances at my empty hands, then at Joe's.

'Gordon's not there,' he says. 'His car's gone too. And the place is locked up.'

'So we take the Land Rover, drive to the other side of the island.'

I shake my head. 'The road's flooded.' I step backwards, into the lobby, then head for the dining room.

Christine, still in her slippers, pads after me.

'Would you like me to come with you?' she asks softly.

I want to say no, that I'm fine by myself, but I'm not. I feel like I'm slipping back into a nightmare, the one where a nurse talks to me with sorrow in her eyes and a break in her voice.

'Here.' Christine opens the door then moves aside to let me in first.

For one glorious, hopeful second all I can see are chairs, tables and the deep green carpet and I listen for the sound of David crashing around in the kitchen, singing Rod Stewart hits in his deep baritone voice. But then I see it, the mound of his body shrouded in white, at the foot of the kitchen door.

I'm too scared to peel the sheet back from David's head but I do uncover his hand. I touch his palm tentatively, my heart pounding in the base of my throat, my eyes fixed on the smooth blank shape of his face. I stroke my fingers against his warm, rough skin and watch for a reaction from beneath the sheet, a twitch, shiver or groan. He doesn't move. I can hear myself breathing and voices in the lobby: Malcolm saying something about the Land Rover, Joe raising his voice and Christine telling them both to calm down. There are footsteps, clattering and banging, swearing, the jangle of keys and the sound of the front door slamming.

Then silence.

David's hand lies still in mine, his fingers curled, his nails clipped short and clean, dark hairs creeping from beneath his white shirtsleeve, reaching for his knuckles but not quite making it.

'David?' I slide two fingers into his shirtsleeve and press them into his skin, where his pulse should be. I wait, expectantly, for his blood to throb beneath my fingertips. Christine could have got it wrong. She must be nearly seventy, her first aid skills could be rusty. David might just be unconscious and we're treating him as though he's already dead.

'David!' I whip the sheet from his body and touch a hand to his cheek. It's warm, just like his palm. I touch a hand to his chest and stare at his stomach, shirt buttons straining, waiting for the soft rise and fall. Out of the corner of my eye I think I see his eyeballs roll under his closed lids.

'David! It's Anna. Open your eyes.'

I lean over him and lower my ear to his gently parted lips but there's no breath on my skin, not even a whisper.

'Come on, David!' I place a clenched fist in the centre of his chest and fold my other hand over the top. 'Come on!'

Nellie the
Elephant
packed her
trunk and
said good-
bye to the . . .

'Anna!' Strong hands pull at my shoulders as I continue to pound David's body. 'Anna, what are you doing? Anna, stop it. Stop it! He's dead. Anna, he's dead.'

In Memoriam

In Memoriam

Remembering Adam Vincent Falkirk who bravely battled until the end.
Gone but not forgotten. May you rest in peace.

It's extraordinary, really, that in such a small, select group of people there should be so much misery and pain. Have you noticed it, Anna, or are you too locked in your own head to see out? I don't think there's a single person in this hotel who doesn't long to sleep. Take poor David, for example. Did you ever think to ask him why he bought the hotel? Grief led him to Rum. When his partner died he felt lost and adrift, a rudderless soul. Do you know how you get someone to open up to you, Anna? You ask questions and then you listen and wait. Most people will open up to you if you give them enough time. And that's something we have plenty of now. Why play board games when you can talk? David talked to me, Anna, and I listened. What a nice man he was. May he rest in peace.

Chapter 20

David is dead.

I push myself up from my bed into a sitting position and say it aloud to the empty room: 'David is dead.'

My voice rings in my ears.

Nothing.

Inside me, still nothing. No hurt. No pain. I feel like a child in a play, making an emotionless announcement to an invisible audience.

'David is dead.' Cross to stage left.

When Joe lifted me up from the dining room carpet and half carried me up the stairs he continually asked if I was okay, his pale brown eyes searching mine as he waited for an answer. I told him that I was fine, I could walk, and that I didn't need his help. When we reached the guest floor I wriggled out from his arm, hooked around my back and under my armpit, and told him that he should go back down to the others. I was absolutely fine, I said. I just wanted to be alone.

He looked at me in disbelief. 'It's the shock, Anna. It hasn't sunk in yet. You really don't want to be alone when it does.'

I am alone, I wanted to scream at him. *And you staring at me won't change that.* Rage had descended from nowhere, hunching my shoulders and stealing my breath.

'Please,' I said. 'Go back downstairs and leave me alone.'

'Would you like me to send one of the women up?'

'Why would I want that?'

He stared at me for a second and his lower lip dropped, as though he was about to say something, then seemed to think better of it and nodded instead. I didn't wait for him to go. I turned and walked up the stairs to the staff quarters, feeling the burn of his eyes on my back.

Now, I swing my legs over the edge of the bed, cross the room, step onto the landing and turn the handle to David's bedroom. It's locked. Of course it is. I walk back into my room and sit on the stool in front of the dressing table. In the mirror my reflection stares back at me. I do my make-up here every morning but the face staring at me now isn't sleep-lined and puffy. It's gaunt, almost completely free of make-up – washed off by rain and sweat – and with no concealer under the eyes the dark circles are purple and deep.

'David is dead,' I whisper to the woman in the mirror.

I barely knew him. We'd been working together for less than two weeks but I was fond of him. There was something so solid and predictable about his presence in my life that made me feel safe. How could he be gone? One minute he was chatting to me in the kitchen and the next he was on the floor. How could the life be snuffed out of such a big personality so quickly? Tomorrow morning he won't knock on my door and shout at me to get up. He won't be in the kitchen, bustling around, when I trail downstairs. He won't laugh that hearty laugh of his when I inadvertently do something that amuses him. He won't catch my eye across the room and raise his eyebrows. He won't . . .

A tear trails down the cheek of the woman in the mirror.

'He's dead,' I whisper again.

Her eyes fill with tears. They glisten and shine, shallow puddles along the lash line.

'Dead.'

They spill and fall, winding and curving around the nostril, down to the lips, then dripping off the chin.

My stomach knots, my chest aches and a strangled sob escapes from my lips. I press my hands to my mouth and turn away from the mirror, bent over, crippled by the pain that rips through me like a blade.

This isn't a play. It's not make-believe.

On shaking legs I rise from the stool and take a step towards the bed. I take another, and another, and then I fall onto the mattress, gathering my knees up to my chest, and I howl in pain.

Someone else is dead.

A gentle tapping sound wakes me and my eyes fly open.

'Anna?' a soft voice calls.

The wooden door on the other side of the room slowly creaks open and a face appears in the gap.

'I'm sorry if I woke you,' Melanie says, her eyes soft beneath the hard red shape of her glasses. 'How are you doing?'

I feel around inside my brain for the correct response. Tired? Destroyed? Broken?

'I'm fine,' I say instead.

Clearly emboldened by my reply, Melanie pushes at the door and slips into my room but she doesn't venture far. She stands with her back against the wall, uncertainty etched into every line of her small, heart-shaped face. 'I know you probably don't want to think about this . . . and none of us . . . we didn't want to have to bring this up but . . .'

'It's okay,' I say. Whatever's making her feel uncomfortable is having the same effect on me.

'David . . . he's still lying in the doorway to the kitchen,' she says, wincing. 'And if the door's open to the dining room you can see him. He's still covered by the sheet of course, but Katie . . .'

'It's upsetting her.'

'Yes.' She nods gratefully. 'We were wondering if we could move him . . . David . . . until help arrives. We thought maybe . . .' Her eyes flick in the direction of his room.

'Of course.' I prop myself up on my elbows. 'Of course.'

'You don't need to get up,' Melanie says hurriedly. 'If you need more time to yourself we're absolutely capable of fending for ourselves.'

'No.' I sit up and run my hands over my face. 'I should be there. Just give me a second and I'll come down.'

It was horrible, watching Joe and Malcolm lug David up the stairs. I was unconscious when they pulled us from the wreckage of the car but the weight of David's limp body and the sag of his head made me think about Freddy and Peter and how they would have looked. The moment Joe and Malcolm lifted David off the dining room floor it was all I could do not to run and hide but I forced myself to stay. Malcolm took his feet and Joe, the younger and wirier of the two men, took most of the weight, his arms under David's shoulders as he gingerly stepped backwards up the staircase. The blanket kept slipping off, threatening to trip Malcolm, so I squeezed up beside them and carefully removed it.

'He's just sleeping,' I told myself as my gaze flicked to David's grey, expressionless face. It was the only way I could stop myself from running back down the stairs.

'Be careful,' I said as they neared the top of the second set of stairs that led to the staff quarters. 'There's a loose floorboard. Don't trip.'

David had pointed it out to me on my first day, after he'd carried my suitcase to my room. It was on his 'to do' list, he reassured me. The only trouble was he kept adding new items that would knock it down to the bottom.

Joe and Malcolm manoeuvred their way over the dodgy floorboard then, after I removed the master keys from David's pocket and unlocked his bedroom door, they carefully angled him inside and gently lowered him onto his bed.

'Thank you.' I pressed my hands lightly on their shoulder blades and felt the dampness of their clothes under my palms. 'That can't have been easy.'

'Least we could do,' Malcolm said, backing out of the room.

Joe hung back.

'Are you okay?' he asks now.

'Not really.' I lift David's arm and fold it across his chest. It is heavy and unwieldy and I feel a strange sense of disconnection as I move around the bed to do the same with the other arm. I know he's dead but I can't accept the finality of it. I keep expecting him to open his eyes and ask what on earth I'm doing.

Joe watches from the doorway, his arms crossed over his chest, his hands on his shoulders. He looks pale and uneasy. 'I haven't seen a dead body before.'

'Me neither.' I avert my eyes from David's face. Whenever I look at him I want to burst into tears.

'He was a nice man, I really liked him.'

'Me too.' As I shake out the sheet and re-cover David it suddenly occurs to me that, when the storm's over and the phones are working again, I'll have to let his relatives know what happened. My heart twists in my chest as I remember the phone calls I made to Freddy and Peter's parents. I can't believe I have to do that again.

'Anna,' Joe says as I turn away from the bed and wipe the backs of my hands over my eyes. Rain is still lashing at the dormer window and the sky is so grey it's almost black. 'What happens if we can't cross the river?'

'We sit it out, I suppose. There's food in the fridge and as long as we've got power and heat we'll be fine.'

I hear him laugh softly. 'Don't jinx us, Anna.'

Jinx us? A cold weight settles in my stomach. David is the third person I know who's died this year. And I was with them all when it happened.

Chapter 21

Steve

Steve Laing pushes his chair back from his desk and crosses his office to stand in front of the huge picture window that makes up one wall. He looks out at London, with its tower blocks, modern builds and historic architecture, tips back his head and takes a deep breath. For the last hour he's been staring at his computer screen, trying and failing to make sense of the figures his accountant sent him last night. It's not that he's no good with numbers – he wouldn't have a million-pound business if he weren't – but his concentration span is shot. He's felt like a stripped nerve ever since his meeting with Jim. He can't settle and he can't sleep. Whenever a phone blinks he snatches it up, certain it's a message from Jim. Whenever there's a knock at the door he thinks it's the police. If he's at home he flicks from news station to news station, searching for her face and never finding it. He does the same at work but with news websites, tabbing away from whichever document he's supposed to be working on to see if there's been an update. Whenever the word 'murder' flashes up on screen his guts twist painfully. But it's not her, it's never her.

It's the not knowing that's the worst. He doesn't know when it's going to happen, or how. He keeps snatching his burner phone out of his drawer, tapping out a text to Jim and then deleting it. He can't let on how nervy he feels. If he doesn't chill the fuck out and play by the rules there's a chance Jim might get spooked and call the whole thing off.

Steve stretches his arms above his head and unfurls his fists, holding his open palms out to the ceiling. 'Please,' he says to the empty room. 'For the love of God, get it over and done with. And get it done soon.'

Chapter 22

Anna

When I walk back down the stairs with Joe, Fiona Gardiner and Malcolm Ward are waiting in the lobby. They've both got their coats and walking boots on and Malcolm has a look of grim determination on his face.

'How are you doing?' he asks.

'Okay,' I lie. I step behind the reception desk, unhook the keys to the Land Rover and hand them to him.

Malcolm looks puzzled. 'You're not driving?'

Joe also looks blank before understanding slowly dawns on his face. He's remembered the conversation we had about my car accident.

'I'd rather not,' I say.

'Nervous driver, eh?' Malcolm smiles and nods. 'Melanie's the same. Won't go on the motorway unless she absolutely can't avoid it.'

'Is there any reason,' Fiona asks, one eyebrow arched, 'why

you gave the keys to Malcolm rather than me? Is it because he's a man?'

'No. I gave him the keys because he was closer.' Before she can reply I add, 'Is it just the two of you attempting the crossing?'

'Yes.' She smiles tightly but it doesn't reach her eyes. 'Christine's gone for a nap. Melanie's looking after Katie. Trevor's God knows where, out there somewhere.' She waves a hand towards the front door. 'And Joe . . .' Her eyes linger on the man standing beside me. 'Seems like he's looking after you.'

There's something about her tone that I don't like. Her voice *sounds* pleasant enough but the undertone is disapproving and mocking. I don't rise to it. She wouldn't be the first person to dislike me.

'Okay, then.' Malcolm pockets the keys. 'With any luck we'll be back with reinforcements in an hour or so.'

They return, empty-handed and dejected, twenty minutes later and trail into the lounge.

'There was no way.' Malcolm slumps into a chair and runs his hands over his bald head. 'We would have flooded the engine.'

I look at Fiona, standing by the window staring desolately out at the storm. She turns, as though sensing me watching.

'That'll be why Gordon hasn't come back. We're cut off from the other half of the island.'

'We're stuck here?' Katie says, her green eyes widening with alarm. 'We're supposed to go back in four days. What if we miss the ferry?'

'We're not going to miss the ferry.' Melanie, sitting beside her on the sofa, lays a hand on her arm. 'The storm will be over by then. Won't it, Anna?'

She gives me a pointed look and I nod, even though I don't have the first clue.

'Yeah.' I smile reassuringly at Katie. 'You'll all be on your way home on Saturday.'

The room falls silent. I've got no idea what the others are thinking about – warm, dry houses and their loved ones, I expect – but I'm thinking about David, lying all alone in his room upstairs. It doesn't feel right, all of us sitting down here, drinking cups of tea and chatting. It still doesn't feel real. Whenever I hear a noise, I find myself listening out for the heavy plod of his footsteps or the loud boom of his voice. I glance at my watch. It's twelve o'clock. Normally at this time he'd be shouting for me to make sure the dining room was laid out for lunch, or to help with the prep.

'I'm going to get the lunch ready,' I say, slightly too loudly.

Melanie looks up. 'Would you like a hand?'

'No, I'm fine, but it's kind of you to ask.'

I burst into tears before I even reach the kitchen, swallowing back sobs as I run through the dining room. Once inside, I slump over the food prep counter and bury my head in my arms. I feel like death's trailed me from London to Rum, throwing guilt, pain and regret at me, shaking the ground beneath my feet as it waits for me to crumple. There are three voids in the world now, dark shadows where Freddy, Peter and David once stood. Three lives snuffed out in the blink of an eye. What do we do with the spaces they left behind? We can't fill them. No one can and this isn't right, me in the kitchen making lunch. This is David's kitchen, his collection of aprons hanging on the hook by the fridge, his knife block, his favourite frying pan. He *was* the hotel. He was its heart and soul. Now it's just a building with a bunch of people whirling around in a storm, looking to me to tell them what to do. I didn't want that kind of responsibility but I either take control or I fall apart.

I push myself back from the counter and wipe my eyes and face on a tea towel.

'You'd better put that in the wash now,' David says in the back of my head.

I'll put it in the machine, David, I reply. *And if you're lucky I might even wash my hands before I prep the vegetables too.*

A little under an hour later, with thick vegetable soup bubbling away on the stove, I carry the bowls into the dining room and arrange them on the place mats. David was a fan of serving lunch from the pan so I'll do the same.

I put a hand to the lobby door and take a steadying breath. The guests need me to hold it together, especially Katie, who looked terrified when Malcolm said they hadn't been able to cross the river.

I glance at my watch then open the door. It's nearly half past one. The guests must be starving. As well as the soup, there's fresh bread cooling in the ovens from breakfast and there's still plenty of cheese and ham that—

I freeze.

Condensation has misted the narrow windows on either side of the front door and something's been written on the window directly opposite reception. Four words curve through the moisture.

TO DIE, TO SLEEP.

I stare at the window, too stunned to move, then scrub at the glass with my sleeve, rage boiling inside me. Who'd write something so crass just hours after David died? It makes me feel sick that someone would find that funny.

The guests turn to stare as I burst into the lounge.

'Who wrote that?' My hand shakes as I gesture at the open door.

No one says a word and my stomach knots as I look from one confused face to another. Christine and Trevor are absent but the other five guests stare at me blankly.

Finally, Joe speaks up: 'What's happened, Anna?'

'Someone wrote . . .' I shake my head, disgusted that anyone could be so callous. 'Someone wrote "TO DIE, TO SLEEP" on the window in the lobby.'

'What?' Fiona jumps up and peers out of the door then looks at me in confusion. 'There's nothing there.'

'I wiped it off.'

I look back at the guests. This is where one of them tells me that I got it all wrong, that it's a joke, written on the window because they were tired and wanted to sleep.

'Was it you, Katie?' I look at the youngest guest, sitting on the sofa with her legs curled up beneath her and a Nintendo DS in her hands.

She stares back at me.

'Of course it wasn't Katie,' Melanie says, leaning in to her. 'She'd never graffiti private property.'

'It wasn't graffiti. It was written in the condensation. Katie, did you . . . did you write it as some sort of . . .' I search for the right word. '. . . some kind of tribute to David?'

'No.' She wrinkles her nose. 'Why would I do that?'

Melanie gives me a look as though to say, *told you*. I look from her to her husband, sitting in the armchair by the fire, strangely quiet, and then to Joe and Fiona.

'Is anyone going to confess to writing it?'

'Anna,' Joe says. 'No one in this room wrote anything.'

'How do you know?'

'Because we haven't moved from here since you went to make lunch.'

'So no one went into the lobby to use the toilet?'

Malcolm, Fiona and Melanie all shift in their seats.

'So that's a yes, then.'

'Maybe it was Christine,' Malcolm says, 'or Trevor.'

'What was Christine?' says a voice from behind me. The oldest guest, her eyes bleary with sleep, smiles up at me. 'What have I missed?'

'Anna's on a witch hunt,' Malcolm says as he slides past me. 'Apparently, one of the guests wrote something inappropriate on the window of the—'

'Witch hunt?' Fiona says, looking riled. 'She's upset, Malcolm, and you're trivialising it.'

'Would you all just shut up! You're doing my head in.' Katie's screech echoes around the room.

For a split second no one reacts, then Melanie shakes her head in disbelief.

'Katie, screaming like that is not acceptable.'

'Oh, fuck off.' She scrambles off the couch and stomps towards me.

'Katie, get back here right now.'

'Leave me alone. You're not my mum.'

'Katie!' Melanie springs after her as she pushes past me and runs towards the stairs. 'Katie! Wait.'

Malcolm sighs heavily, gets up from his chair and follows them. As the door clicks shut behind him the three remaining guests look at each other, and at me, and raise their eyebrows.

'Anyone for a cup of tea?' Christine says, picking up Malcolm's dirty mug.

Chapter 23

There's a strange mood in the lounge, as though a thick grey smog has filled the room, wrapping around each of us, sealing us into our own little worlds. Christine is sipping her tea over at the window, staring out at the rain. Joe is flicking through a magazine. And Fiona is stacking dominos into a pyramid. There's no attempt to make conversation and the silence is loaded. Or perhaps that's just my interpretation. Now the adrenaline of my discovery has worn off, a dark thought has wormed its way into my head: what if the 'TO DIE, TO SLEEP' message wasn't written in reaction to David's death? What if whoever sent me the 'sleep' messages in London followed me to Rum and they're a guest in the hotel? What if they're in this room?

The thought makes me feel sick with fear. The messages in London were unnerving but they felt like an attempt to make me feel guilty about the accident. This message is the first one to feel like a threat.

To die, to sleep. That's from *Hamlet*. Whoever wrote it thinks I want to kill myself, or that I'm at least contemplating it. Or . . . a shiver runs through me, despite the heat from the fire . . . they think that I should.

I look from Joe to Christine to Fiona. What do I really know about any of the guests? Christine's a retired primary school teacher, Fiona's a call centre manager and Malcolm's a semi-retired psychology professor but I've got no idea what Joe, Trevor or Melanie do for a living. I don't know anything about any of their lives, not really, only what they've chosen to share with me. And that's not very much. I assumed Malcolm and Melanie were Katie's mum and dad and I was wrong about that. I'm guessing they're her uncle and auntie. My gut instinct told me that all the guests were decent people, apart from Trevor who made me feel uncomfortable the moment we met.

Assuming. Guessing. Gut instinct.

If someone in this hotel has followed me from London I can't rely on any of those things. I need to find out who they are.

Dinner is a tough lamb stew that could have done with another couple of hours on a low heat. Trevor came in first and sat alone by the window. Malcolm, Melanie and Christine came in next. Malcolm and Christine take seats opposite each other but Melanie doesn't sit down. Instead she strolls across the dining room with a look of quiet determination on her face.

'Hello, Anna.' She forces a smile. 'I was wondering if I could take two bowls of stew upstairs. Katie's not feeling well and I don't want to force her to be sociable.'

Since Katie's outburst earlier the Wards have hidden themselves away upstairs.

'I'll be honest with you, Anna.' Melanie presses her glasses into her nose and looks up at me from beneath her thick fringe. 'I don't know what's going on in her head. I've tried to get her to open up but she won't talk to me.' She sighs heavily. 'We thought she'd enjoy this break but she's like a tightly coiled spring.'

I nod sympathetically and wait for her to say more.

Instead she raises her eyebrows and says, 'So is it okay? For me to take our dinner upstairs?'

I hand her the food and tell her to give me a shout if there's anything else she needs. She nods her thanks then heads back out of the dining room, catching Malcolm's eye as she passes his table. He doesn't comment. Instead he continues to spoon his stew into his mouth.

Christine, opposite him, catches me watching and flashes me a smile before she returns to her dinner.

As Christine, Malcolm and Trevor finish their food, Fiona and Joe enter the dining room. Fiona walks in first, carrying a battered paperback, and takes a seat at a table near the door. When Joe enters a couple of seconds later, Fiona looks up from her book and flashes her eyebrows at him, signalling for him to join her, but he walks straight past and takes another single table. Fiona's smile melts instantly and she looks back down at her book.

She glances up as I bring her the food and says thank you, but when I ask her if there's anything else she'd like she shakes her head wordlessly. Joe couldn't be more different. He shoots me a smile as I approach his table, a steaming bowl of stew in my hands.

'How are you bearing up?' he asks as I place it in front of him. 'You look tired.'

'I've been better.'

He glances towards the kitchen door. 'Even though I helped carry David upstairs I keep expecting him to walk in.'

He dips his spoon in the stew and stirs it, releasing a cloud of steam. 'Have you tried the landline and Wi-Fi again?'

'About an hour ago.'

'And?'

'No joy.'

He sighs. 'There has to be someone on the other side of the island trying to sort it.' Before I can say *let's hope so*, he adds,

'There's no mobile signal anywhere. I went out earlier to check but . . .' He shrugs. 'Nothing. None of the others have had any luck either.'

As I turn to look out at the weather, the lights flicker and Christine yelps in surprise.

I stare at the bulbs, praying we're not about to lose the electricity too, but after a couple more seconds the flickering stops and the lights remain on. There's a collective sigh of relief around the room.

'Is there a generator?' Malcolm asks, twisting round in his seat. 'If the electricity fails.'

'Yes, in the basement.' I shoot him what I hope is a reassuring smile but the truth is I haven't got the first idea how to work the generator. David told me it was in the basement but he didn't get round to showing me how to use it.

Oh, David. As the guests return to their food, it strikes me again quite how alone I am.

12.15 a.m. and I can barely keep my eyes open.

After dinner Trevor went straight up to his room and the rest of the guests retired to the lounge. I was about to disappear into the kitchen to tidy up but Malcolm came after me, insisting I join them for a drink. I tried to get out of it. I needed time alone to think but he wouldn't take no for an answer. They were going to toast David's memory, he said. The dishes would have to wait.

One glass of whisky soon became three and the alcohol warmed my blood and took the edge off my nerves. A little after eleven, I forced myself up and out of my chair and went into the kitchen to make coffees. Once they'd been drunk, Fiona and Christine yawned, said their goodnights and went upstairs. Joe hung around for a bit longer, insisting I let him help tidy up. When I continued to refuse, he finally relented and went upstairs.

No such luck getting rid of Malcolm. He insisted on having 'one more before bed' and has only just disappeared up the stairs. As his footsteps reverberate above me I wander from room to room on the ground floor, checking everything is in order, idly noting what I need to do tomorrow. If David were alive to see the state of the kitchen – the crumbs and scraps on the food prep area and dirty marks on the floor – he'd go mental, but I don't have the energy to tidy it now. I walk into the utility room, sighing at the loaded washing machines. If I don't get the linen in the tumble dryers tonight it'll stink and I'll have to re-wash the lot. I open one machine and pull the damp linen into a basket. As I carry it to the tumble dryer, a movement in the corner of my eye makes me turn sharply.

'Hello?' I look towards the kitchen. 'Is there someone there?'

No one answers.

'Hello?' I put the basket down and walk through the kitchen and into the dining room. One of the guests must have popped downstairs to get something. 'Hello, can I help you?'

I pop my head round the lounge door.

Empty.

I rub my hand over the back of my neck. It's back, the feeling I'd had in London: the prickle down my spine telling me someone is watching me. I stand at the bottom of the stairs listening for the sound of creaking floorboards but the hotel is silent.

I'm too creeped out to go back to the kitchen alone so I make my way up to my room, pausing in the stairwell of the first floor. It's pitch black apart from an eerie orange pool of light cast by the emergency exit sign. Someone's crying. There's a muffled sob coming from one of the rooms. I head for Katie's door but there's no sound from her room. Fiona then? As I cross the corridor the sobbing grows louder. It *is* Fiona. I raise my fist to knock on her door then lower my hand. I shouldn't intrude.

I linger for a few more seconds, reassured as the crying grows softer and softer before it stops completely, then I pad back down the corridor and up the stairs to my room. I slip inside, lock the door behind me and, too exhausted to get changed, crawl into bed, still fully clothed.

There's someone in the room. My eyes are closed but I know I'm not alone. I can feel the weight of their gaze, the pinprick crawl of my skin. What are they waiting for? For me to open my eyes? I want to ignore them and go back to sleep but I can't ignore the churning in my belly and the tightness of my skin. They want to hurt me. Malevolence binds me to the bed like a blanket. I need to wake up. I need to get up and run.

But I can't move. There's a weight on my chest, pinning me to the bed.

'Hello, Anna.'

A voice drifts into my consciousness then out again.

'Help me!' But my voice is only in my head. I can't move my lips. I can't get the sound to reverberate in my throat. The only part of me I can move is my eyes.

Someone's walking towards me, their cold blue eyes fixed on mine.

'Don't be scared.'

They draw closer – staccato movements, like a film on freeze-frame – move, stop, move, stop. Closer and closer. I screw my eyes tightly shut. This isn't real. It's a dream. I need to wake up.

'That's right, Anna. Close your eyes and go back to sleep. Don't fight it. Let the pain and guilt and hurt go.'

No! No! Stop!

I scream, but the sound of my voice doesn't leave my head. I can't move. I can only blink frantically – a silent SOS – as I'm grabbed by the wrist. They're going to hurt me and there's nothing I can do to stop them.

Chapter 24

Alex

Alex holds his breath as he peels his hand from Becca's and hears a soft squelching sound as their naked bodies separate and he rolls away. Only their third date and they've already slept together. He hadn't expected it, particularly as she'd seemed in a strange mood when he'd met her from work. Not that he knows her well enough to read her moods, they barely know each other, but she was definitely off with him. The flushed excitement of their first date was gone and she hadn't even put any lipstick on. She'd smiled as she walked down the corridor towards him and didn't pull away when he reached for her hand, but the worried expression didn't leave her face until they reached the restaurant and her wine glass touched her lips.

'Tough day?' He'd already asked her that once as they left the hospital and again on the tube journey where they'd been crammed into a corner of the compartment by a huge crowd of foreign students. Both times she'd nodded and then changed the subject. Instinct told him to let it drop but he'd never been very good at holding his tongue and besides, whatever it was that was bothering her was ruining their date. Instead of being a welcome distraction her stress was making him reflect on his own worries. Debbie, Anna's mum, had rung him earlier to ask if he'd heard from her recently. She couldn't get through to Anna on her mobile or the hotel landline, she'd said, and Anna hadn't replied to her emails or Facebook messages. There was a storm raging the coast of West Scotland, apparently, and Debbie was worried. Alex had to admit that he hadn't heard from his ex-girlfriend for a few days, then, at a loss to know what else to do, he'd suggested Debbie try ringing the ferry company to see if they could shed any light on what was happening.

Becca set her glass down on the table and sighed. 'Yes, Alex. It was a tough day.' She gazed at him as though willing him to push her further.

'Did um . . . did someone die?' he ventured. He knew that wasn't exactly unusual in critical care and they'd spoken about it before, the types of deaths that particularly upset her and those that didn't cut as deeply.

'No,' she said lightly. 'Nothing like that.'

'So . . .' He reached for his own glass and took a large mouthful. He might have to rethink whether to continue dating Becca if they were going to struggle like this every time she had a hard day at work. Her conversational reticence reminded him of Anna. Why couldn't she just spit out what was bothering her instead of making him guess?

'So why was it a bad day?' He was like a dog with a bone now. He wasn't going to let it drop until she told him what was wrong, then he'd help her to find a solution and they could get on with having fun.

Becca took another swig of her wine. 'There's some kind of investigation going on at work.'

'What kind of—'

'I don't know. That's why it's so worrying. Management have been wandering around the wards and huddling in corners. No one knows what's going on.'

Alex shrugged. 'Why are you so bothered? Have you done something wrong?'

She fixed him with a look that said *did you really just ask me that* then rolled her eyes to the ceiling, giving him a glimpse of white eyeball above her heavily lined lashes.

'Did you ask them what was going on?' Alex ventured.

'No, but the ward sister did. She was told we'd find out soon enough.'

'Was she worried?'

'Well, obviously. If there's some kind of issue with the work we're doing it'll reflect badly on her. Jesus, Alex, are you normally this dense or are you completely lacking the empathy gene?'

He started at the ferocity of her tone. This was new.

'Sorry.' She reached across the table and took his hand. 'I'm awful when I'm in a bad mood. I knew I should have cancelled tonight but I really did want to see you.' Her tone softened. 'I'm not normally such a bitch, I promise.'

'No, no,' Alex lied. 'It's fine.'

But it wasn't. Doubt had hooked itself into his mind like a burr and it remained there all the way through the meal. There was something about Becca that was making him uncomfortable. On their second date, just yesterday, she'd spent a good part of the evening asking him about Anna: how long had they been together? How had they met? Why had they split up? When had he realised he no longer wanted to be with her? She'd moved on to asking him how he felt about her: when had he first realised he fancied her? Was the uniform a turn-on? Did he feel different about her now they were spending time together outside the hospital? There was something vaguely unattractive about her lack of self-confidence and he'd never been into needy women but he'd tried to push away his prickle of unease. Maybe she was struggling to come up with topics of conversation. Or perhaps it was nerves.

But now this, a spikey side to her personality that she hadn't shown him before. Maybe he'd have to rethink the way he saw her; perhaps she wasn't girlfriend material after all. But she was incredibly attractive, with the loveliest little bottom and . . . his mind had wandered over dinner as he imagined what she looked like naked, with her blue skinny jeans and low-cut top stripped away. If Becca had noticed a change in his attitude she didn't let on. The more they drank, the more relaxed and joyful she became, and as they lingered outside the restaurant at the end of the night it was Becca who leaned in for a kiss then whispered, 'I don't have to go home, you know.'

Alex wipes a hand over his brow, then slides out of the bed he used to share with Anna and pads out of the bedroom to get a drink of water. As he reaches the door, Becca makes a noise that makes him turn back.

'No,' she mumbles in her sleep. 'No, I promise. I didn't do anything wrong.'

You probably didn't, Alex thinks as he reaches into the cupboard for a glass. But I did.

Chapter 25

Anna

Katie?

She's standing in the doorway to my room, one side of her face in shadow, the other lit by the orange glow of the emergency exit light. My breath catches in my throat as I shuffle backwards on the bed, my heels slipping on the sheet before I slam up against the headboard. She looks so small in the doorway, so thin and fragile in her oversized nightdress. Her eyes are open but her face is expressionless, her skin slack, her lips slightly parted.

'Katie?' My voice is a rasping whisper. 'Are you okay?'

She doesn't respond but she keeps her strange, vacant eyes fixed on mine. Her hands clench and unclench at her sides and a slow smile creeps onto her lips.

'Katie, can you hear me?' I shift off the bed and cross the room. Katie doesn't move; she barely blinks. As I approach her she looks straight through me. She's sleepwalking.

I deliberate: do I leave her here and go and get Melanie or do I help her back to her room? If I leave her here and she wanders off and falls down the stairs I'd never forgive myself, but I haven't got the first clue how to get her back downstairs. You're not supposed to touch sleepwalkers, are you? My mind flits to David, still and silent in the room beside mine. He'd know what to do. He wouldn't stand here dithering and worrying.

'Katie,' I say, making a decision, 'it's Anna. I'm going to help you back into your own bed.'

She continues to look straight through me but her mouth slackens and her smile fades.

'I'm going to touch your arm now, Katie. And I'm going to help you down the stairs.'

Tentatively I graze the bare skin of her arm with my fingers. When she doesn't flinch or scream I slip my arm through hers.

'Okay?' I take a breath. 'We're going downstairs now. Let's get you back in bed.'

I have to tap on Melanie and Malcolm's door several times before I hear a low groan and the creak of a bed. The door opens a crack and Melanie peers out at me, her hair sleep-ruffled and her eyes small and squinty without her glasses.

'What time is it?' she croaks.

'A little after three. Sorry to wake you but Katie just sleep-walked into my room.'

'What?' She blinks and rubs a hand over her eyes.

'Katie. She was in my room. I managed to get her back into her bed and she seems to be sleeping now, but I thought I should tell you.'

'Really? Oh my gosh! I didn't know she did that. Thank you. I'll go and check on her.'

As Melanie heads over to Katie's room, another door opens and Joe raises a hand in my direction.

'Everything okay?' he asks as I draw closer. 'I heard voices and—'

'Katie was sleepwalking.' I keep my voice low. 'She came up to my room.'

'Up the stairs?'

'Yeah.'

'Jesus.' He raises his eyebrows. 'She all right?'

'Yeah, she's in bed now.'

'Cool. Night then, Anna.' He moves to close his door then pauses. 'Is everything okay with you? How come you're dressed?'

'I passed out like this.' I glance at my watch: 3.21 a.m. I might get another two hours if I go back to bed now. 'I'll see you for breakfast. Goodnight, Joe.'

For the second time, I climb the stairs to the staff quarters on weary legs. I step into my room then walk back out again, a vague feeling of unease stirring in my stomach. There's a key sticking out of the lock on the outside of my door. But it's not mine.

'Joe?' I tap gently on his door, desperately hoping he hasn't gone back to sleep. 'Joe, are you awake?'

The door opens and he stares at me in surprise.

'Sorry,' I say, 'to disturb you again.'

'No, no. It's fine. I was reading . . .' He tails off, a frown forming between his brows. 'What's up?'

I glance over my shoulder. All the bedroom doors are closed but that doesn't mean no one's listening. 'Do you mind if we talk in your room?'

'Course not, come in.' He steps back into his room, apologising for the mess, then scoops a pile of clothes off the armchair near the door and gestures for me to sit down. 'What's going on?' he asks as he perches on the end of his bed.

'I found this in my door.' I hand him the key.

He looks at it then shrugs.

'It's the spare master key. It opens all the rooms in the hotel. It went missing yesterday.'

'I . . .' He shakes his head. 'I don't get it, sorry.'

'I locked my bedroom door when I went to bed last night. When I woke up, Katie was standing in the doorway. The only way she could have got in is if she'd used this.' I gesture at the key in his hand.

'You think she stole it?'

'It would explain how she got into my room, but can you even unlock doors when you're sleepwalking?'

He shrugs. 'I don't see why not. When I was a kid I sleepwalked down the stairs. I had my bin in my hand, my mum said. When she asked me what I was doing, I told her I was going to empty it. She watched me walk into the kitchen, empty the bin and then walk back up to my room again.'

'And you didn't remember doing it?'

'Nope.' He laughs softly. 'And it's not like I have neat-freak tendencies.'

'But if Katie did take the key it also means she let herself into Trevor's room and stole something.'

Joe raises his eyebrows. 'What did she steal?'

'I don't know. He refused to tell me.'

'Wow.' He stretches his arms above his head, then apologises as he stifles a yawn. 'Sorry. I guess you should talk to Mel and Malc about it.'

'I don't want to get Katie into trouble though. She doesn't seem very happy as it is.'

'I've noticed that too.' He shrugs. 'Talk to her first thing maybe? See what she says.'

'Yeah.' I stand up. 'I think you're right. Anyway, I'll let you get some sleep.'

'Thanks, Anna.'

'Goodnight then, again.' I open the bedroom door and I'm just about to step out into the corridor, when Joe touches the back of my arm. I turn sharply and smack straight into him.

'Careful.' He puts a steadying hand on my shoulder but he doesn't pull away. His abdomen presses against my chest, rising and falling with each breath as he looks down at me, his gaze steady. The atmosphere changes, suddenly loaded with expectation and tension. His lips part. He's going to kiss me.

'Don't forget your key.' He presses it into my hand. 'Goodnight, Anna. Sleep well.'

In Memoriam

In Memoriam

Steven 'Curly' Morris

It's been a year since you passed, Curly. It still feels wrong whenever anyone else sits at the bar on 'your stool'. We'll be raising a pint of mild in your memory tonight. With best wishes, John, landlord at the Dog and Duck.

I left you a little message, Anna. I know you saw it but I'm wondering now whether I was a bit too obtuse, if perhaps I should have left you a note with the full speech instead of a small extract.

'To die, to sleep. To sleep, perchance to dream. Ay, there's the rub, for in this sleep of death what dreams may come . . .'

You're a clever girl. You know that's from Hamlet *and he's asking himself if it is better to give up and die rather than face his troubles. He's scared, dear Anna, just like you are, that he'll dream when he's dead and never get any peace from his earthly woes.*

You are both wrong to worry. Death is a dreamless sleep. It's an end to pain.

I'm going to have to be a little less subtle. It seems my little hints aren't enough. I've left you a gift, Anna, and a decision to make. It'll be like Alice in Wonderland, *my favourite childhood book. Only you won't shrink or grow. You'll die.*

Chapter 26

Anna

Wednesday 6th June

Day 5 of the storm

I'm woken by a soft tapping at my door. For a second I think it's David, but then a soft feminine voice calls my name and reality settles in my chest like a rock.

'One second, Christine.' I swing my legs out of bed then jump to my feet when I see the time. It's nearly eight o'clock. I should have been up hours ago.

Christine takes one look at my face as I unlock the door and laughs. 'Oh, Anna, there's no need to look so panicked. I just wanted to let you know that breakfast is ready.'

'Breakfast?'

'Yes. When you didn't come down we decided the least we could do was give you a lie-in. There's a bacon sandwich and a cup of coffee with your name on it when you're ready. Malcolm did a fabulous job.'

'Malcolm cooked breakfast?'

She laughs lightly. 'He commandeered the kitchen. None of us could get a look-in.'

An hour later, with a stomach full of warm food, I get up from the dining room table to start servicing the rooms. As I head for the door, Melanie pops out from the kitchen wearing one of David's favourite aprons and a pair of rubber gloves.

'I hope you're not planning on doing any work.'

'I'm sorry?'

'The rooms. We had a little chat before you got up and none of us need our rooms cleaning or changing. We can cope with the same sheets and towels for two days.'

'But . . .' I stifle a yawn.

'Anna,' her face softens, 'you had a hell of a day yesterday with . . . with what happened to David. We want you to take it easy today. I know you're in charge and we're the guests but we're all human. You need time to grieve. And sleep.'

I'm so touched by her gentle tone and the kindness in her voice that my eyes fill with tears.

'Anna . . .' She takes a step towards me, her arms spread wide, and I ready myself for a hug but then she stops and looks at her rubber-gloved hands. 'You probably don't want these all over your jumper, do you?'

I shake my head, still too moved to speak.

'Go and rest,' Mel says. 'We'll call you down when it's time for lunch.'

As I step into the lobby, Katie comes out of the toilet. She visibly jumps then drops her chin and seems to fold into herself. It takes me a second to register what she's embarrassed about, but then I realise: Melanie must have told her what she did last night.

'Katie.' I move towards her then stop, reading her body language. 'You're not in trouble. I just wanted to have a chat with you. See how you're doing.'

'I'm fine,' she says from beneath the long dark hair that hangs over one eye like a pirate's patch.

'Can we talk?' I gesture towards the lounge but she shakes her head.

'Malcolm's in there.'

I imagine she probably doesn't want to talk in the dining room with Melanie within earshot either, so ask if she'd like to chat in the porch.

'It's raining,' she mumbles.

'We could put our coats and boots on. We won't get wet in the porch, it'll just be a bit cold.'

I take her shrug as agreement and when I hand her coat to her she pulls it on then slips her feet into her boots and follows me out of the front door.

We stand in the porch, Katie pressed up against the wood so there's as much space between us as possible, and stare out at the rain. Her eyes light up as a gull wheels around in the wind.

'Amazing, isn't it,' I say, 'the way they surf the air currents?'

She shrugs and turns to stare at the sea instead, as though my comment just ruined her fun. So much for small talk. I cut to the chase instead.

'What can you remember about last night, Katie?'

She shrugs again. 'Nothing.' Her small voice is almost carried away by the wind.

'Do you often sleepwalk?'

There's a pause, then: 'Sometimes. When I'm stressed.'

She looks stressed now, standing outside with me. Her body's so rigid there may as well be a flashing neon sign above her head that reads 'I WOULD RATHER BE ANYWHERE ELSE THAN HERE'.

'I imagine it was upsetting for you, seeing David . . . seeing what happened to him.' When she doesn't respond I add, 'I'm sorry if I upset you in the lounge yesterday. I wasn't accusing you of anything. I was just trying to understand why someone wrote on the window.'

She moves her head minutely, as though she's about to look at me, then seems to think better of it and turns back to the sea.

'Melanie's your auntie, isn't she?' I venture. 'And Malcolm's your uncle.'

'Yeah.'

I think back to the conversation I overheard on the stairs on the guests' third day: Melanie and Malcolm talking in hushed voices about how worried they were about her.

'Is your dad not around?'

She sighs heavily, but whether it's through frustration or sadness I can't tell. I can sense that this line of questioning isn't going to be helpful so I change tack.

'Katie, did you take the master key from reception?'

She swings round to face me, her eyes small and dark beneath the shadow of her parka hood. 'What?'

'When you opened the door to my room last night, you left the key in the lock.'

'What?'

'You unlocked my room in your sleep.'

'No I didn't.'

'You didn't unlock my room?'

'I didn't take a key.' She stares defiantly up at me. 'Why would I? I've got my own key.'

'So you didn't let yourself into Trevor's room?'

'What?!' She steps out of the porch and into the driving rain, a look of incredulity on her face. 'Who said that? Who told you I did that?'

'No one. But the key went missing, Katie, and it didn't reappear until last night.'

'Well, I didn't take it! I can't believe you're accusing me of something I didn't do again!'

'I'm not accusing you of anything. I'm just trying to understand what happened.'

I want to believe her. Her reaction seems genuine. She'd have to be a hell of an actress otherwise. But I don't know what to believe. Trevor wouldn't say what was stolen from his room so there are no clues there. And if she didn't take the key, how else would it end up in my door?

'Katie,' I soften my tone. 'You won't get in trouble. I just need to know the truth. Did you take the key?'

'No. My God!' She spits the words into my face then shoulders her way past me and storms back into the hotel.

I follow her inside but I don't charge up the stairs after her. Instead I take off my coat and boots and walk over to the reception area, where Fiona's ducked down behind the desk.

'Everything okay?'

'No.' She runs her hand over the base of the radiator. 'I think there might be a problem with the boiler. None of the radiators have come on.'

'I'll check.'

She follows me through the dining room and into the kitchen then hovers in the doorway of the utility room as I open the boiler cupboard.

'Well?' She runs her hands up and down her arms. Now I haven't got my coat on I can feel the cold too. There's definitely a sting in the air. 'Do you think you'll be able to get it back on?'

When she first arrived at the hotel I'd pegged her as being the same age as Joe and me but she's slightly older. Mid to late thirties maybe, with a crease between her eyebrows that makes her look stern, even when she's not frowning. Her blonde wavy hair falls to her shoulders – shoulders that seem to have been permanently hunched ever since she arrived. I watch her out of the corner of my eye as I check the display pane on the boiler. Fiona was in the lounge when I discovered the message on the window. She could easily have written 'TO DIE, TO SLEEP' after telling the others she was going to the toilet.

'I'm not sure.' I close the cupboard door. 'I think we might be out of oil. David told me he gets a delivery from the mainland once a month and if we've run out then—'

'We're screwed.'

'Pretty much, yeah. I'll need to check the tank in the garden.' I touch a hand to the key in the back door then pause, remembering something else about her. 'I heard you crying last night. Is everything okay?'

'I wasn't crying.' She looks at me defiantly, as though daring me to contradict her. 'Have you ever lost anyone you love, Anna?'

I'm so surprised by the sudden switch in topic and the emotion behind her question that, for a second or two, I can't speak. Then Freddy, Peter and David's faces swim in and out of my mind.

'I've lost people,' I say after a pause, 'people I cared about.'

'A boyfriend? Ever lost one of them?' There's a strange expression on her face: hurt but aggressive at the same time. Ever since she arrived she's seemed to swing from one emotion to another. Warm and friendly one minute, defensive and prickly the next.

'Lost a boyfriend . . .' I repeat, drawing out the words as my brain whirs, trying to anticipate where she's going with this. She's trying to tell me something but she's being obtuse instead of coming out and saying it. A cold, prickling sensation travels down my back. Did Fiona's boyfriend die? Is that what she's hinting at? 'I . . . I split up with someone a few weeks before I moved here.'

She laughs dismissively. 'It's all right for you.'

'What is?' Irritation is starting to bubble within me.

'Women like you never have to worry about a relationship ending because there's always another man waiting in the wings to step in.'

'I don't know what you're talking about.'

'Joe.'

'Joe and I aren't together.'

'*Yet*. I'm pretty sure if you gave him the green light he'd make a move.'

My hand drops from the door handle. 'Why do you care if Joe and I get together?'

'I don't.'

'So what's all this about? Why are you so angry?'

'You tell me. I spent the last two years of my life with someone I thought loved me and it turns out he never did, or at least not in the way I loved him.'

'Oh, God, I'm sorry. I had no idea.'

Her mouth twists bitterly. 'He just ended things. He said it wasn't fair to keep me dangling when he knew he was never going to marry me and that it would be better for both of us if we went our separate ways. I tried to talk to him, to find a way to save the relationship, but he refused to listen. He just kept saying it was over.'

She sighs and runs her hands over her hips. 'I've lost nearly a stone since he finished it. I can't eat, I can't sleep and I'm shit company. I thought by coming away on my own it would help me get over him but it's like I packed his ghost in my suitcase.'

'I'm sorry,' I say again, 'it sounds like you've been through a tough time.' She's definitely hurting. I can see it in her eyes. But I don't know if I believe her story, not completely.

'It pisses me off that I still feel like this, you know? Little things are really getting to me.'

'Like what?'

'You and Joe flirting. Mel and Malc's sham of a marriage.'

'Their marriage?'

'Don't tell me you haven't noticed? "Mel do this, Mel do that." He talks over her all the time. Totally winds me up.'

'But she seems happy enough, don't you think? And she stands up to him when she has to, like the other day when he wanted to go out for a walk and she didn't.'

'Seriously?' She laughs. 'You think she's happy? She's playing the part of the contented wife, Anna. It's all an act. She can tell herself over and over again that she's happy but it's a lie. She's knows the truth about her relationship but she won't face up to it. God knows why. Probably scared of being alone.'

And you're not, I think but don't say. What other secrets are the guests hiding that I can't see? I used to think I was a good judge of character, but now I'm not so sure.

As I turn the key in the back door, Fiona points down at the cat flap in the base. 'I didn't know there was a hotel cat.'

'There isn't.' The cat flap is dusty and speckled with mud, but when I tap it with the toe of my boot it swings open.

'The previous owner must have had one,' I say as I open the door and take a step back. 'There's no cat now . . .' The wind swallows the rest of my sentence as rain blasts into the small room.

'After you,' Fiona says, gesturing for me to walk into the garden first.

I take a step forwards, then think better of it. 'No, no. After you.'

Chapter 27

Steve

Steve Laing pushes his chair back from his desk, stretches his arms above his head and yawns loudly. Beyond the glass windows of his office his PA, Vicky Fratton, is pulling on her coat. She picks up her handbag, lifts the strap over her head and twists the bag so it lies on her left hip. She notices Steve watching and gives him a tight smile. Probably worried that I'm going to ask her to do something, Steve thinks as he lowers his gaze to the photograph of Freddy on his graduation day. Other than the photo of Freddy as a toddler, his face and hair dripping with baked beans, it's his favourite photo of his son. It's just so bloody joyous: his gown askew, his right hand reaching above his head, his black cap a blur in motion. He'd never been prouder of his son than he had been that day. The first Laing in his family to go to university and get a degree. And not just a degree, a bloody first in marketing.

'I'm off now, Steve.' Vicky sticks her head round the door to his office. It's a question rather than a statement and he can hear her unspoken prayer for freedom.

'All right then, Vicks. Have a good evening. See you tomorrow.'

She smiles, properly this time, and raises a hand in farewell. 'You too. Don't work too late.'

'I won't.' He waits until he hears the ping of the lift, then reaches into the top drawer of his desk and pulls out his mobile. He lays it on the polished mahogany desk, then reaches for Freddy's photo and places it next to the phone.

'What do you reckon, Son?'

Steve yawns again, not bothering to smother the sound with his hand. He can't remember the last time he had a good night's sleep. He'd been existing on five to six hours for months, but the last couple of weeks it's been more like two or three and he's lost count of the number of times he's fallen asleep in his chair, only waking when Vicky shakes him by the shoulder, to remind him about a phone call or a meeting. It was grief, he told himself. He couldn't sleep for thinking about Fred. And that was true, certainly initially. But recently it hasn't been his son's face imprinted on his closed eyelids, it's been someone else's. A woman's. *The* woman's. She is haunting him.

He's tried to ignore the dreams, to block out the discombobulation that clings to him from waking until sleep, but it won't go away. He's tried turning to his son for help. *What should I do, Freddy? Am I doing the right thing?* But the more he stares at his late son's photograph, the more uneasy he feels. For most of his adult life Steve Laing had been in control of his emotions. Freddy's death was an emotional body blow he didn't see coming and it had knocked him clean off his feet. He remained floored as he cycled through the first few stages of grief – shock, denial, pain and guilt – then dragged himself up again as anger took hold. At first he felt angry with Freddy, then God, and finally her. He couldn't take his anger out on Freddy (and he wouldn't have anyway) and God was studiously ignoring him, so *she* took the brunt of his rage. He'd accepted Jim's offer of help and then sat back, satisfied that justice would be done.

But Freddy doesn't appear to be smiling back at him in his graduation photograph any more. His lineless brow is creased and his smile has slipped.

I don't want this, he whispers wordlessly. *Dad, I never did.*

Steve snatches up his phone then puts it down again. He can't ring from his own mobile. He might be desperate but he's not stupid. He roots through the pocket of his suit jacket and pulls out his burner phone instead. There's only one number listed in the contacts and he jabs at it with a stubby forefinger.

Jim picks up after three rings. 'Hello?'

He doesn't say his name, doesn't say Steve's either, but Steve can hear the surprise in his voice. Jim hadn't expected to hear from him again. In fact, he'd made it very clear, after they'd met in the pub, that the only other contact they would have would be a short text message confirming the job had been done.

'I . . .' Steve falters. He has to be careful. He doesn't know who might be privy to their conversation. 'I need to cancel my order.'

Jim doesn't respond.

'Did you hear me?' Steve says. 'I need to cancel—'

'It's too late.'

'But—'

'Don't make me repeat myself again. Your order has gone through.'

'Can't you stop it?' Steve cringes at the desperation in his voice. This isn't him. This isn't how he built up a million-pound business. He doesn't plead or beg.

'No. Mobile contact cannot be established. Your order will be dispatched in the next twenty-four hours.'

'No! I've changed—'

Steve stares into his son's worried eyes as the conversation ends and the line goes dead.

Chapter 28

Anna

Fiona and I share a look as I pull on the plunger on the side of the oil tank and no oil appears in the gauge tube.

'That's bad, isn't it?' she shouts as the wind whips her hair around her cheeks; neither of us bothered to go back to get our coats before we stepped into the garden and we're both wet through.

'Empty!' I shout back.

'What do we do?'

'Nothing we can do! Let's get back inside.'

We set off at a run, speeding round the trees and bushes that hide the oil tank from view, buffeted by the wind as we jog down the path towards the utility door. I come to a stop as I near it and a short woman, swamped in a man's waterproof jacket, appears at the far end of the building.

'Anna!' Christine shouts, trotting towards us. 'There you are!

Sorry to bother you but there's a bit of a situation with the downstairs toilet.'

'I don't like to point fingers,' Christine says as we follow her back through the kitchen and dining room and into the lobby. 'But I'm fairly certain Trevor was the last person to use it. And I'm pretty sure he was drunk,' she adds, lowering her voice.

There's a splash as I step inside the toilet cubicle. Water is dripping over the edge of the toilet and the bowl is an ugly mess of water, loo roll and . . . urgh . . . I turn away and press a hand over my mouth. Why would someone flood the toilet and just leave it like that?

I back out of the cubicle, hurry across the lobby to the reception desk and grab a pen and a piece of paper. As I slap an 'Out of Order' sign on the toilet door Christine heads back towards the kitchen to continue making lunch, satisfied that the situation is now under control. She signals to Fiona to go with her but raises a hand when I move to follow.

'You're under strict instructions to rest today,' she orders. 'You've done too much already.'

As the door closes behind them I linger in the lobby, unsure what to do. There's no way I can sit down and relax with a book, not after what happened yesterday. Instinctively, I glance towards the window where I saw 'TO DIE, TO SLEEP' but, although the glass is misted up again, nothing's written in the condensation. I lift the phone at reception – no dialling tone – then crouch down behind the desk and reset the router. Thirty seconds pass, then a minute. I shift my weight into the chair, log on to the laptop then raise my eyes to the ceiling in silent prayer and try to connect to the Wi-Fi. Nothing. Damn it.

As I wheel the chair back from the desk, raised voices drift down the stairs. Something's going on in the guest corridor.

*

Melanie is standing outside Katie's room, her hands on her hips and a tense expression on her face. She glances across at me as I approach and holds out a hand, warning me not to come any closer.

'What's going on?' I mouth.

She shakes her head and looks back towards the bedroom. 'I'm sorry, Katie, but I really don't think it's appropriate for a strange man to be in your room.'

'Trevor's not a stranger,' her niece snaps back. 'And we're *just talking*.'

'Trevor,' Melanie beckons him with a finger. 'Come on. You know this isn't right.'

I ignore her advice to stay back and step around her so I can see into the room. Katie is sitting on the bed, her oversized woolly jumper pulled over her knees. Sitting on the chair nearest the door, with a bottle of Bowmore whisky in his hand, his head resting on the seat back and his eyes closed, is Trevor. He opens a weary, bloodshot eye and looks at me, then closes it again.

'She's the only one who'll talk to me,' he slurs.

'That's not true,' Melanie says. 'I think you'll find we'd all talk to you if you actually spent some time with us instead of traipsing off on your own.'

He lazily raises a hand and gestures in my direction. 'She stole from me.'

'What did I steal, Trevor?'

He stares at me contemptuously, then closes his eyes again.

'And you accused *me* of stealing!' Katie says, a look of smug triumph on her face as she waggles a finger in my direction. 'Talk about hypocritical.'

Melanie gives me an exasperated look. 'This is what happens when a child doesn't have a father figure,' she hisses under her breath. 'No sense of boundaries whatsoever.'

'Come on, Trevor,' she says, louder this time. 'Let's get you back to your room. You can drink to your heart's content in there.'

'You can't tell him what to do,' Katie says. 'He's an adult. He's not doing anything wrong.'

I can tell from the defiant look in her eyes that this has absolutely nothing to do with wanting to chat to Trevor and everything to do with control. I was the same as a teenager, trying to stake a claim on my own life. Only in my case it was a battle with my mum about tidying my room. It was my personal space in the house so why couldn't I keep it how I wanted to keep it? If the door was closed, why should she care how messy it was?

'Come on now, Katie.' Melanie's fighting to keep her tone light but I can hear the stress in her voice. 'You and Trevor can have a chat later but let's get you downstairs for a drink. I could make you a hot chocolate.'

'Do I look like I'm ten?'

'No, you don't. You—' She screeches in surprise as Trevor lurches unsteadily up and out of his chair. 'Trevor, would you mind sitting down so Katie can leave the room?'

'What the hell's going on up there?' Malcolm's voice booms from the staircase.

'I've got this under control, Malc,' Melanie shouts back. 'Trevor's going back to his own room, aren't you, Trevor?'

'What's he doing in Katie's room?' Like a bull, Malcolm charges, thundering down the corridor as Melanie freezes in the doorway. Trevor makes his escape, shoving Melanie out of the way as he bursts from the room. As she tumbles backwards, arms flailing before she hits the ground, he sprints into his room and slams the door shut.

Malcolm reaches his wife before I do.

'Mel.' He cradles her limp body in his arms. 'Melanie, are you okay?'

*

'Did you see that?' Malcolm glares up at me as he helps his wife to his feet. 'Did you see that animal assault my wife? I knew he was dodgy. I just *knew* it. Right from the moment I laid eyes on him.'

'Please, Malc.' Melanie touches a hand to her cheek. There's a red raw patch on her cheekbone, about the size of a fifty pence piece, from where her skin grazed the carpet. 'I don't think he meant to hurt me. You startled him when you shouted.'

'Me?' His hand falls away from her elbow and he stares at her with a look of utter incredulity. 'You're blaming this on me?'

'I'm just . . . I'm just saying . . .'

'Melanie.' I wrap an arm around her waist as she sways on the spot. 'Can you make it across to your room?'

'I only came upstairs to use the toilet and I heard voices from Katie's room. I didn't expect to see Trevor . . .' She sighs wearily and rests her head on my shoulder.

'Let's get you onto your bed.'

Malcolm takes a step towards Trevor's room. 'I'm not letting him get away with this.'

As I reach out an arm to stop him, Melanie's legs crumple from beneath her and she slips out of my arms and onto the carpet. As she stares up at me with dark, uncomprehending eyes, a shiver runs through me. Someone just walked over my grave.

Chapter 29

Dani

Dani Miller sits ramrod straight on her bunk, her back against the wall, her feet dangling off the side, and stares at the photos on the wall opposite until they smooth and blur into a kaleidoscope of colour. Unlike her cell mate, Dani hasn't got any photos stuck to the wall with toothpaste. She doesn't want anyone to know her vulnerabilities or any dirty skanks to see what her daughter looks like. Doesn't trust herself not to react if they say something that pushes her buttons. She imagines her three-year-old daughter's face amongst the smudge of colour; focusing in on her until she can clearly see her curly blonde hair, round brown eyes, little squirrel nose and impossibly soft skin. She imagines her mum, grey roots showing against her dark brown hair, leaning over Maisie's pink princess bed and scooping her up for a hug and a kiss. She'd better not be telling Maisie to call her Mummy or Mama or anything like that. She can call herself Nana or Nini or Nona but not

Mummy. Dani is Maisie's mummy and that's never going to change.

That's why she's doing this. Not because she's a psycho, although she's glad that the other women think she is. It keeps her safe, stops anyone from fucking with her. She's never going to make anything of her life. She's been told that enough times. When she was a teenager it fucked her right off but now she's older . . . well . . . sometimes you can't fight what you can't change. But it's not going to be like that for Maisie. Maisie's different. She's clever and she's about as beautiful as they get. You need cash though, to make it in this life, and when she's eighteen a fat lump of cash will be coming her way. That's if her arsehole of a father doesn't rob it. Dani hasn't heard from Del once since she was sent down. Probably got someone else to go on the rob for him so he can get a hit four times a day. Jesus, what was she thinking, buying all that crap about her being the only woman for him? She can see through it all, now that she's clean.

She gets up, glances over her shoulder to check no one's walking past her cell, then reaches into the gap she's dug into her thin mattress and pulls out the toothbrush. She runs her thumb over the pointed end, the plastic burnt and rough. She didn't make the shank. It was given to her by the same fat dyke who asked her if she wanted to make some money. She tucks it under the band of her bra, then bags out her sweatshirt and steps out of her cell, shoulders back, chin up. It's just a job, she tells herself as she crosses the corridor. Just a job, a means to an end.

The prisoner jolts as Dani walks into her cell and closes the door behind her. The book she's reading falls from her hands and she backs up against the wall, her eyes wide and fearful. The knot in Dani's stomach loosens a little. Scared is good. This woman's not going to fight back. She's not going to do her any damage. Not if she acts quickly. But she needs to make sure she stays quiet.

'You Donna?' she asks.

The woman nods. She's a big bitch, huge tits sitting on her equally big stomach, thinning hair pulled back into a ponytail and no neck to speak of. She looks like the sort that sits on her arse all day, shovelling sausage rolls into her enormous gob.

'Donna Farrell?' Dani asks.

The woman nods again. She's got her hands up by her face, her fingers tapping on her doughy cheeks. Morse code for 'fucking help me!' Dani thinks, making herself smile. Dani's smile fades. 'You killed two people,' she says.

'I . . . I . . .' Her target's eyes flit from Dani to the door. Dani can sense her panic rising, smell the fear beneath the honk of body odour and sugary snacks. She needs to act quickly, before Donna finds her voice, or her legs.

'You could have killed a kid,' she says. 'You could have killed my kid.'

It's not true. Maisie's never left Crawley but saying it makes Dani feel better, stronger, more justified.

'Two years,' she says, repeating what she was told. 'I got more for doing what I did and I didn't hurt no one. That's sick, innit? It's wrong.'

'No,' the other woman says as Dani pulls the shank from her bra and grips it tightly. 'No. No. Don't do this.'

Dani weighs up her options. If she lunges forwards and stabs Donna where she is – scrunched up into a fat ball in the corner of the bed – the other woman might have time to grab her, maybe even wrestle the shank off her. She needs her to get up and expose the tender spot under her massive tits – that's if she can find her stomach beneath all the flab.

'Get up,' she barks. 'Get off the bed.'

Donna does what she's told, shuffling across the bed then heaving herself up and onto her feet. Her lips part as she turns to face Dani and her chest expands as she takes a deep breath but the scream doesn't leave her throat. It's smothered by Dani's hand, then silenced by the long shard of plastic that pierces her clothes and her skin and buries itself in her stomach.

Dani keeps her hand pressed to Donna's mouth, pinning her head to the wall as her legs crumple beneath her and she sinks to the ground.

'It's nothing personal,' Dani says, pulling the shank from Donna's guts, jumping back as blood gushes from her stomach and pools between her legs.

She pulls off her blood-splattered sweatshirt and wraps the homemade weapon in it, then takes one of Donna's sweatshirts off her shelf and puts it on. It swamps her but she nods in satisfaction as she turns to leave the cell. 'Sometimes you've gotta do what you've gotta do.'

Chapter 30

Steve

Steve Laing is having dinner, alone, in front of the TV, when a phone vibrates on the table beside the sofa. He tears his eyes away from the screen (it's one of his favourite scenes in *The Sopranos*, the one where Tony sits outside the family house at night with a gun, protecting his family from a bear) and places the slice of pepperoni pizza he's been eating back in the box. He licks his fingers then wipes them on a napkin before he reaches for his mobile.

It'll just be one of the lads, he tells himself as he picks it up. But there's no new message showing on the screen. His throat tightens as he reaches for the other phone and the pizza churns, thick and greasy, in his stomach.

It's only a four-word text message but it makes him heave so violently his mouth fills with undigested pizza and bile.

Order dispatched as requested.

It's over. Justice has been done. Donna Farrell, the lorry driver who fell asleep at the wheel and murdered his son, is dead.

Part Three

Chapter 31

Anna

After Melanie's collapse, Malcolm and I helped her into their room and onto the bed. I tried not to panic as she lay there, pale, silent and wan. After what had happened to David I was terrified that, if she became gravely ill, we might lose her too. Katie, standing in the doorway, looked equally scared. She apologised over and over again about letting Trevor into her room, eventually bursting into tears. As Malcolm comforted her I gave Melanie water and a bar of chocolate I found in the top of a rucksack. I'd noticed her picking at her food during meal-times and assumed she was a fussy eater, but as I held her hand I could see how thin her wrists were. After five or ten minutes her cheeks began to pink up again and when she snapped at Malcolm to stop fussing as he tried to layer another blanket on top of her, I knew she'd be okay.

'Are you all right, Anna?' Malcolm says now. 'You look exhausted.'

'I'm fine,' I say, but the yawn I fail to stifle gives me away.

'Go and have a nap.' Melanie props herself up on an elbow. 'You were supposed to be taking it easy today.'

I glance at my watch. 'But it's nearly lunchtime.'

'We'll save you some.'

'It'll probably just be soup. Not that I'm complaining,' Malcolm adds swiftly.

'Okay.' I look from the pair of them to Katie, her eyes red-rimmed but no longer crying, curled in the armchair by the door.

'You're not going to start anything with Trevor, are you, Malcolm?' I say as I get up from the end of the bed. 'What happened was an accident.'

Melanie raises her eyebrows. 'He wouldn't dare.'

I don't bother to undress when I get back to my room. Instead I lock the door and throw myself onto the bed fully clothed, then flip onto my side so I'm facing the door. It's been less than a day since David died and I'm completely drained, physically and mentally, but there's no way I can sleep. I'm waiting for the handle to turn and the door to my bedroom to swing open. Logically, I know there's no way that can happen. It's locked and I've got David's master keys and the spare in the pocket of my trousers. But someone let themselves in last night and I'm pretty certain it's the same person who wrote 'TO DIE, TO SLEEP' on the lobby window. I want to believe Katie when she says it's not her but I don't see who else it could be. Unless someone else unlocked my door before she came up the stairs. But why? To stand in the doorway and watch me sleep? The thought makes me shiver and I lift the duvet over my shoulder and pull it tightly around my body.

Whoever it was is determined to make me suffer for what I did.

I'm sorry! I want to scream. *I'm sorry I killed them. I'm sorry they're dead. I would bring them back if I could. I'd rewind time. I'd do anything. I'd—*

The thought stalls as a new one cuts in front of it.

They don't want me to suffer. They don't want me to say sorry. They want me dead. Whoever's been leaving me the messages wants me to kill myself. It's the only thing that will make them stop.

I bury my face in the pillow but Freddy and Peter's faces swim in and out of my mind.

How can you sleep, Anna, after what you did?

I press my hands against my ears.

You did this, Anna, you destroyed our lives.

I shake my head. I'm sorry. I didn't mean for any of this to happen. I didn't want you to die.

And yet we're still dead . . .

I hug the pillow to my face, pressing the soft, white cotton into my mouth to stifle my terrified sobs. I just want it to stop. Please, please, just stop.

I cry until my throat is raw and I feel as though I'm suffocating on each inward breath, then I hurl the pillow across the room and thump the mattress until I collapse, numb, raw and spent. I curl into a ball and lie still, my breath raggedy and my heart pounding in my chest. My eyes are open but I'm not really seeing. I'm not looking at anything. I'm just staring at the distance that stretches between me and the wardrobe. The space between me and the world.

I lie there for a long time, doing and seeing nothing, until my right shoulder begins to twinge and ache. I try to ignore it. I want to lie here forever, not feeling, not moving. But the pain increases, gnawing at my muscles and nerves, and the voice in the back of my brain grows louder and louder. *You're going to have to move. You need to turn over.*

Out of the corner of my eye I see my mobile phone on the bedside table, the light blinking green. I grab at it, sending a glass of water tumbling onto the hard wooden floor. But it's not a message or a missed call. It's just a notification from Samsung Health that I haven't met my activity targets for this week. There's no signal in the top right corner and no Wi-Fi symbol. As I open my bedside drawer to tuck it away, out of sight, I see something that wasn't there the last time I opened it. Something that's definitely not mine.

Joe is bent over the toilet bowl, a plunger in one rubber-gloved hand and a straightened coat hanger in the other. The water on the floor has been mopped up but it looks as though the blockage remains. He glances over his shoulder at me and gives a sharp shake of his head.

'You might want to come back when all this is finished.'

'I don't want to use the loo. Have you got time for a chat?'

He grimaces. 'Can it wait?'

'Not really.'

'Okay.' He sighs as he straightens up. 'Give me a second to get cleaned up.'

I point across the lobby. 'I'll wait in there.'

Five minutes later Joe strolls into the lounge, his shirtsleeves still pushed up to his elbows but his hands rubber glove-free.

'What's going on?' He parks himself in the armchair opposite me and leans forwards on his elbows.

'Is this yours?' I uncurl my hand.

He looks down at the capped piece of plastic lying on a sheet of paper in my palm. 'It's a syringe.'

'I know. And according to the leaflet it's got insulin in it.'

'Insulin?' He plucks the rolled piece of paper from beneath the syringe. His confusion turns to concern as he reads it.

'Have you seen this?' He turns it towards me and points to

one sentence that's been picked out in bright yellow highlighter pen.

May result in death.

Of course I've seen it. It made me gasp and slam my bedroom drawer shut. Another message from my tormentor. Another reminder that they want me dead.

'Where'd you get it?' Joe asks.

'Is it yours?'

'What? No.' He looks at me with genuine confusion. 'I use cartridge insulin. You saw the packet when you cleaned my room. Remember?'

'I know but I thought you might use syringes too.'

'No.' He shakes his head. 'Never. Where did you find this?'

'In my room. In my bedside drawer. The instruction leaflet was wrapped around the syringe.'

He runs a hand over his beard, tugging lightly at the wiry hairs. 'It wasn't there before?'

'No. Definitely not.' I point at the piece of paper in his hand. 'Is that normal? For a sentence to be highlighted like that?'

'Not in my experience.' He looks at it again. 'It's not been printed on the page, it's pen. Look, it bleeds through to the other side. I don't understand why you'd do that unless . . . it's not Katie's, is it?'

'Why'd you say that?'

'It's the sort of thing you might do for a teenager, I guess, make sure they remember how dangerous an insulin overdose can be. My parents always used to drum it into me how important it was to test my blood sugar and keep a Mars bar close at hand when I was away on school trips.'

I'm trying to read his reaction. He does seem genuinely surprised by my discovery but he's the only guest with diabetic medication in his room – that I've spotted, at least.

'I suppose it would make sense for it to be Katie's,' I say.

'She's the only other person who's been in my room, other than me.'

As far as I know, I think but don't say.

'When she sleepwalked last night, you mean?'

'Yes. But if it is hers it means she let herself into my room, put her insulin and the instruction leaflet in my drawer and then walked back to the doorway.'

'It's possible.' He shrugs. 'Remember my sleepwalking story about the bin?'

I do remember, but it still seems like such a strange thing to do.

'So what do you want to do?' Joe asks. 'Are you going to have a word with her?'

That didn't exactly go well when I asked her about the sleep-walking earlier.

'No.' I shake my head. 'Not yet. I'm going to have a look at the medical questionnaires first.'

Joe follows me into the lobby then hovers by the reception desk as I search through the drawers for the guest folder. When they made their walking tour bookings, the agent in London had them each fill out and sign a medical questionnaire which was then forwarded on to us. David preferred to keep it paper-based, he told me, because you couldn't trust the Wi-Fi. He was right on that count.

I find the folder and flick through the forms. Trevor's is on the top. He's ticked no to all the major medical issues – asthma, high blood pressure, diabetes, heart disease, etc – and scratched a line through the question 'Have you ever had any serious illness not listed above?' The box for listing prescribed medication is blank too. Malcolm's next, he's ticked high blood pressure, Christine has ticked thyroid disease in 'current conditions' and cancer in the 'medical history' section, Melanie's ticked anaemia (which might explain her collapse earlier), Joe has ticked diabetes, and neither Katie nor Fiona have had any major medical issues and aren't on any medication.

'Well?' Joe says from across the desk.

I don't reply. Instead I flick back through the forms. He's definitely the only one who's ticked diabetes but why would he lie about the syringe being his? Unless . . . my breath catches in my throat and a cold shiver passes through me.

'Well?' Joe says again. He's taken his hands out of his pockets and crossed his arms over his chest. There's an intensity to his gaze that wasn't there a few seconds ago.

I force myself to look him straight in the eye. 'It's Katie's,' I lie. 'You were right. She's diabetic too.'

Chapter 32

Mohammed

The best thing about the spinal rehab centre, Mohammed thinks bitterly as cheerful voices drift into his room from the corridor, is that he's no longer tortured by having to watch other people's visitors come in. It was hell, scanning their faces, looking for his girlfriend – half hoping she'd come to see him, half hoping she hadn't. He told her not to visit, via his parents at first, then, when he was brought a mobile phone, via text.

He took a while planning what he'd say (time was something he had plenty of) and he finally settled on:

Please don't come and visit me. I've had a lot of time to think and I've realised that we don't have a future. You aren't the type of girl I could marry. I'm sorry, but there's no changing how I feel.

It hurt him, writing something so stinging, but he had to be cruel and go for her weak spot to keep her away. She replied immediately:

I know you don't mean that. You're just saying it because of the accident. It doesn't matter to me if you can't walk. I love you and want to be with you.

That made him cry but he swiped at his tears and typed back:

Well I don't love you any more. There's someone else. I met her at work. We've been having an affair for a while and if you come to the ward you're going to run into her.

It was a lie, of course, and his girlfriend kept fighting back, insisting she come and see him. In the end he told her that he'd have her kicked out if she tried to visit, that he wasn't the man she'd fallen in love with and she'd have to learn to accept that (that much was true at least). In the end she acquiesced. She said she could tell he was in a lot of pain and that, if he changed his mind, she'd be waiting. And that made him cry again.

Chapter 33

Anna

As predicted by Malcolm, lunch is soup and bread. It's surprisingly tasty but I haven't had more than a couple of mouthfuls. I was still sitting behind the desk at reception when Christine poked her head round the door and said it was lunchtime. I told Joe to go on in but he insisted on waiting for me as I locked the medical forms in the drawer and pocketed the key. He's sitting next to me now – chatting away to Melanie, who's opposite – seemingly oblivious to the fact that I flinch each time his elbow brushes mine. I want to trust him but he's the only diabetic on the medical forms. Why would any of the others have a syringe containing insulin if they don't have the condition? It doesn't make sense. I still don't know what to make of the medical forms. There's a chance one of the guests could be lying. They could be diabetic but chose not to put it on the form. But why? Did they know before they came that they were going to gift me a syringe and a dark instruction? Is that me clutching at straws because I don't want to believe that Joe's my stalker? My gut tells me that he's a good person, but how do I know for sure? I need to ask him if he knows Freddy and Steve and then study his reaction. If he *is* behind everything I'll see it in his eyes when I say their names, I'm sure of it. I glance around the table. Other than Trevor, who hasn't left his room since he fled Katie's, everyone else is having their lunch. Anxiety twists at my gut. I need answers but my heart's beating so hard I can feel it in the base of my throat.

'Joe.'

Almost in slow motion, he breaks off from his conversation with Melanie and turns to look at me.

'Do you know someone called Freddy Laing?'

A frown creases his brow, just for a second, and I feel sure I'm about to be sick.

'No,' he says flatly. 'Doesn't ring a bell.'

He looks back at Melanie. 'Sorry, what were we—'

'What about Steve Laing or Peter Cross?' My voice takes on a strange, uneven pitch and some of the other guests, further down the table, turn their heads. 'Do you know them?'

'No.' There's a flash of irritation on his face. 'Why, who are—'

He's interrupted by the dining room door crashing open. Trevor, still clutching his bottle of whisky, sways through the room and kicks open the kitchen door.

'Trevor!' Christine gets to her feet. 'There's food—'

But her voice is drowned out by the sound of glass smashing and the low clang of metal being hurled against walls.

'Trevor!' Joe reaches the kitchen first but pulls up short as he opens the door. Malcolm smacks up against him and tries to push him away but Joe reaches an arm across the doorway, barring him from entering. I stand on tiptoes and peer over Joe's other shoulder. Inside the kitchen Trevor is whirling around, swiping at pots, pans and dishes, sending them scuttling along the surfaces and onto the ground.

'Where are they?' He throws open a cupboard and scoops out the glassware. Wine, brandy, cocktail and whisky glasses fly across the kitchen, exploding as they hit the wall, the oven and the floor.

I watch in horror as he yanks open the cutlery door and upends the tray, sending knives, forks and spoons crashing to the ground.

'Trevor, stop it!' Joe shouts, then ducks as a frying pan is hurled in our direction. Before I'm fully upright again, Trevor pulls open the fridge door and scoops the food off the shelves and onto the floor, stamping it into the tiles.

'Not the food!' I scream as he reaches behind the fridge and pulls with both hands. The fridge tips forwards then lands with a crash in front of the oven, forming a barrier between us.

'Malcolm, help me!' Joe shouts as he picks his way through broken glass and smashed crockery. Malcolm squeezes up beside him as they approach the fridge. They bend their knees, grunting as they take the strain.

'Trevor!' I shout as he moves on to the freezer. 'Please! Stop! We need the food.'

He ignores me and wrenches it open, still muttering about finding something. Joe inches towards him, one hand raised, palm out.

'Trevor, mate. Whatever it is you've lost, we can help you look—'

But before he can finish his sentence, Trevor lunges at him, right elbow raised, hand clenched. Joe reels backwards as the fist connects with his jaw. He falls like a stone, hitting his head against the fridge before he drops to the floor.

Christine, Fiona and Melanie all press up against me, trying to see what's going on, all talking at once, shouting at Trevor to stop. As I turn to tell them to move away, Malcolm hunkers down like a rugby player going in for the tackle and launches himself at Trevor. For an older man he's surprisingly fast and his shoulder connects with Trevor's stomach. The force of the blow makes Trevor stumble backwards, into the utility room. He loses his footing and falls heavily, smacking against the cold stone tiles. He lies still, winded and silent, for a second, maybe two, then roars in anger and shifts onto his side. Before he can get up Malcolm slams the door to the utility room shut and slides the bolt across.

'Malcolm, you can't do that!' I start to pick my way through the destroyed kitchen but he blocks my route, standing between me and the locked door. Behind him, Joe groans as he gets up from the floor.

'Malcolm,' I say again. 'You can't lock him in there, he's not an animal.'

'Then maybe he shouldn't act like one.'

'He's drunk. He doesn't know what he's doing.'

He crosses his arms over his chest. 'I'm just giving him the opportunity to cool off.'

'Let him out!'

'He knocked my wife off her feet earlier and now,' he gestures across at Joe, who's upright again, rubbing at his jaw, 'he's hit another of the guests. Who's he going to hit next if we open that door? Me? Christine? Katie? Someone could get seriously hurt.' He touches a hand to the utility room door. 'Do you want to take that risk, Anna? Yes or no?'

I look from Malcolm to the women huddled together in the doorway and then to Joe. He gives me a strange, pointed look and lightly shakes his head.

'Well?' Malcolm says. 'Are you going to put us all in danger or not?'

I meet his gaze. 'I'm not putting anyone in danger. And I'm not going to be told what to do. Could everyone please return to the lounge? Yes, Malcolm,' I say as he backs up against the utility room door, 'even you.'

Over by the fire Katie, Joe and Fiona are gathered together on the sofa. Fiona is dabbing at Joe's jaw, face and neck with a blood-stained tea towel, while Katie looks on in horror. I catch her eye.

'Are you okay?' I mouth.

She pulls the blanket that's around her shoulders up over her head. 'Yeah.'

She's not though. There's fear and confusion written all over her face. Not that Malcolm seems to care. He hasn't stopped pacing up and down by the window, ignoring Melanie's pleas to sit down, since we all came into the lounge.

Everyone falls silent as I stand up and clear my throat. The whole building seems to be holding its breath.

'After what happened in the kitchen I just wanted to reassure you all that I take your safety seriously. Unfortunately, one guest's behaviour has—'

'Just say it as it is,' Malcolm snaps. 'Trevor's behaviour.'

'Trevor, who's still *locked* in the utility room,' Fiona says tightly.

'Only until this meeting is over,' I say, 'then I'll have a word with him. I'm sure once he sobers up he'll be horrified at what just happened.'

Malcolm puffs out his chest. 'You seriously think you can reason with that man?'

'Why not?'

'Because he's dangerous! He punched Joe, knocked Mel over and destroyed most of our food. And you want to let him out? Why, so he can burn the whole place down too?'

'Maybe we should keep him in the utility room until we can get help,' Christine says.

Fiona raises her eyebrows. 'And how long do you think that will take? Another day? Two? A week? You can't seriously think we should keep him locked up that long? The man had too much to drink and lost his shit. He wouldn't be kept in a police cell longer than twenty-four hours for that.'

'No one's suggesting we keep him locked up for a week,' I say. 'And we're not the police.'

Joe shifts position on the sofa. 'How long do storms normally last here, Anna? At this time of year?'

'I don't really know. I only arrived ten days ago.'

Malcolm stops pacing. 'You've worked here for less than two weeks. And you didn't think to mention it?'

'I just have.'

'Oh, for goodness' sake, Malcolm,' Melanie says. 'Can you just let her speak?'

'Why should I? She obviously doesn't know what she's doing.'

'And neither do you,' Fiona says, the base of her neck flushed red. 'Ex-policeman or prison guard, are you?'

'Actually,' Malcolm says, 'I'm a professor of psychology. I know how to read people and that man—'

'Please!' I hold up my hands. 'This isn't getting us anywhere.'

'I think we should have a vote,' Malcolm says.

'Vote?'

'About whether Trevor stays locked up until the storm passes.'

'No.' I shake my head. 'That isn't up for debate.'

'I hate to say it but I agree with him,' Christine says. 'I think we should vote.'

I look at Joe and Fiona but they avoid my eye. I do a quick tally in my head. It's close but I think there are enough sensible people in the room to put an end to this ridiculous debate. Trevor's not the loose cannon, Malcolm is, and he's not going to let this drop until he realises he's in the minority.

'Okay then. We'll vote on it,' I say decisively. 'Who thinks we should leave Trevor in the utility room until after the storm passes?'

Malcolm raises his hand. After a pause, and a swift look from her husband, Melanie does the same. I stare at her in disbelief. I'd have put money on her voting no. After a nudge, Katie raises her hand too.

Fiona half raises her hand. 'I'm not voting. I just want to ask a question.'

'Only if it's relevant.'

'It is. If there's no running water in the utility room, how's Trevor going to eat and drink? Or use the toilet for that matter?'

'There's a cat flap,' Christine suggests. 'We could post food and drink to him.'

'But not a toilet presumably.'

'We're not letting him out for toilet breaks if that's what you're suggesting, Ms Gardiner,' Malcolm cuts in. 'There's a bucket in there. He can use that.'

'You can't be serious?'

Anxiety gnaws at my guts. Three guests are in favour of keeping Trevor locked up. I'll vote no, so will Joe and Fiona. If Christine votes no too, this stupid charade will be over. I smile at her. 'Any more votes for yes?'

She looks up at me. Considering all eyes are on her, she appears remarkably unperturbed.

'I'm sorry,' she says. 'I'm loath to agree with Mr Ward over there but, for all our safety, I vote to keep Trevor in the utility room until the storm passes.'

Malcolm raises his fist. 'Four. Majority win.'

All the blood in my body seems to sink to my feet. We can't do this. The storm might not end for days. We'd essentially be keeping someone captive.

'Another suggestion,' I say quickly. 'We have another vote and decide whether to let Trevor move into the cottage instead.'

'Gordon's cottage?' Malcolm says.

'Yes.'

'But it's locked, isn't it?'

'So we break in.'

'And how do you suggest we get him down there? Offer to hold his hand? You're assuming he'd go willingly.'

Joe, still staring into the fire, mutters something under his breath.

'Sorry,' I say. 'What was that, Joe?'

He doesn't turn to look at me but he does raise his voice. 'You can't let this happen, Anna.'

I'm gripped by a wave of uncertainty. What do I do? Overrule the vote? Let Trevor go so he can hole himself away in his room with a bottle of whisky again, not knowing when he'll come out or what he'll do? Or do I get someone to pack him a bag and ask him to leave, hoping he'll find a way into the cottage? Anything could happen to him and we'd never know. He's as much my responsibility as the rest of the guests. But if I let him go I'll have a mutiny on my hands. I turn back to the others and look at each of their anxious, expectant faces in turn. I'm going to have to pretend to go along with this, at least until Trevor sobers up. Then I'll let him out and make up some kind of excuse.

'I'm sorry, Joe,' I say. 'It was a majority vote. Trevor stays in the utility room for now.'

Chapter 34

Walking out of the front door is like stepping into a monsoon. Rain lashes at my face and the wind hits me full force in the chest, almost shoving me back into the building. I lean into the gale and run round the hotel until I reach the utility room door. The back of the building is more sheltered from the elements than the front, with the upwards curve of the garden, trees, bushes and sheds offering some protection from the storm.

'Trevor?' I tentatively push at the cat flap, bracing myself to snatch my hand back if it's slammed back down again. I push a little harder until it's fully open. Water seeps through the thin denim of my jeans, wetting my knees as I peer inside.

Trevor is sitting with his back to the kitchen door, his knees pulled up to his chest and his head lowered onto his folded arms. He groans softly.

'Trevor, it's Anna, the hotel receptionist. I just wanted to check that you're okay.'

The groaning increases in volume.

'I'm really sorry this happened, Trevor, but you're not going to be in there forever. We just need you to calm down and sober up. You can't go round smashing up the hotel and assaulting people.'

Trevor's lips move but I can't catch what he's mumbling.

'Can you say that again? A bit louder?' I angle my head so my ear is closer to the cat flap.

'Someone took my medication.' Trevor's shout is slurred and the words run together but this time I understand.

'What medication?'

'My medication!' He scrabbles to his feet and charges at the door. The cat flap slaps shut and the door vibrates on its hinges as he slams himself up against it. 'Let me out!' he shouts as he forces the handle up and down. 'Let me out! Let me out!'

I jump back, willing the door to hold as he continues to throw himself at it. I want to run away. But I don't. I force myself to stand and wait.

After what feels like forever the pounding stops and all I can hear is the drumming of the rain on the paving stones, the gushing of the gutters and the howl of the wind. I rip a branch off the bush behind me and use it to push the cat flap open. But there's no sign of Trevor. He's not by the door any more. I shuffle to my right and lean forwards so I can see the left of the room where the washing machines and tumble dryers are, but the branch slides off the plastic and the cat flap rattles shut.

'Trevor!' I reach a hand towards the cat flap. 'You need to tell me what kind of medication it was.'

I tap at the plastic then snatch my hand away, startled by the cawing of a gull. Rainwater drips off my nose and my eyelashes, and my jeans and jacket cling to my skin.

'Was it in a syringe?' I push at the cat flap again, forcing it fully open. But Trevor's not standing beside the washing machines and tumble dryers and he's not—

His face appears in the cat flap, making me scream.

'Find my medicine,' he says as I scrabble away from the door, my heels slipping on the wet patio tiles.

'WHAT KIND?'

He slurs a word at me, his eyes fixed on mine.

'Try again,' I say. 'Say it again.'

He sighs heavily, takes a deep breath and screws his eyes tightly shut.

A second later he opens them again.

'Valium,' he says.

Other than the smell, an unpleasant combination of body odour and rotten food, Trevor's room isn't at all how I imagined it. I expected total devastation: belongings all over the place, a dirty toilet, crumpled bed linen and broken fixtures. Instead the room is neat and tidy. The bed has been made, the duvet straightened, and there's nothing in the bathroom apart from a stick of deodorant, a toothbrush, a travel-size tube of toothpaste, a bottle of Head and Shoulders and some supermarket own-brand shower gel. There's nothing on the bedside table. Nothing in the wardrobe either, or in any of the drawers. The only sign that someone's been staying in this room is the large blue rucksack propped up against the radiator under the window. I lift it and look underneath. There's nothing there.

Trevor's medication has to be in the rucksack. I unclip the top and loosen the toggle. Inside is a plastic bag containing what I assume are his dirty clothes. Underneath are more clothes, clean and neatly folded. I carefully place them on the bed, then look back in the rucksack. I lift out a pair of binoculars, a compass, a map of the Scottish Isles and a heavy roll of material bound with a leather lace. I carefully untie it and unroll the bundle. Inside are five knives with wooden handles and long, sharp blades, tucked into letter pockets. One pocket is empty: a knife is missing. I lay them down on the bed and continue my search. I find waterproof matches, a sleeping bag, rolled tight, some black plastic bags, a first aid kit, a canteen of water, canned food, some wire, a sharp piece of metal that looks like the end of a spear, a torch, a can opener, a sewing kit, a length of cord, sunscreen, cotton wool balls and petroleum jelly. There is also a camping gas stove and a gas canister. I've never seen anything like it. Trevor seems to have packed for a camping trip, not a hotel stay.

I check the side pockets, the hood of the rucksack and all of the zipped nooks and crannies but there's no medication in any of them. I rifle through the first aid kit but there's nothing in there either. I check under the bed, in every single drawer and in the bin. Again, nothing.

I take one last look around the room, then start packing Trevor's things back into his rucksack. I pause as I reach for the roll of knives. Where's the missing one?

The hairs prickle on the back of my neck and my skin tightens against my scalp. Someone's watching me. I swing round, expecting to find someone in the doorway.

But there's no one there.

In Memoriam

In Memoriam

Akhtar Begum

Remembering my friend Akhtar (1990–2012). You were the best friend I could have ever wished for. I still miss your smiling face. You will always be beautiful to me.

You're not taking the hint, are you, Anna? Your obsession with the guests – those frantic bleating sheep – has distracted you from your guilt. It's not good to bury your feelings, Anna. You need to face up to what you did. I wasn't going to do this again, I wasn't going to step in and make that decision for someone. I wanted your passing to be gentle. For you to lie down, close your eyes and drift away. I wanted it to be perfect, but it's not going to be that way now. You've ruined it. And that makes me very cross indeed. Almost as cross as I was with my mum.

Chapter 35

Anna

When I returned from checking on Trevor I was met by the sound of sweeping, tinkling glass and low groans. Melanie and Christine were in the kitchen, sweeping the floor, wiping the surfaces and cleaning up. Almost everything Trevor had wrenched out of the fridge was beyond saving. He'd even emptied the last of the milk by stamping on the plastic bottle. All we had left to eat were a few industrial-sized bags of pasta, a bag of potatoes, some tinned tomatoes, fish and meat, flour, spices and whatever was in the freezer. Melanie took one look at my stricken face as I surveyed what was left and said that she and Malcolm would make dinner. I didn't put up a fight. Instead I joined in with the clean-up effort.

For the first half an hour or so the utility room shook on its hinges as Trevor threw himself at the door, screaming to be let out. It was almost more than I could bear but, with Christine and Melanie voting to keep him in, there was no way I could let him out. After a couple of hours the kitchen looked almost normal again.

Melanie shooed me and Christine out of the kitchen once it was tidy and I had no choice but to leave. I turned down Christine's invitation to play backgammon and went up to my room instead, hiding away, unable to sleep, rest or read, until finally Malcolm shouted up the stairs that it was time for dinner.

The atmosphere couldn't be tenser. Fiona and Joe, sitting at the far end of the table, seem to be pretending that I no longer exist. Fiona looks away whenever our eyes meet and Joe is studiously ignoring me. There's a divide in the group now – us and them and, to those two, I am most definitely 'them'.

After dinner, a very bland tomato pasta, I sneak out to check on Trevor again. Hope flares in his eyes as I peer through the cat flap and explain that I've searched his room for his medication, then dies just as quickly when I admit I haven't been able to find it. He buries his face in his arms and doesn't look up again, not even as I post three blankets, a pillow, a bottle of water, some biscuits, tinned meat and apples through the small gap. I move to stand up but I can't bring myself to leave. It doesn't feel right, leaving him in there all alone when he's in such a bad state. Whatever the Valium has been prescribed for, he's a nervous wreck without it, shaking and rocking and muttering to himself. I touch a hand to my jeans pocket, feeling the shape of the back door key under my palm. I could get Trevor's rucksack from his room and leave it propped up by the bush, then post him the key to let himself out. Other than a tent he has everything in his rucksack that he needs to survive and I'm fairly certain he'll be able to break into the cottage without too much of a problem. But what about the missing knife? Has he got that on him? I'm pretty certain he wouldn't use it on me if I let him go but what if he ran into Malcolm or Joe? I've got no way of predicting how he'll act. Sighing, I get to my feet. I'll wait until the morning, when he's sober, then I'll talk to him again and let him out.

Malcolm's baritone rumble greets me as I open the front door to the hotel. The lounge door is ajar, just a couple of inches but enough for me to be sure that Malcolm and Melanie are the only two people inside. He's striding back and forth in the centre of the room with whisky sloshing around in the tumbler in his hand and an exasperated look on his face. Melanie's sitting on the sofa, her glasses in her hand, wearily rubbing her eyes.

'All I'm asking,' she says, 'is for you to think before you speak. I don't think you have any idea how offensive some of the things you say are to the other guests.'

'I don't give a crap what they think.'

'What *I* think, then. I can't bear hearing you refer to Trevor as an animal. You were the Head of Psychology, for God's sake!'

'And?'

'And you should know better!' Her voice takes on a strange, strangled tone. 'I can't believe you'd be so insensitive.'

'The man's a drunk.'

'He *was* drunk. There's a difference. What you said is offensive, dangerous and incredibly uneducated.'

'You're calling me uneducated?' He guffaws. 'Says the woman who barely scraped a 2:2.'

'Oh, for God's sake.' She grabs the corner of the cushion beside her and, for a second, I think she's going to throw it at him. Instead she smacks it against the seat of the sofa. 'Don't you dare start playing that game. This isn't about education—'

He smirks. 'You just said it was.'

'Arrrgh.' She grabs her hair at the roots and screams up at him. 'You can be a complete arsehole sometimes. I have never, ever met a more pig-headed man in my life.'

'Resorting to name-calling now, are we?'

'Yes, I am. Because you're not listening to me, Malcolm. I am *trying* to let you know that your behaviour is unacceptable and I'm not the only one who thinks so. We're on the verge of being completely ostracised by the other guests.'

'And I should care about that why?'

'You might not care but I do. The way you act reflects badly on me.'

'Oooooh.' He raises his eyebrows theatrically. 'That's what this is about. You're embarrassed to be associated with me.'

A second passes, then another as Melanie stares up at him and her fingers twitch on the cushion in her lap. Go on, I silently urge her. Tell him how you feel. Don't be scared.

'Fiona been having a word in your ear, has she?' Malcolm plonks himself down on the sofa beside her, sloshing whisky all over the carpet. 'Been schooling you, has she? Telling you to speak up for yourself?'

His voice has changed tone. It's thin and nasty, loaded with danger.

'No one's been schooling me, Malcolm.' She shifts away from him, backing up against the arm of the sofa. 'This conversation has been a long time coming.'

'It has, has it?' His top lip thins, revealing his teeth. 'But you chose now – NOW – to bring it up.'

His shout makes me jump and Melanie flinches.

'Yes,' she says quietly. 'I'm speaking up now and it's up to you to choose whether you listen or not. I'm sick of the way you treat me, Malcolm. I don't like the way you snap at me, speak over me and order me around. It's disrespectful and I won't have it.'

Malcolm says nothing but his grip tightens on the whisky tumbler and his left foot swings back and forth.

'I only voted for Trevor to stay locked in the utility room,' Melanie continues, 'because I knew you'd start an argument if

I disagreed with you. I've been feeling terrible all evening. That poor man. He needs our help, not to be ostracised.'

'I'd probably have more respect for you if you had disagreed with me.'

'What?' She holds herself very still as Malcolm reaches forwards and swipes the whisky bottle from where it's propped up against the base of the sofa. He unscrews the lid and fills half his glass.

'You think I enjoy it?' he says. 'Being married to someone who isn't my intellectual equal? The reason I'm occasionally controversial, my dear, is because I enjoy the fallout. It keeps me on my feet, mentally. God knows you don't.'

'I see.' She studies him silently, then her spine straightens and she raises her chin. 'Well, if that's the case you won't object if I ask you to sleep down here on the sofa tonight rather than share my room.'

'Our room.'

'*My room.*' Her voice takes on a steely note. 'I paid for the holiday, Malcolm, just like I pay for the house, the food and your bloody walking boots. You might have a PhD but your consultancy work doesn't pay the bills. *I do.*'

I scuttle across the lobby and hide behind the desk as Melanie walks stiffly out of the lounge and up the stairs. She pauses halfway up and turns back. I hold my breath, terrified that she's seen me, but her gaze is fixed on the open lounge door.

'We made a mistake locking Trevor in the utility room,' she says, loud enough for Malcolm to hear. 'We should have locked you in instead.'

I wait for the sound of Melanie's footsteps on the first floor to recede, then I speed up the stairs, covering my mouth and nose with my sleeve as I reach the second set of steps. The air's so pungent it makes my stomach turn. If the storm goes on much longer we're going to have to think about moving David somewhere else. That's a job no one's going to volunteer for.

The time glows red – 11.34 p.m. – on my digital alarm clock as I push open the door to my room. I throw myself onto my bed and bury my face into the pillow. I'm so tired I'm not sure I could move if the hotel burned down. I just want to go to sleep and wake up when this is all over. I'm not sure how much more I can take.

I wake with a start, propping myself up on my elbow as I stare into the darkness, sleep-dazed and confused, caught in the haze between dream and reality.

'Alex?'

I search the gloom for his boxes full of vinyl, the fifty-inch television and the hideous seventies-style curtains the landlord insisted we leave up at the windows. As my eyes adjust to the darkness the dream slowly fades, leaving behind the faintest trace of unease. My ex-boyfriend isn't in the room with me and we didn't just have a blazing argument about the amount of time I spend at work. I'm not back in the flat. I'm in a small attic room with low beams, a beast of a wardrobe, a chest of drawers that has seen better days and a man lying dead in the room next door.

I slump back onto the pillow and pull the duvet up around my shoulders. It's 3.55 a.m. I need to go back to sleep.

The sound of a floorboard creaking on the landing forces me up and onto my elbow again. I hold my breath, my heartbeat thudding in my ears.

There's another creak. And another. Someone's walking around outside my room. I don't move. I don't speak. I keep very, very still, all my attention focused on the door handle. There's no way anyone can get in. I locked the door and the other keys are in the pocket of my jeans.

My breath catches in my throat as, very, very slowly, the door handle tips towards the floor.

'WHO'S THERE?'

The handle swings back into position with a click and I hear the thudding of footsteps on the landing as whoever just tried to get into my room makes their escape. Rage courses through me and I throw back the duvet and run across the bedroom. As I fumble the key into the lock, the staircase creaks under the weight of whoever just tried to get into my room. They're going to disappear before I can catch them.

'Come on, come on.' I twist the key in the lock, then slap my palm against the light switch in the landing. Nothing happens. The only light is the eerie orange glow of the emergency bulb.

'I can hear you,' I shout as I run across the landing. 'I know you were trying to get into my room.'

As I reach the top of the stairs a shadow disappears into the guest corridor. They're going to get away.

'Stop!' I reach for the banister and take a step forwards. My heel hits the floor but the ball of my foot drops into nothing and I lurch forwards, arms wheeling and reaching as I fall through the darkness. One second I am at the top of the staircase, screaming and flailing. The next the stairs are rushing up to meet me. I land heavily, the heels of my hands scraping against the carpet runner, my ribs smacking against wood, thumping the air from my lungs as my head ricochets off the wall. I lie still, too shocked to move, to speak, to breathe, then an ocean of pain washes through me and everything goes black.

Chapter 36

Anna

Thursday 7th June

Day 6 of the storm

'Anna? Can you hear me? Can you open your eyes?'

I feel hands touching me, stroking my hair and my cheek, and I force my eyes open. Colours blur and swirl together. I blink them away then close my eyes again. When I open them, the colours have separated, revealing a peach-tinged cheek and metal glasses hiding pale eyes ringed with purple shadows. I focus on the nose and the red patches beneath each nostril, then the face vanishes.

'Malcolm,' the voice hisses as a white light burns into my eyes and I screw them tightly shut. 'Don't shine the torch in her face.'

'I was just checking her for injuries.'

'I think we should let Christine do that, don't you? She's the first aider. Where is she, anyway? Joe, bang a bit louder!'

'Anna, can you open your eyes again?'

'Well done,' she says as I force them open. 'Careful,' she adds as I try to move. 'We don't know if you've broken anything yet.'

'Melanie?' My voice is little more than a croak.

She smiles tenderly. 'You've had an accident and you're lying at the bottom of the stairs. There was an almighty thump and—'

'It woke me up,' Malcolm says. 'I thought it was Trevor, escaped and on the rampage.'

'Seriously?' Melanie glares at him. 'How is that kind of comment helpful – oh, Christine, you're awake.'

A small, squat silhouette appears in the doorway. Christine draws closer and peers into my face. An eye mask is pushed up into her white hair and her face is crumpled with sleep.

'What happened?' She glances up at Melanie, who's sitting on the bottom stair, beside my legs.

'I . . .' I try to push myself up from the ground into a sitting position but an agonising pain rips through my shoulder, making me howl.

'I think she might have dislocated her shoulder,' Melanie says. 'Look.'

There's a weird lump at the top of my arm. Just looking at it makes me feel faint.

'With any luck it's only partially dislocated,' Christine says. 'Can you move your legs, Anna?'

'Jesus Christ!' Malcolm breathes as I flex my feet and for one horrible moment I think he's seen a bone protruding through my skin but it's not my feet he's looking at. 'This hotel is a bloody death trap.'

'What is it, Malcolm?' Melanie presses herself up against the wall as he steps over me and makes his way carefully up the stairs, using his phone as a torch.

'A board's come free,' he shouts. 'No wonder you tripped.' He steps over it and disappears towards the bedroom. 'Light's gone. No, wait. There's no lightbulb. Jesus Christ, it stinks up here.'

'Your legs feel okay.' Christine ignores him and runs her hands lightly over my knees, ankles and feet. 'Did you lose consciousness at all?'

'Yes,' Melanie says. 'She was unconscious when I found her.'

'She's going to need that arm in a sling,' Fiona says from the corridor. 'There's a first aid box in reception. I'll go and get it.'

I lie still as Christine continues to run her hands over me, murmuring to herself under her breath.

'Does she know what she's doing?' Malcolm asks Melanie, loud enough for everyone to hear.

'Not really.' Christine looks up at him. 'I had to take a first aid course when I did my teacher training and it's been a while since I've had to use it. But you're in no immediate danger, Anna,' she adds quickly. 'I don't think you've broken your legs or hurt your spine but you'd need a scan to know that for sure.'

'Should we try the Land Rover again?' Malcolm asks. 'See if we can get her over to the village?'

'I don't know. Even if we do get through the river she'll be in a lot of pain. Every lump and bump in the road will be torturous.'

'She looks like she's in a lot of pain now.' Melanie peers at me. 'She's very pale.'

They're all referring to me in the third person, talking over me as though I'm still unconscious.

'Can you pop the shoulder back in?' Malcolm asks.

Melanie shrugs. 'Possibly.'

'My brother's hypermobile,' she says to Christine. 'I learned how to put his limbs back in as a teenager. Anna's a lot bigger than an eight-year-old boy, though.'

Malcolm ignores the hesitancy in her voice. 'Go on then, pop it back and let's get going.'

'It's been a long time, Malcolm, and if I get it wrong . . . ' She shakes her head. 'No, I'd rather someone qualified did it if I'm honest.'

'But what if we can't get across the river?'

'Then I'll have no choice.'

'Here you go.' Fiona leans over her and hands Christine a green first aid kit, a pillow from the sofa and what looks like a tablecloth. Behind her, Joe has his arms crossed over his chest, his hands gripping his shoulders.

'Okay, Anna,' Christine says. 'If you're going in the car we need to get that arm strapped up. It's going to hurt so brace yourself.'

I'm not a screamer but when Christine took hold of my elbow so she could slip the cushion between my body and my arm I howled with pain. I pleaded with her not to put the sling on my arm – and gratefully knocked back two ibuprofen with a large measure of whisky that Fiona handed me – then sobbed as Christine tied a knot behind my neck. By that point Malcolm wasn't the only one commenting on the smell drifting from the second floor and when Joe suggested we all go down to the lounge there weren't any objections.

'Coffee,' Fiona says now, placing a mug on the table beside me. 'Sorry there's no milk but I added extra sugar to make up for it.'

I smile gratefully up at her but she's already turned away and is heading for Joe, who's sitting alone by the window.

'How's Trevor?' I ask Melanie as she walks into the lounge.

She glances behind her, at Katie who's biting into an apple, then flashes her eyebrows at me. She doesn't want to talk about Trevor in front of her niece but I can't let the subject drop.

'Is he still in there?'

She nods.

'Back door and utility door locked?'

'Yeah.'

'And he's alive?'

She nods again. 'Alive but incoherent.'

'Tell me later,' I mouth as Katie nudges her and says, 'Who's incoherent? What are you talking about?'

Malcolm, studying a Land Rover maintenance book, closes it decisively and gives me a nod.

'You ready to give it a go? See if we can get you out of here?' he asks.

'Absolutely.'

I shiver, despite the blankets heaped on my shoulders and the fire crackling away in the grate. Now the shock of the fall has worn off and the whisky has dialled down the pain in my arm and shoulder the reality of what happened to me has slowly sunk in. Someone deliberately unscrewed the plank, removed the lightbulb from outside my room and then turned the door handle. They weren't trying to get into my room, they were trying to lure me out, into the darkness at the top of the stairs.

Christine's sitting opposite me with the first aid box on her lap, unwinding and rewinding bandages. Melanie's sipping her coffee with Katie beside her, still nibbling at her apple, and Joe and Fiona are sitting quietly at the table by the window. Another shiver courses through me, more violent than the last. Whoever lured me out of my room didn't want to scare me. They *wanted* me to trip and fall. They've given up waiting for me to kill myself. They want me dead.

Chapter 37

'I really don't think you should do this, Anna.' Christine adjusts the hood of David's coat so it doesn't hang over her eyes. 'If Joe has to brake suddenly it could do irreversible damage to your shoulder.'

'I'm sure it'll be fine.' I clamber awkwardly into the back seat of the Land Rover, shivering in my wet clothes. I was only able to get one arm into my coat and had to drape the other side over my damaged shoulder and leave it unzipped.

'Okay then,' Christine says, closing the door behind me. 'If you're sure.' She takes the seat beside me, leans over and reaches for my seat belt. 'Let's get you buckled up.'

She carefully pulls the strap over my body, taking care to manoeuvre it under my sling.

Joe, in the driver's seat, waits until Christine has her seat belt on too, then starts the engine and the car crunches over the gravel driveway, quickly leaving the hotel and the remaining guests behind. The further we drive the less anxious, and more hopeful, I feel. All we have to do is cross the river, then it's a fifteen-minute drive to the safety of the village on the other side of the island. There's a pub there that David told me about. I'm sure they'd let me use their phone to ring the police on the mainland. It's not just threatening messages any more, it's attempted murder and I've got proof – a bloody great hole where a floorboard used to be, for one. Once we're over the river I won't have to see any of the guests ever again.

But when we do reach the Glen Duian river the hope in my chest deflates like a balloon. The water level is even higher than it was two days ago. It's going to take a small miracle to get us across.

'Slow down,' Malcolm barks to Joe as we get closer. 'You need to be in first or second. If the water goes over the bonnet you're going too fast. You need to make a wave in front of the car.'

'I have driven a Land Rover before, Malcolm.' As Joe's grip tightens on the wheel I find myself staring at his hands.

'Aha,' Malcolm says. 'But have you attempted a river crossing?'

The knuckles of Joe's right hand are swollen, red raw and split. The wounds look fresh, as though he punched someone recently or . . . a jolt of fear zaps through me . . . or he grazed them prising a piece of wood out of the top of the staircase.

'Brace yourselves,' he says as he changes gear from second to first and the Land Rover creeps towards the water.

As the car rolls down the bank we all tip forwards. A wave of pain courses through me as the seat belt strains against my body but I don't cry out. Christine, watching me, grimaces.

'Easy now,' Malcolm says as the river swells around the bonnet. 'Easy.'

'Joe,' Christine says as the car creeps further into the river. 'There's water coming through the doors.'

She's right. There's dirty river water squeezing through the trim and pooling beneath our feet.

'Nothing to worry about,' Malcolm says. 'We're all going to get our feet a bit wet before—'

Without warning we suddenly drift to the left and the nose of the car points further down the river instead of straight across.

'We're going to get swept out to sea,' Christine screeches.

'It's okay,' Joe says. 'If I accelerate a bit we can—'

'Reverse the car!'

'Trust me, Christine. I can do this.'

'If we have to get out and swim Anna will drown.'

'I can swim. Keep going, Joe. We'll be fine.'

His eyes meet mine in the rear-view mirror but I can't read the emotion behind his fixed stare.

Malcolm twists round in his seat. 'It'll be easier to keep going than to reverse back up that bank.'

'You don't know that,' Christine snaps. 'Reverse the car. Unless you want to be responsible for the death of three people?'

Joe continues to stare silently at me, forcing me to look away.

'All right,' he mutters after a pause. 'Fine.'

The wheels whir and skid as Joe changes gear and for several terrifying seconds I'm convinced we're stuck, but then we lurch backwards and slowly reverse up the bank.

No one says a word as the car creeps back up the driveway but when the hotel comes into view my throat tightens and my eyes sting with tears. I thought I was finally going to escape but I'm right back in the nightmare.

'I'm sorry, Anna.' Christine shoots me an apologetic look. 'I know you're disappointed, we all are. Please don't be cross with me. It was too dangerous and I couldn't let them take that kind of risk with our lives.'

Malcolm unbuckles his seat belt. 'I vote we try again, Joe. Leave Christine and Anna here.'

'No.' Joe shakes his head. 'Even if we manage to cross the river I don't think we'd make it to the village. There's barely any petrol left. We'd be cutting it fine driving straight across the island, never mind continuously revving the engine to get across the river.'

Malcolm twists round in his seat to look at me. 'Did David keep any petrol cans anywhere, do you know?'

'I don't think so.'

'Mind if I look?'

'Not at all.'

'Let's get you back in the hotel, Anna,' Christine says as she reaches across to unbuckle me. 'See if Melanie can get your shoulder back in. Brace yourself. I've heard it hurts.'

Melanie pulls out the chair next to me and sits at the dining table, crossing one leg over the other. Beneath her jeans she's wearing a pair of very pink, very fluffy socks. For such a no-nonsense woman they seem incongruous.

'Secret Santa,' she says, catching me looking. 'Not the sort of thing I'd normally buy but they're surprisingly comfy. Anyway,' she fixes me with a look, her eyes unusually bright behind her glasses, 'how are you, Anna? You look . . . oh, sweetheart, have you been crying?'

'I . . .' My throat tightens and I have to cough to find my voice again. 'I'm just . . . I really thought we were going to make it.'

'I know. Malcolm told me.' She lays her hand over mine. 'And you're in a lot of pain too, aren't you?'

I nod, pressing my lips together to stop myself from crying.

'I will try my very best to help you. I know I said it's been a long time since I've done this,' she gestures towards my injured shoulder, 'but I do remember. How are you doing otherwise? Emotionally I mean. I've heard you pacing the hotel late at night.'

'I . . . um . . . I've taken David's death quite badly. I've been having trouble sleeping.'

'Yes,' she nods, 'of course you have. But you were up at all hours, even before the storm hit. What is it you're worried about, Anna?'

I sit back in my chair, stunned by her perceptiveness. Unnerved, too, that I wear my unhappiness so visibly. David hinted that I was running away from something as well. Or maybe I read too much into his comment about the reasons why people move to Rum.

'Would you like to talk about it?' Melanie says now. 'Whatever it is that's stopping you from sleeping? Malcolm might disagree but I'm a good listener, you know.'

I look into her soft, gentle face, her eyes so full of concern, and feel a pang of homesickness. It's been five days since I last spoke to Mum and Dad. They've probably tried to ring me countless times, only to get my voicemail. They must be so worried.

'It's okay to cry,' Melanie says, touching the back of my hand as a tear rolls down my cheek. 'You've been through a lot.'

'Melanie, can I ask you something?'

'Of course.' She tilts her head to one side. Her fingers, still on the back of my hand, press a little firmer into my skin. 'Anything.'

'I . . .' The words dry up on my tongue. I don't know what to ask. Do you think Joe could be capable of murder? Or Fiona? Christine? Your husband maybe? Do either of you know Steve Laing? Did you lose a relative in a car crash recently? Have you been following me around, leaving me creepy messages? Did you mean to kill me last night?

Even if she did, she's not about to hold up her hands and say, 'Well done, you got me.' This isn't an episode of *Columbo*.

'I don't suppose you know if . . .' I shift my hand from beneath hers. '. . . if any of the guests are recently bereaved?'

She raises her thick eyebrows.

'I'm not being nosy,' I add. 'But I realise that David's death has stirred up a lot of emotion in everyone and . . . I just want to be sensitive if anyone—'

'Joe.'

The room suddenly feels very still.

'His brother,' Melanie adds. 'That's all I know.'

She stares at me, waiting for me to respond, then stands up decisively and smooths her hands over the dining room table. 'Let's get you up here, shall we? Get that shoulder back in.'

It's Joe.

It has to be.

He's Freddy's brother, sent here by Steve. Joe's probably not even his real name. My stomach clenches as I remember the moment in his room when I thought he was about to kiss me. The flirting and kindliness were all a charade. He's been biding his time, waiting for the right opportunity to take his revenge. And last night he nearly did.

'I'm not sure which of us is more nervous,' Melanie says as she helps me onto the table and eases me down onto the wood. 'Sorry, that's probably not very helpful, is it?'

I grit my teeth as she removes my sling, then cry out in pain as she takes hold of my hand and moves it away from my body.

'Sorry, sorry.' She swipes the back of her hand over the sweat beading on her top lip. 'I know it hurts and it's going to get worse, unfortunately, but I will try to be as quick as I can. Um . . . right . . . okay . . . ' She pauses and looks towards the kitchen. 'Maybe we should have got you a wooden spoon to bite down on.'

I push down a wave of panic. By her own admission she hasn't put a dislocated shoulder back in for years. What if something goes wrong? We've got no way of calling for help. But I can't stay the way I am. 'Just do it quickly, Mel,' I beg. 'Please.'

'I need you to be brave. Ready?' She puts her other hand on my elbow and moves my arm so it's at a ninety-degree angle from my body, then seems to steady herself against the table. 'Three . . . two . . .'

I screw my eyes tightly shut and brace myself.

'One!'

'FUCKKKKKKKK!'

The most excruciating pain I've ever felt in my life radiates from my shoulder to my chest and all the way down my arm, then there's a terrifying crunching sound and my whole body jolts. My shoulder throbs and burns as Melanie moves my arm back to my side and releases my hand and elbow. I pant against the pain, then open my eyes as it slowly ebbs away and a wave of relief washes over me.

'Are you all right?' She leans over me. 'Oh God, you've gone very white.'

I nod, too scared to speak in case I'm sick.

'I . . . I think it's okay.' She gently slides her fingers over my arm and shoulder. 'Yes,' she sighs with relief. 'It's gone back in.'

I stare up at the whitewashed dining room ceiling and tentatively wiggle my fingers and rotate my wrist.

'Careful.' Melanie presses a hand to my back to support me as I try to sit up. 'We're still going to have to strap the arm up to protect it.'

'Thank you,' I whisper as she retrieves the tablecloth sling and uses it to cradle my arm. 'I don't know what I would have done if—'

She stiffens. 'Can you hear that?'

I don't immediately but then something reaches my ears – a low, repetitive thump-thump-thump sound, coming from the kitchen. We share a look.

'Trevor,' we say at the same time.

Chapter 38

Alex

Alex Carter kicks off his shoes, wanders into the kitchen, opens the fridge and takes out the gin. It's a routine that's become so ingrained over the last few weeks that he barely registers what he's doing as he takes ice from the freezer and tonic from the cupboard, slices a lemon and fixes himself a drink. He knows it's not wise, self-medicating with booze, but it takes the edge off his day and it's something he looks forward to during the hot, cramped, gruelling forty-five-minute commute home on the Northern Line.

He takes a long gulp of his drink, draining half the glass, then tops it up, grabs a bag of Doritos and wanders into the living room. He puts the drink and snack on the coffee table then drops onto the sofa, groaning as he stretches out, and folds his hands behind his head. When Anna left him, over a month ago, he felt strangely buoyant, as though the anchor that had been weighing him down for so long had finally been raised.

He felt lighter, happier, and he no longer woke feeling as though a dark cloud had settled in his brain. When he went on the first date with Becca he felt like a new man. He was an attractive, intelligent bloke who could still be entertaining and amusing if he put his mind to it. But almost ever since he hasn't been able to shake the unsettled feeling in his stomach or the vague sense of unease that descends whenever he spends time alone. He tried passing it off as guilt. Thing weren't going brilliantly with Becca and it had made him reflect on the way he'd treated Anna. But it wasn't just guilt. There was something else he couldn't put his finger on.

He turns on the TV, hoping the background burble will fill his brain and block out his thoughts, but when a news reporter appears on the screen, he moves his thumb over the remote, primed to switch to a different channel. As the reporter is replaced with footage, he pauses. There's something very familiar about the man walking into a police station with a police officer either side of him. Alex turns up the volume.

Earlier this afternoon, the voice-over says, *one woman and two men were arrested on suspicion of attempted murder. The victim, forty-seven-year-old lorry driver Donna Farrell, was serving two years in HM Prison New Hall in Wakefield for the deaths of two people after she fell asleep at the wheel of her HGV and crashed into a car containing four colleagues on their way back to London after a team-building weekend in the Brecon Beacons. Donna Farrell was attacked in her cell by fellow inmate Danielle Miller and is in a critical condition in Pinderfields Hospital. It is believed that one of the two charged men, Steve Laing, fifty-three, father of Freddy Laing who died in the M25 crash, financed the revenge attack that was orchestrated by Jim Thompson, forty-nine. In a statement Laing gave on the steps of Inner London Crown Court after Farrell's sentence was announced, he said, 'I would like to say that justice has been done today but the sentence meted out is an insult to my son's death and the colleague who died with him. Farrell will probably be out on parole in twelve months' time. She will be free to get on with her life whilst my son had his cruelly stolen away from him because of Donna Farrell's actions.'*

Alex presses pause on the remote and stares into the dark, angry eyes of the man freeze-framed on the TV. He recognises him from the trial where Anna gave evidence. Steve Laing was sitting a couple of places down from them on the public viewing bench and spent the whole trial hunched forwards, staring at Donna Farrell as she twisted her hands together in the dock. And he tried to have her killed. Jesus Christ! Alex's thoughts flick from the trial to Anna and he snatches his mobile out of his back pocket and searches for her number. Has she even heard about this yet? She'd been so nervous about giving evidence, convinced the defending barrister would try to pin the accident on her. She barely slept after she came out of the hospital. Whenever she closed her eyes she'd be right back in the car, listening to her colleagues screaming as it tipped over and skidded down the bank. And when she did finally fall asleep she'd have terrible nightmares that would make her wake up screaming. It was horrible, watching her fall apart over what had happened, constantly blaming herself when she was as much of a victim as her colleagues who'd died. She'd always been so strong and ballsy and he didn't recognise the nervy, paranoid woman she turned into. She was convinced that someone was out to get her. He could have happily throttled the person who tried to freak her out with those stupid 'sleep' messages but it was hard to support her, not least because he was riddled with guilt about his behaviour before the accident.

He'd only signed up to Tinder because he was curious, not because he was actively planning on cheating on Anna. He'd heard so much about the dating app that he wanted to see what all the fuss was about. He certainly hadn't expected anyone to swipe right on him or send him a message and he hadn't bothered to reply to the first few women who did. But then someone wrote something that made him laugh and he couldn't help replying. It was just banter, he told himself. He wasn't doing any harm because he had no intention of meeting up with her. And he wasn't cheating on Anna if he wasn't having sex or falling in love. It was just a bit of fun, a distraction from all the crap that went round his head the rest of the time. He liked who he was on Tinder. He was a funnier, wittier, more erudite version of himself and he got a kick out of it whenever he made the other woman laugh. He did feel guilty though, when Anna came back from work saying how tired she was and then went straight into the kitchen to make the dinner. He felt like a shit then; a miserable, slimy excuse for a human being. He knew he should end things with her so she could go and find someone else, and the weekend she was in the Brecon Beacons with her team he primed himself for the awkward conversation he'd initiate when she got back. Only she didn't walk through the door on the Sunday afternoon, weighed down with her suitcase and stress. She didn't come back at all and a tiny part of him hoped that maybe she'd decided to leave *him* and he was off the hook. And then her stepdad called from the hospital with the news.

Alex places his phone on the coffee table and picks up his gin instead. He's got no right to ring Anna and talk to her about what he just saw on the TV. The chances are she's already seen it and if she hasn't . . . he swigs at his drink . . . someone else is bound to get in touch. She made it clear in her last text that she didn't want to hear from him and that's okay. She deserves to move on and get on with her life.

He takes another swig of his gin then sets it back on the table. As he does his mobile vibrates, making him jump. He snatches it up. It can't be Anna, surely. That would be too weird. But the WhatsApp message isn't from his ex-girlfriend, it's from Becca.

Sorry if I've been a bit off with you. The investigation's still going on at the hospital. I found out yesterday that it's to do with an abnormally high number of patient deaths and it's got everyone worried, me included. There's something I need to tell you but I'd rather do it in person. When can we meet?

In Memoriam

In Memoriam

Elizabeth Harding 1946–2016

God saw the road was getting rough
The hill too hard to climb
He gently closed her weary eyes and whispered
'Peace be thine'

I liked my mum best when she was asleep. Her skin, normally pinched tight between her brows, would smooth and soften and her pursed lips would slacken and part. She'd give a little sigh as she drifted off, a gentle 'ooh' of contentment, and her long lashes would flutter then lie still. I'd hold her hand as she slept, something she wouldn't let me do when she was awake, and stroke her hair back from her forehead.

As a child I didn't think there was anything unusual about having a mum who was as stiff emotionally as she was physically. She was so highly strung it was as though she was bound with wool from head to toe. She rarely left the house but, if she had to, to buy groceries or visit the dentist, she'd make polite conversation, her red lips lifting with the occasional smile. She only ever addressed me in short, sharp sentences – Leave me alone. Go and play. Not now. I'm busy. She was always busy – sweeping and polishing, wiping and cleaning. 'In case we have visitors,' she told Dad if he suggested she leave the hoovering for another day. Visitors? I'd never seen anyone other than us three walk into the house.

I could never predict Mum's moods. Sometimes she'd burn the dinner and burst into tears. At other times she'd rage at my dad, screaming that he didn't understand her, that he didn't care about her, that he had no idea how much she was suffering. Whenever she said the word 'suffering' she'd give me a pointed look and then continue to rant. And if she wasn't ranting she'd lie on the sofa and stare at the ceiling. I don't remember being saddened by her behaviour. More annoyed and perturbed.

When I started school, Mum was forced to leave the house in order to walk me there. I was delighted to find myself surrounded by so many potential playmates but I was confused by the way they interacted with their mothers. I'd watch from the sidelines as women of all shapes and sizes would wrap their arms around their children, squeeze them to their chests and press their wet lips against their cheeks. I looked up at my mum, wondering if she'd do the same, but when the bell rang she gave me a curt nod and hissed, 'Off you go then.' Some of the other children cried when we were told to line up to go in. They clung to their mothers and sobbed to be taken back home. I didn't look for my mum. My eyes were dry as I took my place at the front of the queue.

Chapter 39

Anna

'Trevor?' My whole left side throbs as I crouch down at the utility room door and push at the cat flap. Melanie is at my side, holding a piece of tarpaulin over our heads, panting after our sprint round the house.

'You should be resting,' she hisses. 'Anna, you could damage your shoulder. Be careful.'

'Trevor,' I say again. His hands are balled into fists, held in front of his body like a boxer as he repeatedly kicks the door that leads to the kitchen. 'Trevor, the door won't open. It's bolted on the other side. Please calm down, you're going to hurt yourself.'

He ignores me and continues to kick at the door. He's breathing heavily and there's a sweat stain on the back of his T-shirt. His fleece is in the corner of the room with the crumpled blankets, his glasses, several empty bottles of water and some food wrappers.

I look at Melanie. 'He needs more food and water.'

'You go,' she says. 'I'll talk him down.'

'No, I'll do it. I think he trusts me.'

Trevor makes a low grunting sound as he continues to hammer the door and Melanie hurries back round the building in her makeshift tarpaulin tent.

'It's Anna! I want to help you. Melanie's gone to . . .'

Trevor stops kicking the door and stands still, his hands clenched at his sides, his back rigid. He's listening to me. He wants to hear what I have to say.

'She's gone to get you some more food and water. We're trying to get you out of there, I promise. We tried to cross the island earlier but nearly got swept away by the river. The phone signal could come back at any time. I just need you to hold on for a bit longer, then we'll get you back home. We all want to see our families.'

The wind whips my hair into my face, wrapping it around my nose, mouth and eyes. As I push it away Trevor sinks onto his knees.

'Talk to me,' I say. 'Tell me how I can help you.'

He makes the grunting sound again as he slowly turns to face me and the air is knocked from my lungs.

His face is almost unrecognisable. His lips are swollen and bloodied, there's a dark red-black gash on his cheek and his eyeballs are slits sitting in blue-black eggs.

Someone has beaten him up.

'I'm going to get help, Trevor. I'll be back.'

My stomach clenches and a wave of nausea flows through me as I run through the rain to the front door. This is my fault. I should *never* have agreed to keep him locked up.

Melanie is in the kitchen, filling a bottle at the tap. She jumps as I slam open the door.

'Lounge. Now!' I say. 'Someone's beaten Trevor up.'

She gawps at me as the bottle overflows onto her hand, but I don't wait for her to reply. Instead I haul myself up the stairs and thump on the bedroom doors.

'Downstairs! Now! Urgent meeting!'

As everyone slowly congregates in the lounge I pace back and forth in front of the fire, cradling my injured arm. My thoughts are all over the place – zipping from Trevor's bloodied face to the loose floorboard at the top of the stairs, to David's limp body, to Joe gripping the Land Rover steering wheel with battered knuckles. I stop pacing and stare at him, sitting by the window, slumped forwards, his elbows on the table and forehead resting on his wrists. He must have beaten Trevor up. But why? Did he think Trevor was going to warn me about him? But how would he know?

'What's this all about?' Malcolm, standing in the doorway in a white towelling dressing gown, crosses his arms over his chest. 'I was having a bath.'

Melanie, who's sitting beside Christine and Fiona on the sofa, rolls her eyes and sighs. Katie, perusing the bookshelf at the back of the room, doesn't so much as glance at him.

'Someone has beaten Trevor up,' I say. 'Melanie and I went to check on him after we heard him kicking the door to the kitchen and . . .' I shake my head. 'His face is such a mess he can't speak.'

'Jesus Christ!' Fiona presses a hand to her mouth.

Joe raises his head from his hands.

'Are you sure?' Melanie asks. 'He might have done it to himself. I mean . . . it's a possibility, isn't it?' She glances over at Malcolm, whose expression and stance haven't changed.

'I'd be very surprised if that were the case,' I say. 'He's got two black eyes and his mouth's pretty badly smashed up.'

'Dear God.' Christine's lips are thin as she shakes her head.

'Melanie was the last one to check on him,' Fiona says, more to herself than anyone else. 'This morning, after we brought Anna downstairs.'

Mel looks affronted. 'I did. I posted some food and drink through the door and asked him how he was but he didn't reply. He just grunted.'

'You didn't see his face?'

'He was curled up in the corner of the room under a blanket. He had his back to me.'

'And you didn't ask him to turn around?' Fiona asks accusingly.

'What is this? Why are you all looking at me like I had something to do with it?'

'We're not,' I say. 'We're just trying to work out when this could have happened.'

'Who cares when it happened?' Joe gets up from the table and stares around the room. 'Our first priority should be getting him some medical care.'

My gaze flickers from his face to the battered knuckles of his right hand. It's terrifying how easy it is for him to fake concern.

'He is in a bad way,' I say tightly. 'Christine, do you think you could see to him?'

She presses a hand to her collarbone. 'Me? You want *me* to go in there?'

'Yes. He's—'

'According to you he was kicking a door down.'

'Well, yes, but he's not going to do anything to you.'

'How do you know?' Malcolm gestures at his wife. 'He didn't have any compunction about knocking Melanie over.'

Fiona rolls her eyes. 'He didn't mean to do that!'

Malcolm steps closer, creating a tight ring of people around the fireplace and me. 'No? Well, he certainly meant to punch Joe.'

'Doesn't mean he'd hurt a woman.'

'I'd offer to go in,' Fiona says. 'But I'm not medically trained.'

'I'm hardly a surgeon.' Christine raises her eyebrows. 'Anyone can dab a bit of antiseptic on someone's face. And anyway, he might be armed.'

'Armed?' The word comes out louder than I intended it to. I've suddenly remembered the missing knife in Trevor's rucksack. I backtrack quickly. 'If he had a weapon don't you think he would have used it on whoever attacked him? For God's sake. The important issue here is not whether he's armed or not. It's . . .' I look directly at Joe, '. . . which one of us let themselves into the utility room and beat his face into a bloody pulp.'

Silence falls again as everyone stares at me, shock etched on their faces. Everyone, that is, apart from Malcolm. He's staring around the room.

'Did anyone see Katie leave?' He walks to the door and pokes his head out into the corridor. 'Katie?' he shouts. 'Where are you?'

The room falls silent as Malcolm walks into the lobby. 'Aha! There she is!'

Melanie, across the lounge, catches my eye and smiles tightly. Joe retakes his seat by the window, sighing heavily as he stares out at the rain.

'Where've you been?' Malcolm's booming voice carries into the lounge. 'Did you go and get a snack or something?'

'No,' Katie says loudly. 'And don't even bother telling me off because I don't care.'

There's a pause then. 'Telling you off about what?'

'Letting Trevor out.'

Chapter 40

We are all congregated in the lobby, staring at the diminutive figure standing in the doorway to the dining room.

Melanie crouches down so her eyeline matches her niece's. 'You let Trevor out of the utility room?'

'Yeah.' Katie shrugs. 'I felt sorry for him. It's not his fault he's ill. Someone took his medicine.'

I feel a jolt of surprise. 'You know about that?'

'I know about lots of things.' She tosses her head dismissively. 'I know he was a soldier in the army and he went to Iraq. I know he saw his friends getting blown up. I know he tried to save their lives and they died in his arms.'

'How do you know all this?' Melanie puts her hands on her niece's shoulders. 'When did he tell you?'

'When he was in my room. He heard me crying and tapped on the door. I told him I was upset because Mum can't walk any more and he said he had friends in the army who lost the use of their legs.'

'Why didn't you tell me?'

'Because you were too busy shouting at him to get out.'

As Melanie gasps I look from Fiona to Christine. 'Did

either of you know about this? About Trevor's background?'

They both shake their heads.

'I don't understand why you were all so scared of him,' Katie continues. 'He's not a bad man. He's just confused. Sometimes he doesn't know if what he's seeing is real or not.'

'PTSD,' I say under my breath. 'Did he say if he'd been to the doctor, Katie?'

'He was too scared to so he got some tablets from a friend of his. He said they helped keep him calm,' she shrugs, 'until *you* stole them.'

'I didn't steal anything, Katie. I've already told Trevor that.'

'Jesus,' Joe says from the front door, making me jump. I hadn't noticed him slip out of the lounge. 'What a fucking mess.'

'We need to find Trevor,' I say. 'When did you let him out, Katie?'

'When you were all arguing about who beat him up. I undid the bolts on the door.'

'What happened then?'

'He ran up the stairs to get his rucksack and then he left.'

'Did he say where he was going?' Melanie asks.

Katie shakes her head. 'He didn't say anything, apart from thank you.'

'We need to find him,' I say. 'Now.'

The others peel off in different directions. Malcolm insists on going out alone so, as Christine shepherds Katie into the kitchen for a drink, Joe and Melanie head off together. I'm left standing in the lobby with Fiona. She's staring out of the open front door, rather than at me, but the energy she's giving off is distinctly prickly.

'Fiona.' I gaze up at her ramrod-straight back as I pull on my boots. 'I know you're pissed off with me about the vote. Believe me, it didn't go the way I thought it would.'

'It's your hotel, Anna.'

'I made the wrong call and I'm sorry.'

'Don't you think it's Trevor you should be apologising to, not me?'

That stings but I take it. She's right. Joe wouldn't have had the opportunity to beat Trevor up if he hadn't been locked away. I want to make excuses, to tell her about what happened on the M25 and explain that I never wanted this responsibility. I came to Rum to escape, not take charge. But I can't, and I won't. There are no excuses for the decision I made. I got it wrong. Two of my colleagues were killed because I didn't do my job properly and if we don't find Trevor he could end up dead too.

'I will apologise to Trevor,' I say as I pull on my coat. 'I just hope we can find him.'

Fiona turns and gives me a long, lingering look. 'You and me both.'

We walk silently towards the cliffs. The further we get from the house the stronger the wind becomes and the more we are buffeted. It's almost impossible to walk in a straight line. I have to tighten the toggles on my hood to keep it on my head and bend into the wind as I force one foot in front of the other. There are very few gulls in the sky but there are dozens crouched on the edge of the cliffs, heads curled into puffed feathers. The horizon has disappeared; the sea and sky are the same shade, a great grey canvas that stretches on forever. The sea is angry today, wild and noisy and churning. Huge, dark waves roll into the shore then smash against the rocks, covering them with white surf.

'Let's look over there.' Fiona gestures for us to head towards Gordon's cottage, the whitewashed building next to the mausoleum.

I nod and we both break into a slow jog. By the time we reach the cottage we are both soaked to the skin and breathing heavily. We stand shoulder to shoulder in the small porch, our backs against the door, and stare across the lush green grass towards the mausoleum a few hundred metres away.

'At least they're warm and dry in there,' Fiona says.

'And dead.'

'There is that.'

I turn to look at her. 'Can I ask you something?'

'Maybe.'

'Has Joe talked to you about his brother, the one who died?'

I hold my breath as she continues to stare at the mausoleum. I fully expect her to say no, or to tell me she doesn't know the details. Instead she turns her head to look at me.

'What do you want to know?'

'How did he die?'

She shifts her weight from one foot to the other and I fight to keep my breathing under control. This is when she tells me that he died in a car crash.

'He hung himself. In a prison cell.'

All the air rushes from my body and I double over, gripping my thighs. Fiona says nothing but I can feel her watching me.

'Are you sure?' I straighten up again. 'You're absolutely sure?'

'That's what he told me.'

I pause over her words. *That's what he told me*. It doesn't mean it's the truth.

'What else did he tell you about him?'

She shrugs. 'That his name was Will and he was a drug dealer. Apparently he'd had a gambling problem. It started at university when a few of his friends suggested a poker night and Will got lucky and won the pot. He played again, and again, and then, when his mates lost interest, he started going to a local casino on his own – chasing the high, you know?'

I nod, even though I don't. The only time I've ever gambled was on the Grand National and I vowed I never would again after I found out how many of the fallen horses had to be shot.

'Anyway,' Fiona continues, 'apparently, Will became convinced that he could work the system and he all but dropped out of university to keep gambling. He did okay for a bit, then his luck turned and suddenly he'd drained the last of his student loan and stretched his overdraft as far as it could go.'

'He told Joe all this?'

'Yeah, he asked him to lend him some money but Joe was between jobs and Will was too proud to ask his parents to help him out. That's when he started dealing drugs to make a bit of cash on the side. Only selling drugs and making money was as addictive as the gambling, according to Joe. Will started off selling weed to his mates but there was more money in cocaine, GBH and ketamine, so he started dealing those too. When the police raided his house, they found thousands of pounds' worth of drugs: heroin, crack, the lot.'

'Jesus.'

I don't know if it's the amount of detail in the story or because it seems so plausible but it sounds true.

'Did you believe him? Joe. When he told you all this?'

Fiona brushes her hair out of her face and gives me a look. 'Why wouldn't I?'

'Sometimes people aren't who they say they are.'

'What do you mean by that?'

'Nothing.' I look past the mausoleum and out to sea. I was convinced that Joe was my stalker but everything Fiona's just told me has thrown doubt on that. But if it's not him, then who is it? Maybe it's not even a guest at all. Maybe it's someone who's been hiding out and watching us, sneaking in while we're all asleep.

Fiona touches my arm, making me jump.

'So,' she says irritably. 'What happens now?'

I tap the door behind us. 'We're going to find out if Trevor's in here.'

Fiona twists the door handle. 'Locked.' She shakes her head. 'He's not in here. If he was, one of the windows would be smashed and there's no sign anyone's tried to break in.' She walks over to the window, presses her nose to the glass and cups her hands around her face. 'Nothing looks disturbed inside either.'

I leave her with her face still pressed to the dark glass, then shout her name as I round the cottage. She comes running.

'Look!' I point at a small, opaque window. The glass is smashed and the window is unlatched and open an inch. 'Someone's been in here.'

Fiona pulls her sleeve over her hand, opens the window fully and looks inside.

'It's a toilet and the door's open to the hallway.' She lifts a leg as though she's about to scale the wall. 'I'm going in.'

'No.' I step forwards. 'Trevor trusts me. I'll go in.'

'You sure about that?'

'He won't do anything. He knows I want to help him.'

Her gaze drifts to my sling, visible beneath my half-on, half-off coat. 'What about your arm?'

'It'll be fine. And anyway, you'll be right outside. I'll shout if I need some help.'

Chapter 41

Mohammed

As his parents stroll into his room, positively brimming with positivity and cheery smiles, Mohammed turns his head and looks in the opposite direction.

'You all right, love?' His mum rounds the bed and takes the seat nearest his head, forcing him to look at her. She reaches for his hand and gives it a squeeze. 'Sorry we're a bit late. The traffic was awful. Wasn't it, Ali?'

Mo's dad nods. 'Murder. How are you, son?'

Mohammed doesn't respond. He knows what they're hoping he'll say – that he's feeling well in himself and positive about the future. But that wouldn't be true. He feels like shit in himself, he hates the rehab centre and its crippled, broken people and the future is a big, dark hole. He can't tell them that though. His parents look as though they've aged ten years in the last three months.

'Any word from the doctor about when you might get out?' his mum asks.

He sighs. It's not his mum's fault that she asks him that each time she visits. It's a question he's been asking almost daily and the most he's been able to get out of his consultant is 'it might be a few more months yet'.

'No,' he says. 'Not yet.'

'Any more sensation in your right leg?' his dad asks. 'You said you could twitch the muscles in your thigh last time we were in.'

That development is the only glimmer of hope in Mohammed's dark world.

'I can still twitch the muscle,' he tells his dad. 'But I can't move either of my legs.'

'Did you see the news?' his mum asks, glancing up at the television screen fixed to the opposite wall.

Mohammed's throat tightens and all he can do is nod. He felt sick with fear when the headlines flashed up and he saw Steve Laing being bundled into a police station. For one terrible, horrifying moment he thought it had been Anna who had been stabbed and he was almost relieved when he realised it was the lorry driver, Donna Farrell. Watching the story unfold he remembered Freddy's father sitting by his bedside ranting about the injustice of the trial and how, if Donna Farrell had walked into a shop and stabbed two people, she'd be inside for the rest of her life, not a measly two years. Falling asleep at the wheel wasn't a defence, he told Mo. An articulated lorry was just as much of a weapon as a knife. Mo had no idea, as he'd lain back against his hospital pillows and made sympathetic noises, that Steve Laing wasn't trying to come to terms with what had happened to his son; he was planning a murder of his own.

Now, Mo closes his eyes and a single tear dribbles into the hairline by his ear.

'Mo?' His mum tightens her grip on his hand. 'Talk to me, love. What's upsetting you?'

He shakes his head. He doesn't want to talk but the guilt he feels is burning away at him, charring the person he used to be.

'I'm no better than Steve Laing,' he says, his voice little more than a whisper.

'Sorry?'

'She asked me . . .' He swallows down the lump in his throat. 'She asked me if I wanted to see Anna.'

'Who, love? Who asked you?'

He hears his mother's question but he needs to keep speaking. If he doesn't say it now it'll keep burning away at him, making him feel like the worst kind of person.

'She thought I'd want to see Anna but I said I didn't want to see her, that the crash was all her fault and that I wished . . .' His mother doesn't speak but he can hear her holding her breath, waiting for him to continue. '. . . I wished she was dead.'

Chapter 42

Anna

It's dark and cramped inside the small cottage and when I flick the light switch in the kitchen the faint glow from the bare lightbulb in the middle of the ceiling does little to lift the gloom. The kitchen units were probably white or cream once but they're yellowed with age, or tobacco, and split and peeling. There's a wooden table in the centre of the room holding a bowl of shrivelled apples, a book on birds of the British Isles, a pad and pen and a pile of post. I reach for the letter on the top. It's a letter to a Mr Gordon Brodie from the Bank of Scotland, telling him his ISA containing £2,367 has matured. There's a mug, bowl, plate and assorted crockery on the draining board by the sink, a fridge containing a bottle of milk well past its use-by date, a pat of butter and some cheese and ham that's curling at the edges. And that's it. There's no personality in the small room, no trinkets, photographs or ornaments. It feels unloved. I walk over to the kettle and touch its rounded belly. Cold. Nothing in the room is out of place but one cupboard door is open. I crouch down and look inside: tins of baked beans, soup, chicken curry and tomatoes, their lids grey and dirty. In the space at the front of the cupboard are six circles, ringed with dust, where more cans once sat. From the complete lack of dust inside the circles the cans must been taken recently.

'Trevor?' I push open the heavy wooden door to what I assume is the living room and listen for signs of life before I walk inside. This room is as neglected as the kitchen. There's a thick layer of dust on the television, a saggy green sofa that's seen better days and a rug that doesn't look as though it's seen a vacuum in a while. I touch the vents at the back of the television. Cold. If Trevor did break in he didn't stay long. It's unlikely anyone else has been living here since Gordon left, which discounts my theory that the person who wants to kill me might not be a guest. I don't know whether to be relieved or more scared.

'Everything okay, Anna?' Fiona's voice echoes faintly around the cottage.

'Yeah!' I walk back through the kitchen to the small downstairs toilet.

'Found anything?' Fiona props her elbows up on the white window frame. She looks desperate to get inside.

'I think Trevor might have taken a couple of cans of food but that's the only sign he's been in here. Oh,' I point at the empty toilet roll hook, 'and some toilet roll maybe. I'm going to go and look upstairs now.'

An expression I can't read passes over Fiona's face, then she smiles tightly. 'Good luck.'

I take my time climbing the rickety wooden stairs, gripping the banister as I test my weight on each step. There's a frayed carpet runner up the middle but some of the tacks have come away and it slides around under the soles of my boots. The landing is small and cramped with three doors leading off it. I push at the first one. It swings open to reveal a small bathroom, the shower curtain spotted with mildew and toothpaste stains on the sink.

I push at the next door with my foot but it doesn't open.

'Trevor?' I turn the handle and brace myself.

But there's no one inside, just a double bed with a plain blue duvet, a bedside table holding a lamp, an abandoned hairbrush on an old oak chest of drawers and a pine wardrobe. As I turn to leave a strange scrabbling noise makes me whip back round. I listen for it again, my heart pounding in my chest. It sounded like it came from across the room, beyond the bed.

'Trevor?' I step into the room, keeping my eyes fixed on the space between the chest of drawers and the far side of the bed. Is he hiding down there, lying face down on the floor, out of sight?

'It's Anna, from the hotel. Katie told us what you're going through,' I say as I move closer. But there's no one lying on the threadbare carpet on the other side of the bed. I don't know what I heard but it definitely wasn't—

I scream as something small, brown and furry rushes out from under the chest of drawers and darts under the bed. It was too big to be a rat. I drop to my knees, my heart still trying to beat its way out of my chest, and peer under the bed. Two terrified green eyes stare back at me.

'It's okay.' I reach out a hand as the cat backs up against a suitcase, its fur on end. 'I'm not going to hurt you.'

I like cats but I haven't got the first idea how to look after one. I can't leave it here though. God knows how it got in or how long it's gone without food. I didn't see any food or water bowls in the kitchen and I'd be surprised if Gordon left his pet behind to fend for itself. Unless he didn't mean to stay away this long and the storm has stopped him from getting back.

'Come on.' I make a squeaky, cooing sound but it does nothing to calm the cat, which retreats further beneath the bed. I can't lie flat on my stomach because of my arm so I have to twist onto my side and inch towards it, my good arm outstretched. As I do I hear the squeak of stairs and heavy footsteps pounding the floorboards outside the bedroom. I shuffle backwards but, before I can get out from under the bed, a hand grips my calf.

'Anna?' Fiona says as a gasp catches in my throat. 'Jesus. What the hell happened? I heard you scream, then the next thing I know you're face down on the bedroom carpet.'

'There's a cat.' I get onto my knees and stand up. 'Under the bed. I think it might be Gordon's. We need to take it back to the hotel. God knows when it last ate.'

'A cat.' She presses her lips together and exhales heavily through her nose. 'Great.'

'I can't believe you hate cats,' I say as we leave the cottage and head back towards the cliffs, Fiona struggling to keep the squirming lump in her coat under control.

'I don't *hate* them. I just don't trust them. It's the way they follow you with their eyes. I can't walk past a cat on a wall without worrying that it's going to jump on me.'

'Seriously?'

'No . . .' She gives me a sideways look. 'Yes, but don't tell anyone. If you don't like animals people think there's something wrong with . . . ow!' She unzips her top and glares down at the small, furry brown head that peers up at her. 'The little bugger just bit me.'

'Probably just wanted a better view.'

She doesn't laugh and neither of us says anything for a couple of minutes. After Fiona wrestled the cat from under the bed, I quickly searched the cottage for anything useful. I was hoping for a satellite phone or a mobile with signal. I didn't find either but I did find an empty cat food bowl behind the kitchen door and some cans in the back of the cupboard.

'Do you think there was a satellite phone and Trevor took it?' Fiona asks now.

'Unlikely. There's so much dust in there I think we'd have noticed if anything had been taken and . . .' I freeze and point into the distance. 'Is that him? On the edge of the cliff. Is that Trevor?'

Fiona stops walking too and raises a hand to her eyes. 'Is what Trevor . . . Oh, God.' The expression on her face morphs from confusion to panic. 'I think he's going to jump.'

In Memoriam

In Memoriam

In loving memory of Eileen Cutherbert,
wife, mother, sister and friend. Those who have a
mother, treasure her with care,
for you never know how much you love
her until she is not there.

The older I grew, the bolder I became. I'd sneak out of bed and sit cross-legged at the top of the stairs and gobble up the morsels of my parents' conversations that drifted up from the open living room door. Most of it was mundane gossip about the neighbours (gleaned from my mum's curtain-twitching habit) or tales of woe and illness (from Dad's surgery) but one night, after one of Mum's more difficult days, I swallowed something huge. I discovered why I had no grandparents or aunties or uncles on my mum's side of the family. I'd met my dad's parents when I was three, not that I could remember the event. They lived a long way away, he said, and it was hard to arrange a visit because they were too old to travel and Mum was too fragile.

'Fragile', that was one word for her. 'Neurotic' is another.

'I can smell smoke,' Mum cried one night as I sat at the top of the stairs. 'Gerald, I can definitely smell smoke.'

I sniffed at the air. All I could smell was the faintest whiff of body odour from my twelve-year-old armpits.

I heard the low rumble of my dad's voice in reply. He was my hero. My big, strong father in his tailored suit with his big black bag. There was magic in that leathery case – lotions and potions, pad and pens. He'd let me play with his stethoscope. I'd press it to his chest, then mine, and marvel at the rhythmic thuds of our hearts. But mostly I loved my dad because when he arrived home from work, I knew it wouldn't be long until Mum fell asleep. She called them Dad's 'special pills'. They took the pain and heartache away, she said. I was always so disappointed when she woke up. I think Dad was too.

'The house is not on fire, Dorothy,' I heard him say, as clear as a bell. 'No one is going to die.'

'I miss them,' my mum wailed. 'I wish I'd died too.'

'Dorothy, please,' Dad said. 'Keep your voice down. You can't talk like that.'

'Why can't I? Why can't I express how I feel? I can't be silent. I need to—'

'You're getting hysterical.'

'Please,' my mum begged. 'Please help me, Gerald. I can't live like this any more.'

My dad fell quiet then and I could have sworn I heard the faint click of his medical bag.

'What's that?' I heard my mum ask. 'I don't need an injection, Gerald. I need a pill.'

My dad didn't reply.

Mum screamed, shouted and begged.

Then she was quiet too.

Chapter 43

Anna

I run as fast as I can, my boots slipping in the mud, the rain lashing at my face and my shoulder jarring with every step, but Fiona reaches the man on the cliff top before I do. She stops suddenly, about twenty metres from the edge, her back curved, her head low, bracing herself against the driving wind. Beyond her, sitting with his legs dangling over the edge of the cliff, is Malcolm.

'Don't come any closer!' he shouts. 'Or I'll jump.'

'Malcolm!' I shout back. 'Please move away from the edge. The weather will have made the cliffs unstable.'

'I don't care.'

Fiona looks at me. 'Should I go and get Melanie?'

'No, not yet. I might need you here.'

For what, I'm not entirely sure, but from the hunch of Malcolm's shoulders and the way he's rocking back and forth I'm pretty sure we shouldn't make any sudden movements.

'You know, don't you?' he shouts back at us. 'I can tell by the look on your faces.'

I stare at him blankly. I've got no idea what he's talking about but Fiona seems to.

'You beat up Trevor!' she shouts. 'Didn't you?'

As Malcolm turns to look at us he loses his balance and ends up on his side, his bottom and legs hanging over the edge. He grabs frantically at a clump of heather to stop himself from slipping over completely. 'Don't!' he shouts as I move to help him. He hauls his body away from the edge and lies on his back, his eyes closed against the rain falling from the grey-black sky. When he laughs, it's manic and jubilant. 'You're going to have to do better than that, you fucker! When I die, I get to choose when! Not you!'

'Don't move, Malcolm!' I shout. 'Stay where you are.'

'Does Melanie know what I did?'

Do I tell him or not? I pause a fraction too long and Malcolm roars with anger and scrabbles to his feet, his walking boots slipping in the sodden earth.

'You're not the only one who's done something wrong,' I shout. 'We've all acted in terrible ways. This storm has brought out the worst in us.'

Malcolm raises his arms out to the side, at a ninety-degree angle to his body, and takes a step backwards.

'Stop!' I step towards him but Fiona nudges me sharply.

'Don't. He'll do it. He'll step off the edge. Look at the expression on his face. You need to talk him down, Anna.'

'Melanie's going to leave me!' Malcolm shouts. 'She thinks I'm scum. I've seen it in her face.'

'You don't know that.'

'She doesn't want me anywhere near her. She can't even bear to look at me.'

'You can still put this right.' The rain is so heavy now I have to blink continuously to keep it out of my eyes. 'You've got your issues but don't all couples? This isn't what Melanie would want. It's not what Katie would want.'

'Katie doesn't love me!'

'You're part of her life. She's already lost her dad. If you do this she'll be scarred forever. Mel will be too.'

'They'd be better off without me.'

'How do you know that? You made a mistake, Malcolm, and you did something awful—'

'I beat up a defenceless man!'

'Yes, you did. And you're going to have to live with that for the rest of your life because that's what we do when we fuck up. We say sorry, we try to put things right and we just get on with it. We get on with life and we try not to fuck up again.'

He stares at me – the only sound the roar of the wind and the drumming of the rain – and for a second I think I've got through to him. But then he takes another step back.

'Malcolm, stop! You're not alone! You're not the only person in the hotel wrestling with regret. You're not the only one who's torn up inside because of something you did.'

'What do you know about pain?' he bellows.

'I killed two people and crippled another!' My eyes fill with tears but I blink them back. 'Two people *died* because of me. I should have had my eyes on the road. I should have looked in my wing mirrors. I should have seen the huge, great truck that was thundering towards us from another lane. But I didn't. And do you know why? Because of my pride! Because I needed to show I was in control. That I was the boss. That I was . . .' I choke on my own words.

'It's okay,' Fiona says. 'It's okay, Anna.'

I force myself upright again. 'Don't you fucking dare step off that cliff, Malcolm. Don't you do that to me. Don't give me another life to grieve over. Don't give me another regret.' My voice breaks. 'Don't you fucking dare!'

Malcolm stares at me, his eyes clouded with confusion and despair.

Don't do it, I will him. *Don't do it.*

My heart leaps into my throat as he takes another step backwards.

Then he sinks to his knees, wraps his hands over his head and howls with pain.

Neither Malcolm nor Fiona say a word about my confession as we trudge back up the hill to the hotel, although I catch Fiona glancing at me several times out of the corner of my eye. Malcolm, teeth chattering, seems completely out of it. Christine takes one looks at him as we shepherd him into the lounge and suggests to Katie that they go upstairs for a bit.

'Before you go.' Fiona reaches into her hoody and pulls out the cat by the scruff of its neck. The fight seems to have gone out of it and it hangs limply from her fingers until she supports its weight in her other hand.

Katie, enshrouded in blankets with just her face peeping out, squeals with excitement then wriggles her arms free. 'Where did you get that?'

'We found it in Gordon's cottage.' She carefully transfers the cat into Katie's outstretched hands. 'It's tired and hungry. Here' – she reaches for the pocket of my jacket, still dangling from my shoulders, and pulls out two tins of food – 'give it one of these and see if you can find something to use as a litter tray.'

Katie barely has time to hug Fiona thank you before Christine shoos her, and the cat, out of the room. Malcolm doesn't comment about the cat or the fact that Katie barely gave him a second glance. In fact, he hardly registers that there are other people in the room. He stands lifeless by the window, dripping rainwater onto the carpet, and I have to call his name three times to get him to take a seat by the fire.

Fiona retrieves the whisky bottle and three glasses from the cabinet beneath the bookcase and pours out three hefty measures. Malcolm has two for every one of mine but I don't comment and I don't criticise. But I do slump back in my chair and close my eyes when his jaw finally stops juddering and his breathing slows and settles. Now the adrenaline has worn off, my body feels leaden and amorphous, as though my bones have been stripped out in one swift tug.

'Are you okay, Anna?' Fiona asks. 'Your arm's not hurting, is it?'

'No more than it was earlier.' The dull throb is still there, from my neck to my fingertips. I unhook the sling from behind my neck and experimentally wiggle my fingers then stretch and contract my arm. It hurts, but it's not unbearable.

As I carefully manoeuvre my arm back into the sling, Malcolm shifts in his chair.

'How are you doing?' I ask. 'Is there anything I can get you?'

He slugs at his whisky, the skin pinched and grey beneath his cheekbones, his eyes distant and glassy. He looks old all of a sudden. Late seventies rather than late fifties.

'I guess I should make the most of this.' He drains his glass.

'Why's that?'

'I imagine you'll want to swap me with Trevor and put me in the utility room.'

Fiona catches my eye. He doesn't know that we haven't found him yet.

'Trevor's still missing,' I say.

I brace myself for an explosive reaction; instead, Malcolm's glass wobbles as he sets it back on the table.

'Joe and Melanie are still looking for him,' Fiona says. I join her as she gets up, walks across to the window and stares out.

'It's getting dark,' she says, keeping her voice low so Malcolm can't hear.

'You don't think they'll find him, do you?'

'I'm sure he'll be all right. He's ex-military, isn't he?'

'He hasn't got a tent though.'

'How do you know?' She gives me a quizzical look. She doesn't know I searched Trevor's rucksack for his medication.

'I . . . I don't. I just assumed. Do you think he'll come back? Later? After everything's calmed down a bit?'

She gives me a look. 'Would you?'

Chapter 44

The moment I hear the front door opening and the sound of voices in the lobby I hiss at Fiona to keep an eye on Malcolm, then hurry out of the lounge and close the door behind me. Melanie, her hair plastered to her scalp, shakes her head as she peels off her coat.

'We looked everywhere but there's no sign of him.'

'I know.' I take her coat from her, hang it up on the peg then wipe my wet hands on my jeans. 'Fiona and I searched the cottage. We think he broke in and took a few things but he's not there now. I'm hoping, if he doesn't come back here, he'll stay there tonight because at least that way . . .' I glance at Joe, who's taking off his boots and has avoided eye contact with me ever since they came in, '. . . at least that way he'll be dry, if not warm.'

'This is a bit delicate,' Mel says carefully, 'but Joe and I were talking on the walk back, about David. He's been in his room for a few days now and . . . um . . . nature's obviously taking its course.'

She means the smell.

'We thought it might be a good idea if he were moved,' she

adds. 'Perhaps to the greenhouse in the garden. Just until we can call for help.'

I hate the idea of it, the indignity of David being laid out amongst withered tomato plants and bags of compost, but Melanie's right. None of us have any idea how much longer the storm's going to last and he can't stay in his room.

'That's fine,' I say. 'I understand.'

'Joe very kindly agreed to carry him and, if Malcolm agrees, he could help.'

'I'll go up and . . .' Joe straightens up, rubbing his lower back with his knuckles, '. . . check on David.'

I watch him take the stairs, each step slow and laboured, as though the weight of the world is on his shoulders, and my heart twists in my chest. Moving David isn't a job anyone would actively choose to do, but for Joe to have lost his brother recently it has to be doubly difficult. I want to go after him, to tell him that I understand, but he's still angry with me, I can tell. His brother lost his life locked up in a small room against his will and I sanctioned Trevor's imprisonment.

'Mel, hang on a sec!' I slide between Melanie and the door to the lounge as she moves to go inside. I need to tell her what happened with Malcolm before she sees him. 'Can I have a quick word with you?'

'Sure.' She tries to reach round me for the door handle.

'Not here. In private. Do you mind if we go up to your room?'

'What's this about?' Melanie perches on the edge of her bed, her hands pressed between her knees. 'You look very serious, Anna.'

Serious, and nervous. I push down the panic that bubbles in the pit of my stomach and adjust the sling so it's not cutting into the back of my neck. Now I've pretty much ruled Joe out as my stalker there's every possibility that I'm alone with the person who wants me dead. It's the reason I've taken the seat nearest the door and why I scanned the room for potential weapons the moment I walked in. But there are no weapons to speak of, just a glass of water and a book on the bedside table, two rucksacks and four walking poles propped up against a wall.

'It's bad news, isn't it?' Melanie says.

'What makes you think that?'

She raises her eyebrows above the red rims of her glasses. 'The look on your face.'

'It's about your husband. I'm worried about him. When we were looking for Trevor we found Malcolm sitting on the edge of the cliff. He . . . he threatened to throw himself off.'

Melanie presses the palms of both hands into the bed as though to steady herself. 'You're not serious?'

'I am. He admitted he was the one who beat Trevor up.'

'Oh, God.' She folds into herself, wrapping her arms around her head.

'Melanie? Are you okay?'

She looks up at me, a pained expression in her eyes. 'I thought it might be him but I wouldn't let myself believe it. We had an argument last night. He got drunk and I told him that I hated the way he talked about Trevor. I said I didn't want to share a room with him and he should sleep on the sofa. I went up to bed but I couldn't sleep. When I came down to check on him he wasn't in the lounge. He was sitting on the floor of the kitchen with his head in his hands, crying and muttering.'

'What about?'

'He kept saying sorry, mostly. *I'm sorry, Trevor. I'm a fucking arsehole.* That kind of thing. I didn't realise then what he'd done. I thought he was just feeling sorry for himself, so I crept away without him seeing me. I'm so sorry, Anna. I don't know what to say. I can't believe I married a man like that. I genuinely . . .

I really had no idea that he could do something like . . .' She buries her face in her hands again and sighs heavily.

I ease myself out of the chair and wrap an arm around her shoulders. 'It's not your fault. You had no way of knowing he'd do that.'

'Didn't I?' She pulls away. 'He's never hit me, never hit anyone as far as I know, but he's always so bloody angry. I don't know why. Apart from children he's got everything he ever wanted out of life but he's wound up so tightly and he'll take any opportunity to complain, moan or criticise. It does my head in! I can't watch the news with him any more because he just rants all the way through it.'

She sighs again. 'I wanted children too but you don't see me beating up defenceless men. Secretly I think he resents me, Anna. I was forty-one when we met and time was never going to be on my side. Malcolm's sperm could probably do the job well into his seventies, that's what he claims anyway, but my eggs . . .' She laughs lightly. 'What eggs?'

'It sounds like he's been really insensitive.'

'That's one way of putting it.' She snorts softly. 'Cruel's another. You know this trip was his idea? He thought everything would be hunky-dory between us if we spent some time alone. I can't tell you how pissed off he was when I suggested we bring Katie with us.' She sits back and runs her hands over her face. She looks tired and emotionally spent. 'He wouldn't have done it, you know.'

'Done what?'

'Thrown himself off the cliff. He knew he'd be outed as the person who beat up Trevor as soon as we found him. I imagine he saw you running towards him, assumed you'd discovered what he'd done, and faked being suicidal to get you on side. Honestly, Anna, you've got no idea how manipulative he can be.'

She looks utterly convinced by what she's saying but I can't reconcile it with the man I saw on the cliff top, shaking and rocking and screaming at the sky. Malcolm would have to be one hell of an actor to pull that off.

Melanie sighs. 'Sounds like I'll have to have a talk with him.'

'What will you say?'

'That it's over.'

I start to say something then change my mind.

Her eyes narrow behind her glasses. 'What?'

'I just . . . I just wonder if it might be better to have that conversation once you're back in London. I know you think Malcolm was faking being suicidal but he just seemed very . . . fragile.'

She laughs, then slaps her hand against her mouth as though forcing the sound back in. 'He's as fragile as a brick. Just ask Trevor.'

'Okay, wrong word. Unstable then.'

She shifts back on the bed, leans against the wall and raises her eyes to the ceiling. 'All these unstable men that we have to tiptoe around. Could you imagine this happening if it were the other way round – if me, you, Christine or Fiona went on a rampage, smashing things up and thumping people? Do you think the men would be quite so considerate of our *unstable* feelings? No! Of course they bloody wouldn't. They'd label us neurotic and give us a wide berth!'

'I'm not sure that's—'

'True? Really? I was alone for six years before Malcolm came along. There was no one to catch me if I fell, no one to look after me if I had a nervous breakdown. I had to look after myself, and my ageing parents. It's bullshit, women being the weaker sex. Who looks after us if we have enough of being strong? Huh? Tell me that! Who looks after us?'

The base of her throat is flushed red and her eyes are shining with anger and indignation behind the glint of her glasses. She stares at me, as though challenging me to argue with her, then closes her eyes and sighs heavily.

'Don't worry. I'm not going to say anything to Malcolm that will make him want to throw himself off a cliff. I've got enough on my conscience without adding that too.'

The atmosphere in the room changes in an instant, or maybe it's just my feelings that shift. A second ago I felt overwhelmed with sympathy and sadness for her. Now I'm tense and wary.

'What do you mean? About having too much on your conscience.'

Melanie shakes her head, her eyes still closed. 'I'm not sure I've got the energy to tell you.'

'Try me.' I glance at the door, still closed, and the sharp tips of the walking poles propped up against the wall. Is this where she confesses that she's been stalking me for months? My mind whirs with possibilities – could she be Freddy's older sister? Steve's sister? I don't know what her maiden name is, I've never thought to ask her.

'It's Katie,' she sighs. 'I'm worried about her.'

I hold myself very still, waiting for her to continue.

'She's a carer.' She opens her eyes and looks at me. 'Did you know that?'

'No, I didn't.'

'Her mum, Tracy, my sister-in-law, has got a degenerative neurological condition. She's had it for years but it was manageable, well, as manageable as a chronic condition can be, and Katie's dad took charge of most of her care. But then she got worse, almost overnight it seemed, and now she can barely walk, she's often sick and, really, she can't look after herself when Katie's at school.'

A new thought digs itself into my brain. Could Katie's dad be Peter? I know he's not around but it hadn't occurred to me until now that he could be dead. What if the stalking has nothing to do with Steve Laing and instead it's revenge for Peter's death? He never mentioned a wife and child at work, neither did his parents when I rang them, but he always kept himself to himself. I wasn't the only one who didn't socialise with Freddy and Mo.

'Mel . . .' I'm almost too scared to ask the question but I have to. 'What . . . what happened to Katie's dad?'

She straightens her legs and sits up taller. I grip the sides of the bed, ready to propel myself across the room and out of the door.

'He left.' She shrugs. 'Said the marriage had been over for years, that he'd only stayed because of a sense of duty, but he couldn't cope with it any more and it was either leave or have a nervous breakdown. I was shocked. Graham's a lot of things but that was a new low.'

'Katie's dad left her to look after her mum on her own?' I'm so shocked by what I've just heard that it takes me a second to realise that Melanie just said Graham, not Peter.

'Yeah. God knows where he's gone. Malcolm thinks he might be in Spain, or on a cruise ship. Apparently he worked on one before he met Tracy.'

'Graham is Malcolm's brother, not yours?'

She smiles tightly. 'Bunch of charmers, aren't they?'

I stand up and move over to the window. Outside, lit up by the security lights on the back of the hotel, Joe and Malcolm are struggling to manoeuvre David's body down the path and into the greenhouse. Both men have what look like white tea towels tied around their mouths and noses but there's no tea towel loosely draped over David's head. He's been tightly wrapped with sheets, bound from head to foot like an Egyptian mummy. He no longer looks human. Just *human-shaped*.

That could be you, a voice says in the back of my head. *If you'd died last night they'd be taking your body into the greenhouse with David's and no one would know your death wasn't an accident.* I try to block the voice out but it's too loud and insistent to ignore. *Whoever tried to kill you isn't going to give up until you're dead, Anna.*

'I know Katie's not family,' Melanie continues, 'not by blood anyway, but I feel so responsible for her. She's fourteen years old and she's a carer. That's why she's with us – to give her a bit of a break. I paid for a private nurse to look after Tracy while we're away but I can't afford to do that full time. With Malcolm partly retired we're living on my salary and it only stretches so far. I've tried Tracy's GP and social services to get someone in to help but the bureaucracy's ridiculous. Even the smallest step forwards seems to involve two steps back.'

'That sounds really tough.'

She shrugs. 'What can you do?'

An awkward silence fills the space between us, neither of us knowing what to say next.

'I'll um . . . I'll go then,' I say. 'Give you a bit of space to yourself.'

She laughs lightly, whether through nerves or relief that I'm leaving, I'm not sure.

'Anna,' she says as I reach for the door handle. 'While you're up here I don't suppose you could get me a fresh towel, could you? Or give me the linen cupboard key and I'll get one myself.'

'No, no, of course. I'll get one now. Sorry, it's been forever since I . . .' I pause as I step into the corridor. The last time I cleaned the rooms I had no idea that my stalker was in the hotel. But I do now.

Chapter 45

Alex

Alex looks at his phone and sighs: 9 p.m. and still no sign of Becca, and no text to say she's running late either. Maybe there was an urgent situation at work (she'd forewarned him on their first date that she very rarely left on time after a shift) or maybe – he shifts uncomfortably in his chair – maybe she's stood him up. That would be a bit weird, considering she was the one who wanted to see him in the first place, but she might have lost her nerve. It had to be a dumping, though why she couldn't bring herself to do that over the phone he didn't know. He'd much rather dump someone from the comfort of his own home with a beer in his hand and an 'end call' button to silence any awkwardness. He reaches for his pint, takes a sip and considers how he'll react when Becca breaks the news that she doesn't want to see him any more.

He'll be nonchalant, he decides. Probably make it easier on her by saying that he'd been considering doing the same thing.

That he thinks they'd be great friends (although obviously they'll never see each other again after they've said their goodbyes) and he hopes there's no hard feelings. Yes, he sets his beer back on the table, that's the way he'll play it. Cool, calm and nonchalant. And if she gets to the pub in the next five minutes there's a chance he'll be able to fit in a couple of episodes of *The Walking Dead* before he has to go to bed. He considers the lager level in his pint glass. It's just dipped below the halfway point. Can he risk another trip up to the bar for a second pint before Becca turns up? Running out midway through their conversation would be irritating. Although he might appreciate the excuse to leave the table.

'Hi, Alex.' Becca touches a hand to his shoulder and leans down to kiss him on the cheek. She smells sweet and floral at the same time. It's different from her normal perfume. She's moved on already.

'Hi.' He pushes a glass of Rioja across the table towards her and her face lights up.

'A drink already waiting for me. That's so sweet.'

Her response confuses him. She doesn't seem like she's about to dump him but maybe this is her way, make the dumpee feel so calm and relaxed that when she places the bomb in their hands they barely notice it go boom.

'How's work?' he asks, more out of habit than interest. He just wants her to get to the point and put him out of his misery. Misery? That's interesting. Maybe he's not as nonchalant about splitting up as he thought. She is good company most of the time and there is that great bum.

'Not good.' She knocks back half her glass of wine. When she sets it back on the table there are two tiny claret smudges at the edges of her lips. Alex decides not to mention them. 'Sorry I've been a bit evasive recently but I couldn't say any more about what's going on. I still can't really. The hospital board are terrified that if the press get a sniff of it then . . .' She sighs and takes another gulp of her drink. 'Anyway, sorry I've been a bit distant. I've been really stressed about . . . um . . . something I've done . . .'

'Go on.' Alex takes a gulp of his pint and braces himself.

'I . . . um . . . I did something I shouldn't have, at work. That's why I was so freaked out when the managers started sniffing around. I thought they'd found out and I was going to get sacked.'

Alex leans forwards in his seat, elbows on the damp table. Becca was never anything other than utterly professional when Anna was in hospital. He can't imagine her doing anything wrong.

'What I did was . . .' Her eyes flick away from his. 'I gave someone your home address.'

'What?' He sits back again, unsure and confused. 'Why would you do that?'

'Well . . . it wasn't so much your address. It was Anna's.'

'You gave someone our address? The flat in Woodside Park?'

'Yes.' She nods, still not looking at him. 'And the details of Anna's next of kin.'

'You gave them my details? Which ones? When?'

'Not yours, her parents. You're not . . . you weren't married. It was after Anna was discharged from hospital and before we got together. Someone rang the nurse's station and said they needed to contact her urgently. When I asked why, they said it was confidential.'

'So you just gave them all her details? Are you even allowed to do that?'

'No.' She finally meets his eyes. 'I'm not. That's why I've been so worried.'

'Why do it then?'

She sighs heavily. 'Because of who it was. The person who asked for Anna's details . . . I worked with them.'

Chapter 46

Anna

'Melanie, would you mind going downstairs and telling the others that we need to have another house meeting? Everyone's to wait in the lounge until I come down.'

'But I was hoping to have a shower.' She looks longingly in the direction of the linen cupboard.

'I know, I'm sorry. The meeting won't take long and you'll have plenty of time afterwards.'

'Is it about Trevor? Because I'm not sure there's much more we can do tonight.'

'It's about a number of different issues.' I finger the master key in my pocket, willing her to hurry up and go downstairs. If we stay here much longer other guests will drift up to their rooms. I need Melanie to keep them all in one place so I can start searching.

'Well, if you insist.' Reluctantly, she steps out of her room, pulling the door shut behind her.

I wait until she's disappeared into the stairwell then, key in hand, I let myself into Trevor's room. I'm fairly certain he's not my stalker: he self-medicates his PTSD with Valium and just living day to day must be hell.

Trevor's room is empty. There's no rucksack on the floor and no toothbrush or toothpaste in the bathroom. The only evidence he ever stayed here is the ever-so-slightly rumpled bed. I shut the door and deliberate about where to go next. I've already had a quick look in Melanie and Malcolm's room and I saw the inside of Joe's room after Katie's sleepwalking escapade. Katie's room? I dismiss her as a suspect straight off. If her dad was Peter Cross then maybe there'd be a tiny possibility she could be my stalker but he's not, and she's not. That leaves Fiona and Christine.

Fiona's room is closest so I head in there. Whereas Melanie and Malcolm's room smells of damp clothing, Fiona's room is much more pleasant. The scent of her perfume hangs in the air and her toiletries, make-up and hair products are neatly arranged on the dressing table. Unlike some of the others, she's completely unpacked. Her empty rucksack is in the wardrobe and her clothes are in the chest of drawers. I rummage through them, keeping one eye on the door and freezing whenever I hear the pipes rumble or a joist creak. There's nothing hidden amongst her clothes but I do find her purse in the top drawer. With fumbling fingers I search through her cards. They all say Fiona Gardiner, including her driver's licence, which gives her date of birth as 15 August 1983 – she's nearly thirty-five – and her address as 15A Wimpole Street, London. There's nothing else of interest in her purse apart from a small pre-printed card that says, 'To the world you may be one person, but to one person you're the world.' Underneath, in sprawling handwriting, it says, *Love you Fi, M. x*

M? That has to be the ex-boyfriend she mentioned when we

were checking the oil tank. I move to shove the card back into the purse, then pause.

An image flashes up in my mind, of Mohammed sitting next to me in the car, his head tipped back, his mouth open as he snored softly. Could Fiona be his girlfriend? I know he was seeing someone older than him. I remember Freddy taking the piss when he saw a photo on Mo's phone, saying he was dating a cougar, but I didn't hear a name mentioned and I didn't bother to ask. Why would I? Their private lives were their own. At least that's what I told myself at the time. It's only now I realise how little I knew about my team's lives.

But why would Fiona come after me? She said her boyfriend had dumped her out of the blue. Even if that is Mo, why would she want me to 'sleep' when he's still very much alive? Unless she thinks it's my fault that he dumped her.

I tuck the card back into the purse, return it to the drawer and turn my attention to the bedside table where Fiona's mobile phone lies redundantly next to a glass of water. I snatch it up and press the button at the base. The phone flashes to life but the screen's locked. The background wallpaper doesn't give me any clues. It's a tropical beach somewhere, with a crystal-clear sea. I swipe upwards and try to guess her pin number.

1234.

Incorrect PIN entered.

4321.

Incorrect PIN.

I try the first four digits of her date of birth then freeze as something creaks in the corridor. Holding the phone behind my back I creep to the door and peer out, but there's no one there. I take a steadying breath, look back down at the phone and tap on the screen with my thumb.

1508.

Incorrect PIN.

0883

Incorrect PIN.

Damn it. I could be here for hours, guessing, and I've still got Christine's room to check. Reluctantly, I lay the phone back down on the bedside table and lift the mattress. Nothing. Nothing hidden in the wardrobe either. If Fiona's my stalker, she's hiding it well.

I feel a pang of guilt as I unlock Christine's room and step inside. She's not much older than my mum and she'd *hate it* if a stranger rooted through her things. She gave me an absolute bollocking when I was a teenager and I went through her chest of drawers looking for a hairbrush while she was out at work. *How* she knew I'd been through her things when she got back, I have no idea, but she completely lost the plot.

Christine's room is even tidier than Fiona's. There's nothing on any of the surfaces, not even the bottle of whisky I saw the last time I came in. Unlike Fiona, she's only partially unpacked. There are jumpers, trousers and several floral scarves hanging in the wardrobe but there are still several items in her rucksack: three pairs of socks, a glasses case, a clear pencil case containing several pens and a first aid kit. As I reach for the first aid kit something else catches my eye: a book, the cover curled and battered, the pages yellow-tinged and crinkled with age.

The Book of Sleep: A Poetry Anthology.

My stomach twists as I stare down at the faded countryside scene on the cover: a huge yellow moon peering between the black skeletons of leafless trees.

It has to be a coincidence that the title includes the word 'sleep'. It makes sense that Christine would be interested in poetry, she's an ex-primary school teacher, after all.

Unless she's not.

I open the cover, flick to the index page and scan the contents:

SLEEP

Sonnet 39 – Sir Philip Sidney
Sonnet 27 – William Shakespeare
Golden Slumbers – Thomas Dekker
Cradle Song – William Blake
To Sleep – William Wordsworth

I run my thumb over the pages, scanning the text as one poem blurs into the next, then stop abruptly as something unusual leaps out at me – a flash of yellow against the cream pages:

In Memoriam

Emily and Eva Gapper

Emily Gapper, devoted wife and mother. Passed away on 13.2.2015 to be with our darling daughter, Eva Gapper. Knowing that the two of you are together is my only comfort. Forever in my thoughts, my beautiful girls. Love and miss you always . . .

It's a death notice, a heart-felt tribute published in a newspaper, clipped out and pasted over one of the poems. I find more as I continue to turn the pages: a tribute to a young woman called Akhtar, a farewell to a pub regular called Curly, fond reminiscences about an Auntie Mary and a goodbye to a man called Derek Sanders. There are dozens and dozens of these notices glued into the pages of the book. I feel a strange sense of disconnect as I flick back and forth between the clippings, as though I'm caught in a dream. This isn't Christine fondly remembering a lost relative and pasting their 'In Memoriam' notice into her favourite book, it's a catalogue of death.

My hands shake so violently that the book falls from my fingers and drops to the floor. As it hits the carpet a single piece of paper flutters from between the pages and settles near my feet. It's not a cutting from a newspaper. It's the same size but it's been handwritten on a piece of complimentary Bay View Hotel notepaper:

In Memoriam

David Allan Campbell
? – 5th June 2018

Remembering David Campbell, hotelier, friend and colleague.

He struggled to live, then he fell asleep . . .

It is as though the ground has just disappeared from beneath my feet and I'm suspended in midair, my stomach hollowed against my spine, anticipating the fall. I grip the edge of the mattress but I can't feel the coarse, puckered material beneath my fingertips. I can't feel anything. My heart has stilled in my chest and there is no air in my lungs.

Why would Christine write her own 'In Memoriam' notice for David and what does it mean – *he struggled to live?* She tried to save his life. Didn't she?

With hollow legs, I force myself up from the bed and onto my feet. I pull the rucksack towards me and reach inside. What else is Christine hiding?

The sound of distant voices makes me freeze.

I drop the book back into the rucksack, hurl myself out of the door and, with trembling fingers, turn the key in the lock. My heart hammers in my chest as I turn to run to my room but, before I can take a step, Christine appears at the top of the stairs.

In Memoriam

In Memoriam

In loving memory of Stan Eric Holloway

The world may change from year to year
And friends from day to day,
But never will the one I loved
From memory pass away.

Sleep.

We crave it, that blissful darkness that rocks us in its arms and carries us away from our cares and our worries. Life is struggle but sleep is an escape. It is the womb to which we return when our limbs are heavy and our minds are tired. Sometimes we fight it. We struggle to remain awake. Our guilt, or misplaced loyalty, keeps us rooted to this coil, too afraid to move on to the next.

I was twenty-five the first time I helped someone to sleep. Her name was Eileen Cuthbert and she was eighty-seven years old. She'd been transferred from her nursing home to hospital after suffering a stroke and, in the two days she'd been in critical care, she hadn't had a single visitor. The next of kin listed on her medical records was a Millicent White, manager of Sunshine Care Home. Her next of kin was someone she wasn't related to? That struck me as terribly sad. Eileen wasn't wearing a wedding ring when she came in and, if she had had children they were obviously no longer part of her life, if they were even alive. I couldn't stop thinking about her when I went home from work after my shift. What did she have to look forward to when she returned to the care home? She was paralysed down one side. She couldn't feed herself, she couldn't speak and, in all likelihood, she would never walk again. It was terribly cruel, I felt, for her to have to live a half-life. If an animal were in the same state we'd put it down and end its misery.

The next day, when I returned to work, I held her hand and stroked her thin grey hair back over her flaky pink scalp and I promised her that I would help her. She looked at me with her cloudy blue eyes and her lopsided mouth twitched horribly. She wanted to sleep. I was in no doubt about that.

There was something very beautiful about the speed with which Eileen Cutherbert slipped from consciousness into the blissful arms of a coma. I was by her side as she took her last breath. I held her hand, as I'd held my mother's hand many years before, and I told her to let go. My heart swelled with love as her chest rose and then fell for the last time and her fingers slackened in my palm.

The longer I worked as a nurse the more difficult it became to help people to sleep but I persevered, in memory of my mum, who'd suffered so much in life and only found peace in sleep. I helped a mother who survived a car accident, but lost her child, to reunite with her baby. I helped an acid attack victim escape the pain of her disfigured future and I aided a red-nosed pensioner whose most faithful companion was a pint of ale.

I am no angel of mercy. I am flawed and ugly but I am compassionate and merciful. I am also determined. That is my most admirable quality.

Chapter 47

Anna

Christine doesn't step into the corridor; instead she remains in the shadows of the stairwell, her gaze flicking from her closed bedroom door to my clenched hand, the master key hidden within my fist, and then to my face. The cheery smile she'd normally greet me with is gone. Her lips are a tight, thin line, her eyes narrowed, steely behind her wire-rimmed glasses.

I can't breathe. I can't speak. I can't move. I'm gripped by such a powerful, abject terror that, even though my brain is screaming at me to run, my feet are rooted to the floor.

As she walks towards me she forces a smile, incongruous against the tight set of her face. 'Is everything all right, Anna? You look as though you've seen a ghost.'

She knows I've been in her room and seen her book. She's smiling up at me but, beneath the faux concern of her words, her rage is icy cold. I need to reply, to scream or shout or act, but there's a void in my brain where my thoughts used to be.

'Anna?' She takes a step towards me, narrowing the space between us. I don't know who she is any more. Where once I saw a warm, caring woman, now I see a monster, obsessed with sleep and death. She's the one who's been haunting me since the accident, sending me terrifying messages telling me to sleep and trying to lure me to my death. Why? I want to scream the question in her face and burst into tears at the same time. Why would you do this? Why did you come after me?

'Anna? Christine?' A male voice from the stairwell makes me jump. Christine spins round to see who it is.

Joe, one hand resting on the wall, looks lazily in my direction. 'Is this meeting happening soon? Because Fiona says dinner's ready.'

Meeting? For a second I don't know what he's talking about but then I remember, I sent Melanie downstairs to keep the others away so I could look through their rooms.

'Dinner?' Christine says brightly. 'I don't know about you, Anna, but I'm starving. I'm sure the meeting can wait, can't it?'

The change in her demeanour is astonishing. Her face and voice have softened and she's herself again, or at least the self she pretends to be.

'Anna?' Joe says. 'Is that okay?'

'I . . . um . . . I . . .'

He frowns as I search for the right words.

'I . . . yes, that's fine. Can I have a quick word with you, please?'

I skirt around Christine and half run, half stumble down the corridor towards him. His frown deepens as I get closer and he looks from me to Christine and then back again.

'I'm just going to get a scarf from my room,' Christine says, taking her room key out of her pocket. 'Then I'll be right down.'

Joe moves to walk down the stairs but I'm fixed to the spot as Christine lets herself into her room. My blood freezes as she dips down and picks up a small piece of paper from the floor. It's David's obituary notice. I forgot to put it back in the book.

'Anna?' Joe says as Christine whips round and fixes me with an icy stare. 'Are we going back downstairs or what?'

The second we reach the bottom of the stairs I burst into tears. Joe stands awkwardly at my side as I cling to the banister, pressing my hand over my mouth to try to stifle my sobs.

'What is it?' he asks. 'What's the matter?'

I glance up the stairs, terrified that Christine will walk back down at any moment. Low voices drift from beneath the closed lounge door and the sound of clinking crockery carries through from the dining room.

'Anna?' Joe says again. 'What is it?'

'Not here.' I yank open the front door, not bothering to pull on my coat or my boots.

Joe follows me outside, pausing to grab his coat from the rack. He drapes it over my shoulders as I press myself up against the porch, my legs suddenly too weak to hold me upright. Beyond the glow of the hotel it's pitch black. The clouds, heavy with rain, block out the light of the stars and the moon. Even if I could get the Land Rover across the river I'd be stranded in the dark as soon as it ran out of petrol. There's no way I'd be able to find my way across the island virtually blindfolded.

'Please, Anna,' Joe says, his tone suddenly gruff. 'Just tell me what's going on.'

I shake my head. 'You won't believe me.'

'Try me.'

'Christine's been stalking me.'

'What?' He physically jolts.

'It began in London, after I was in a car accident. I started to receive disturbing messages telling me to sleep. At first I thought a man called Steve Laing was behind them. His son,

Freddy, died in the accident.' I give Joe a long look. 'I was driving.'

'Jesus.' He stares at me in shock. 'You mentioned a car accident but I didn't know people had died. My God, Anna.' He presses a hand to my arm, just the lightest of touches before his hand falls away again. 'I'm so sorry. I had no idea.'

The concern in his eyes makes my throat tighten and tears prick at my eyes but I blink them away.

'You've mentioned those names to me before,' Joe says. 'Steve and Freddy. You asked me over dinner if I knew them.'

I can hear the question in his voice. He's trying to work out why I asked him about them.

'When I came to Rum,' I say, looking back at him, 'I thought the stalking would stop but then that message appeared on the window – TO DIE, TO SLEEP.'

'That was real?'

'Of course it was.'

'Sorry. It was just . . . a bit weird. None of us knew what you were on about. If I'm honest I thought the shock of David's death had . . .' He shrugs off the rest of the sentence.

'You thought I'd lost it?'

'Maybe a bit. I still don't get what makes you think Christine's involved.'

'I found a book in her room just now, a poetry collection, about sleep. There were obituary notices pasted into it.'

He shakes his head.

'The kind of thing people send in to newspapers,' I explain. 'In loving memory of Auntie Laura, that sort of thing.'

'Oh, right.' He nods but I can tell from the look on his face that he still doesn't understand.

'There were dozens of them, Joe, dozens and dozens. And she'd handwritten one for David. I think she killed all the people in that book, including him.'

'Wow.' He runs a hand over his hair and stares out at the rain. He doesn't believe me. Why would he? How many female serial killers in their sixties or seventies make the news? But I *know* Christine was the one who left the insulin in my room and took the floorboard out. I have never been more certain of anything.

'Has she ever mentioned her children or grandchildren?' I ask. 'Has she ever mentioned a Steve, Freddy or Peter?'

Joe shakes his head. 'Not to me.'

'A recent bereavement?'

'No, sorry, no.' He falls silent then sighs heavily. I can't shake the feeling that he doesn't believe me. 'What do you want me to do, Anna?'

'I want you to ask her for the book of poetry. It's the only proof I've got that she's behind all this.'

I wait outside, the front door cracked open, watching as Joe lumbers up the stairs to the first floor. As time ticks by Fiona comes out of the dining room, David's apron fastened around her waist. She doesn't see me watching as she crosses the lobby and goes into the lounge, leaving the door ajar.

I hear Melanie say, 'Where is she? We've been waiting here for ages. Katie's hungry,' then the low murmur of Fiona's reply.

A couple of seconds later she comes back out again and returns to the dining room. As the door clicks behind her Joe's socks appear at the top of the stairs. The tight knot in my stomach loosens, just the tiniest bit, as he steps down into the lobby and I see the book clutched in his right hand. I can't believe Christine's given it to him. She wouldn't dare do anything else to me now she knows Joe knows the truth.

'What did you say?' I ask as he joins me outside, gently closing the door behind him. It's all I can do not to snatch the book out of his hand.

'I told her I fancied reading some poetry and asked if she could recommend any. She gave me this.' He holds the anthology out to me.

I look at the book. The title's the same as the one I found, so's the faded countryside scene on the jacket – a huge primrose moon peering between the black skeletons of leafless trees – but the pages aren't yellowed and the cover isn't curled. I flick through it but, while the book I saw had faded newspaper cuttings glued to the pages, all the poetry is still visible in this book; it's practically pristine.

'It's not the same book. She must have given you a different copy. I know that sounds mental,' I add as Joe sighs heavily. 'But I swear to you, this isn't the book I saw. There's nothing in this one.' I hold it by the cover and shake it. Nothing falls out.

'Anna,' Joe says softly, his eyes clouded with worry, 'I . . . I think you've had a stressful time recently and . . . um . . . I'm not saying you're lying, and I believe you when you say you saw something in Christine's book, but . . . whatever it was you saw, it's not there now.'

'Can you go back up to her?' I beg. 'Please. Go up and ask if you can look through her other books, or we can wait until she's at dinner and search her room together. I've got a master key.'

'I'm not doing that, Anna.'

'What?'

'I'm not searching someone else's room. It's an invasion of privacy.'

'But she tried to kill me! She removed the plank at the top of the stairs.'

'That plank was always loose, you told me as much when we carried David upstairs. What happened to you was awful, but it was an accident.'

'That's what she wants you to think! You don't believe me because you've bought into her nice little old lady act and you think I'm a horrible person for agreeing to keep Trevor locked up in the utility room. I know what happened to your brother, Joe, and I know you're hurting but I could end up dead too if you don't help me and . . . ' The words dry up in my throat as Joe's expression darkens.

'Leave Will out of this, Anna.'

'You punched a wall, didn't you?' I reach for his hand, the knuckles still red and sore. 'I get it. I know all about guilt, Joe. But what happened to your brother wasn't your fault. You have to know there was nothing you could have done to stop—'

He yanks his hand away and opens the front door. 'I can't do this, Anna. I'm sorry. I thought I could help you but I can't.'

Chapter 48

'Joe!' I follow him back into the hotel but, before I reach him, Fiona walks out into the lobby.

'Oh! There you are.' Her gaze drifts down from the oversized coat around my shoulders to the socks on my feet and she raises her eyebrows. 'Dinner's ready. Do you still want to hold that meeting first or . . .' She tails off as Katie comes out of the lounge.

She crosses her feet at the ankles and looks hopefully across at me. 'Can we have dinner now, please?'

It feels so surreal, a conversation about food when upstairs, holed away in her room, is someone who wants me dead.

'Anna.' Joe, standing at the bottom of the staircase, almost barks my name. 'People are hungry. They need to eat.'

He thinks I'm unstable or that I've completely lost the plot.

'Of course.' I force the words out of my mouth. 'Of course we should eat.'

I nearly cry out when Christine walks into the dining room. She smiles warmly at Katie, sitting nearest the door, and takes a seat next to her, opposite Joe. The smile remains fixed on her face as she turns her attention to him.

'Have you read any of that poetry yet?'

I hold my breath. *Please*, I pray as I lean back in my seat so I can see past Melanie, who's sitting between us. *Please, Joe, ask her if there's another copy.*

'Not yet,' Joe says dully. 'Maybe after dinner.'

'I think you'll enjoy it.' Christine's gaze flicks back to me. 'Do you enjoy poetry, Anna?'

Before I can answer, Fiona walks through from the kitchen with a saucepan full of food. Silence falls as she dishes tuna pasta into our bowls then takes her seat at the end of the table. Malcolm, sitting opposite me, keeps his gaze fixed on his dinner as he shovels it into his mouth. I move my food around my bowl with my fork.

'Lost your appetite, Anna?' Christine asks. 'Bagsy your leftovers.'

As everyone laughs I fight back tears. There isn't a single person around this table who'd believe me if I told them the truth about her. She's hoodwinked them all and, without her book, I haven't got any proof. There's no point trying to search her room again. The book won't be there. Now she knows I've seen it she'll have hidden it somewhere I can never find it – that's if she hasn't got it on her.

'Don't go yet,' Fiona says as Joe pushes his chair back from the table and stands up, his empty bowl in his hand. 'I've got a little post-dinner treat for everyone.'

As he sits back down she hurries back to the kitchen. A couple of minutes later she appears with a tray holding eight steaming mugs.

'It's hot chocolate,' she says. 'We found some evaporated milk at the back of the cupboard. I know a lot of us have been craving something sweet so hopefully this will hit the spot.'

The mugs are greeted with indifference by some, curiosity by others and suspicion by Malcolm, who blows on it then dips his little finger in for a taste. I take a sip of mine, then another.

I've got no appetite but I can't remember the last time I had something to drink.

Katie takes a tentative sip then raises her eyebrows appreciatively. 'Quite good.'

Fiona laughs. 'Praise indeed.'

'It's lovely, Fiona,' I say as I drain my mug, grab my full bowl of pasta and stand up. 'Thank you.'

'What are you doing?' she asks as I head towards the kitchen.

'Clearing my things.'

'You've only got one working arm! Sit down, we can do it.'

'It's fine.' I nudge the kitchen door with my good shoulder and it swings open. I head towards the sink but as I step forwards something rushes at my foot, making me trip. As I struggle to stop myself from falling I bash against the bin, knocking it over.

'Sorry, boy.' I drop to my knees and peer between the fridge and the wall where the cat has backed itself up against the legs of the ironing board. It won't come out, despite my coaxing, but it doesn't look injured – just pissed off – so I grab a bin bag from the drawer and tidy up the mess on the floor. I mindlessly shovel vegetable peelings, cans, packets, tubs, tins, a blister pack of pills and some stained cellophane into the black plastic and then reach for a strip of blackened banana skin. I pause and reach back into the bag for the blister pack. Diazepam. That's another name for Valium, the medication Trevor said was stolen from his room.

Keeping one eye on the kitchen door, I shovel the rest of the rubbish back into the bin then look again at the empty blister pack in my hands. I am *certain* it wasn't in the bin earlier. I know because I emptied it and left the back door unlocked in case Trevor wanted to sneak in unnoticed to get food or drink. But who put them in here? The guests have been going in and out of the kitchen all day, helping themselves to snacks and hot drinks. There are three saucepans on the stove: one empty that must have been used to boil the pasta, one with the remains of a tuna tomato sauce smeared over the base and sides, and one with congealed hot chocolate sitting in the bottom. A dark thought settles in the back of my brain. Why take Trevor's medication and keep the tablets unless you were going to use them for something? I pick up the wooden spoon, dripping chocolate onto the counter, and move it through the gloop in the bottom of the saucepan. It's the first time we've had hot chocolate after a meal. It's either a complete coincidence and I'm paranoid or I've just drunk something loaded with crushed Valium.

I pick through the washing-up, piled up beside the sink. There's nothing on the chopping board, other than a few streaks of tomato and the strong scent of garlic, and nothing on the blades of any of the knives. The cat creeps out from its hiding place and winds itself around my legs as I pick up a handful of cutlery then quickly discard it. I look at plates, bowls, pans and dishes, then, out of the corner of my eye, I spot a teaspoon I missed, lying between the draining rack and the tiled splashback. I snatch it up and almost throw it straight back down again but then I see it, fine white power on the back of the spoon. As I run my nail over it, the door creaks open.

'Everything okay in here?' Fiona glances around the kitchen, her gaze flitting from the damp wall to the bin to my mug, sitting on top of the counter. 'I thought I'd come and give you a hand.'

'Who made the hot chocolate?' I ask, pointing at the pan with a shaking hand.

'What?'

'Who made that?'

'Well, I made the pasta, Christine made the hot chocolate.'

'Everything all right, Anna?' she calls after me as I push open the door. I keep my pace slow and unhurried, aware of the guests' eyes on me as I stroll through the dining room, but as soon as I'm out in the lobby I sprint to the toilet.

I shove open the door, flip back the seat then bend over and shove my fingers down my throat.

'Anna?' There's a light tapping on the bathroom door. 'Anna, are you okay?'

'I'm fine, Melanie.' I grab a handful of toilet roll and wipe it over my face. There's sick in my hair, on my hands and down my top. 'I'll be out in a minute.'

'I don't need the loo,' she calls. 'I just wanted to make sure you're all right. It sounded like you were being sick.'

'I was.'

'Oh no.' There's worry in her voice. 'Shall I get someone?'

'No.' I open the door and peer into the lobby. We're alone and the door to the dining room is closed.

'What is it?' Melanie asks. 'What's the matter?'

'Does anyone else know I've been sick?'

'No.' She shakes her head. 'You looked very pale. I thought there might be a problem with your shoulder. That's why I came after you.'

'So no one knows I've been sick?'

She shakes her head again. 'No, I . . . as I just said, I thought you—'

'Don't say anything. The others will worry that it's a bug or food poisoning and I think we've got enough on our plates at the moment. Don't you?'

She looks confused, as well she should. The real reason I want her to keep quiet is because Christine will be expecting me to pass out in the next couple of hours, but there's no way I'll be sleeping tonight. I'm going to leave as soon as it's light. And I'm going alone.

Chapter 49

Anna

Friday 8th June

Day 7 of the storm

It's 1 a.m. now and the hotel is quiet. It's been over an hour since I heard floorboards creaking in the corridor below and the low clunk of doors being pulled shut. My curtains are drawn, the door is locked, the bedside lamp is on and I've got the duvet draped around my shoulders. When I first locked myself in my room I couldn't settle, so I unzipped my suitcase and sorted through my belongings, moving my most precious things into a small tote bag. There's not much in there that I value – just my purse, passport and a framed photograph of my parents. My phone – without 4G or Wi-Fi it's little more than a bedside clock with a torch function – is charging on the chest of drawers. The only other item in the tote bag is the teaspoon, wrapped in a tissue. As far as evidence goes it's pretty pathetic but it's all I've got to take to the police. What else can I show them – a floorboard that may or may not have come loose on its own, a damaged shoulder and a window with a message that I wiped clean? I wish I hadn't left Christine's book in her room. I can't stop thinking about the look on her face when she came up the stairs and the coldness in her eyes. She has to be Steve Laing's mother or sister, it's the only explanation for what she's doing. Does Steve know? Did they decide between themselves that she'd come after me? But why her? She's a sixty-seven-year-old woman, an ex-primary school teacher. It doesn't make sense.

2 a.m. I put down the book I've been 'reading' for the last half an hour. I've turned dozens of pages but nothing has sunk in. Beyond the window, an owl hoots in the darkness and the sea roars in reply. The room seems to have grown smaller over the last hour. I feel like an animal in a pen. If anyone comes through the bedroom door I'm trapped in here.

3 a.m. I've yawned at least a dozen times in the last hour and I'm desperate for a coffee but there's no way I'm risking a trip downstairs to the kitchen. I've tried pacing to keep myself awake but it's barely six strides from one side of the bedroom to the other and the boards creaked with each step. I've tried sit-ups but the effort made me feel even more exhausted so I had to stop. With the silence and darkness comes paranoia. I'm starting to wonder if maybe I jumped to the wrong conclusion about Christine. I assumed the book was hers but what if it wasn't? What if whoever took Trevor's tablets from his room planted the book in her bag to try to throw me off the scent? But that would mean Fiona's behind it all. She could easily have crushed up the Valium in the kitchen, not Christine. I just don't know any more. Either way I'm still getting out of here. I've got the key to the Land Rover in my pocket but I don't know

how much petrol there is left, if any. I didn't think to check after we all got back from looking for Trevor. Could I swim across the river if I had to? I remove my sling and tentatively bend and stretch my arm but it makes me feel sick and I have to stop.

4 a.m. I nearly fell asleep then. It can't have been for more than a second or two and I snapped awake, my heart thumping in my chest. I've written a letter, just in case anything happens to me, but I'm not sure where to put it – under the mattress, in my suitcase, in the pocket of my jeans? I nearly tore it up, after I read it through. I feel like I'm jinxing myself by writing a letter that starts, 'If you're reading this then I am no longer alive,' but I need to document everything that's happened. It has to come from me. I'm struggling to keep my eyes open. I mustn't . . . I MUST NOT . . .

I wake with a start, clutching at the desk as I jolt back in my chair. For a second I don't know where I am but then I see the sun streaming through the gap in the curtains and the double bed, unslept in, and a suitcase on the floor and I remember. Shit. I snatch up the phone: 5.25 a.m. The hotel is quiet; all the other guests must still be asleep. I can still creep away unnoticed. I nip into the en suite to use the toilet but, when I flick the light switch, nothing happens. The bulb must have gone. I wee in the dark, one foot outstretched to keep the door open, then pull up my jeans and pat the pockets to check for the Land Rover key. Still there. With my tote and phone in one hand I slowly unlock and open the bedroom door, slip out onto the landing and step over the missing plank. I run on tiptoes down the stairs. I stop, suddenly, as I reach the stairwell on the first floor.

Smoke. The distinctive, acrid smell floods my nostrils. Not cigarette smoke though. It's much, much stronger.

Instinctively I glance up at the fire alarm but the light's not blinking on the small red box on the ceiling, halfway along the corridor. I was wrong when I thought the bulb had blown in my en suite: the electricity's gone off.

As I run down the stairs to the lobby the smell grows stronger and stronger, but there's no sign of smoke, no terrifying crackle of flames. Is it the lounge? Has an ember started to smoulder on the rug? I tentatively touch a hand to the door. Cold. I turn the handle and peer inside. Malcolm, splayed out, is snoring on the sofa. There's a dead fire in the grate.

'Malcolm.' I lightly shake his shoulder. 'Wake up!'

When he doesn't respond I give him a shove. 'Malcolm, wake up! I can smell smoke.'

His eyelids don't so much as flicker.

I leave him snoozing on the sofa and venture into the dining room but stop short before I reach the kitchen door. Thick, black smoke is twirling and winding its way through the cracks between the door and the doorframe. I tap the door handle with the very tips of my fingers. It's not hot but I'm scared. I've seen films where people yank open the door on confined fires and are thrown across the room in a huge, fiery backdraught. I need to get outside and look through the window.

But when I return to the lobby and pull on the front door it's locked and the key isn't on the hook behind reception. I reach into my pocket for the master key, then stop as my fingers close around cold metal. They only open the inner doors of the hotel. The lock on the front door is completely different.

'Malcolm! WAKE UP!' I slap his cheek, gently at first then harder when he doesn't respond. There's half a glass of whisky on the table. When I hurl it into his face his eyelids flicker and he looks lazily in my direction then closes his eyes again and goes back to sleep. I was right about the hot chocolate, but it wasn't just my mug that was drugged.

I reach through the curtains and pull at the sash window. It only opens three or four inches. I try the next window, and the next, but none of them open more than a couple of inches.

'FIRE!' I run up the stairs and move from room to room, thumping and kicking on the doors.

I pause outside each room, listening for the sound of stirring, of shoes and clothes being pulled on and voices raised in alarm. But there's nothing. The corridor is completely silent.

'Katie!' I bang on her door. 'Wake up!'

When there's no response I slot the master key into the lock and let myself in. Katie is curled up on her bed, fast asleep. I shake her, shouting her name, but she doesn't so much as stir. It's the same in Joe's room, Fiona's and Melanie's. They're all comatose. But when I open the door to Christine's room there's no one inside.

I speed back down the stairs, grab the fire extinguisher from behind reception and then stop abruptly halfway across the dining room. The thick black smoke that was drifting through the gaps in the kitchen door a couple of minutes ago is now billowing out. It hangs in the air above my head like a dark cloud. I pull the sleeve of my jumper over my mouth and retreat into the lobby, slamming the door after me. I need to get everyone out but with the front door locked and the fire raging in the kitchen there's no escape. We're trapped.

Chapter 50

I slip my arm out of the sling and, lifting the fire extinguisher with my left hand, take the weight with my right. All the nerves in my shoulder scream at me to put it down again but I grit my teeth and carry it into the lounge. Our only way out is through a window. Malcolm, still on the sofa, snuffles and shifts from his back to his side.

I rest the fire extinguisher on the table then reach for the curtain. As I pull it back a face looms out at me and a startled scream catches in my throat. Trevor's standing outside the window, the hood of his jacket pulled tightly around his face, his glasses misted with rain. There's a grunt from the sofa as Malcolm stretches his arms over his head, gurning and blinking as he wakes up.

'Don't go back to sleep!' I reach back with my foot and kick the sofa repeatedly. 'Wake up, Malcolm. Wake up!'

Trevor is still watching me from outside, his hands wrapped around the straps of his rucksack, his eyes wary. His lips move but I can't hear a word through the thick glass.

'Move out the way.' I gesture for him to move away from the window. The dank, acrid stink of the smoke is stronger now and loud pops and bangs punctuate the crackle that's growing louder and louder. The fire must have spread to the dining room. There's a fire door between it and the lobby but it won't hold forever. I hack and cough as I take the weight of the fire extinguisher and step towards the window.

'One . . . two . . .' Pain shoots from my shoulder to my neck as I swing the fire extinguisher behind me. 'Three!'

I'm not strong enough to throw it with any power and, for one horrible second, I think it's going to drop to the floor before it hits the window but then – BANG – it smashes against the glass and lands with a clunk outside. I grab an iron rod from beside the fire and smash the rest of the glass away.

'There's a fire!' I shout at Trevor. 'Please, please help me get everyone out!'

Trevor stares at me blankly from beyond the shattered window. Of course he's not going to help me. Why would he, after what we did to him? He looks away, towards the driveway and the river beyond it, and the expression on his face changes. There's a spark of excitement, or perhaps fear. Whatever he's watching doesn't keep his attention for long because he looks back at me, shrugs off his backpack and unzips his coat. He bundles his coat into a pillow shape then steps towards the window.

'Move,' he says as he knocks the broken glass out of the base of the frame with the handle of his knife. 'I'm coming in.'

We leave Malcolm, still struggling to sit upright, on the sofa and run up the stairs. My injured arm throbs with every step but I barely notice the pain when I open the door to Katie's room and see her, so small and fragile in her pyjamas, walking socks and an oversized hoody, curled up on her bed with one hand tucked under her face.

I grab her by the wrist and pull. She slides across the sheets towards me but doesn't wake up. I look back at Trevor, hovering in the doorway. He looks as though the slightest noise might send him scurrying back down the stairs. I wrap Katie's arm around my neck and try to hoist her onto my back but she keeps slipping to one side. 'Trevor,' I shout. 'Please, help me!'

My shout seems to snap him back into himself and he rushes forwards and scoops Katie off the bed and into his arms.

'No, wait,' I say as he turns to leave. 'Let me take her. You can get Fiona.'

'No.' He disappears down the corridor before I can stop him.

The door to Melanie's room is still ajar. Other than Katie she's the smallest and lightest guest and if I'm going to be able to get anyone onto my back and down the stairs it's her. But, unlike Katie, Melanie isn't splayed out on her mattress. She's sitting on the edge of the bed, rubbing her hands over her face and groaning softly. She turns slowly and blinks up at me as I walk into her room. Without her glasses her eyes look small and beady below her thick, unkempt eyebrows. She coughs as she tries to sit up, then collapses back onto the mattress.

'I need to get you out.' I take hold of her hand, loop her arm around my neck and straighten my knees. She's so light she slides off the bed but when her feet hit the floor her legs crumple beneath her.

'You need to stand up, Melanie. Look at me! Melanie, look at me. There's a fire. We need to get out.'

She croaks something about her glasses but I haven't got the strength, or the time, to put her back down again so I can look for them.

'I can't see,' she says, her words slurring together as I half drag, half carry her out of the room, her toes barely making contact with the carpet. 'I can't see without my glasses.'

'We have to leave them. Come on. Please. Try to walk.'

Sweat is pouring off me and we're only halfway down the

corridor. As we approach the stairwell Trevor comes pounding up the stairs, arms pumping, with a piece of material wrapped around his nose and mouth. He reaches out to take Melanie but I shake my head.

'You need to get Fiona and Joe. I can manage.'

He nods sharply and squeezes past me.

It seems to take forever to get down the stairs and each step is agonising. With no free hand to grip the banister I have to press my bad shoulder into the wall to stabilize myself. Melanie is still unsteady on her feet and I screech each time she lurches forwards. Finally, we make it to the bottom stair and I pretty much drag her across the lounge and over to the window. Malcolm is sitting up now, his head resting on the top of the sofa, his eyes closed. I shout his name as we pass him and his eyes flicker and open.

'Mel?' He looks groggily at his wife and frowns in confusion. 'Mel?'

Trevor appears in the doorway with Fiona, awake but woozy, flung over his shoulder. He drops her onto the sofa beside Malcolm then disappears back into the lobby. Beyond the window Katie is lying on the grass outside, still asleep and curled up on her side.

'Mel.' I point to the blanket that Trevor must have wrapped over the base of the frame. 'You need to step over that.'

She lifts her leg, grabbing hold of me as she wobbles and tries to get her foot over the sill, but she's too short.

'Wait here.' I leave her slumped against the wall and drag an armchair across the room. 'Here.' I hold out my hand for Mel to take. 'Step on the chair, then on the blanket, then jump out of the window. There's a bit of a drop on the other side so be careful.'

'Okay.' She rubs at her eyes then takes my hand.

'Careful.' I pat the blanket with the flat of my hand before she steps on it but I can't feel any glass. 'Ready? Three, two, one.'

She falls, rather than jumps, out of the window, her bare feet hitting the patio, her hands smacking against the grass verge. She lies still then lifts her head and drags herself towards Katie, lying a few feet away. The lobby is full of thick black smoke now and flames are licking around the dining room door. Where's Trevor? He's a tall man, ex-military, but Joe is no featherweight. He's probably struggling to move him. I don't know whether to help him or try to get Malcolm and Fiona out of the window.

'Malcolm!' I grab hold of his hands and pull. 'You need to get out. NOW.'

As his bum lifts off the sofa and he lurches towards me I howl with pain. My shoulder's still in its socket but it's unbearably painful.

'Out!' I shove Malcolm in the direction of the window. 'Mel! Help him get out.'

Then, pulling my jumper up and over my nose and mouth, I venture out into the lobby and almost collapse with relief as Trevor's brown hiking boots appear at the top of the stairs.

Chapter 51

We sit on the wet grass, panting, groaning and coughing as the rain speckles our sooty skin and the wind whips at our clothes. Everyone is awake now. Katie is sitting on Melanie's lap, her face buried in her neck. Her soft sobs punctuate the roar of the wind and the low growl of the sea. Malcolm is sitting beside them, his shoulder pressed against his wife's, his face turned towards the hotel. They both look wan and tired, grey with shock. Joe, lying flat on his back on the grass, stares silently up at the grey sky.

'Trevor?' I turn to the man sitting on his rucksack at the edge of the group. His right hand shakes so much as he lifts his water bottle to his lips that he has to use his left to steady it. 'Are you okay?'

He continues to drink, avoiding eye contact.

'You saved their lives.' I gesture towards the other guests. 'They'd be dead in their beds if it weren't for you.'

I jump as Trevor launches the water bottle at the hotel, his face twisted with rage and frustration. It curves through the air and bounces off the wall of the hotel, spraying the patio with water. He's thinking about Christine. After he carried Joe, fireman-style, down the stairs, he dropped him out of the window then helped Malcolm and Fiona to get out too. I waited for him to escape next but, instead of clambering through the broken window, he ran back into the lobby. The paint on the dining room door was blistering and bubbling. It was so hot I felt as though the skin was peeling from my face.

'Trevor, no!' I grabbed at his arm but he shook me off.

'I need to save her.'

'If Christine's in there she's already dead.'

He continued to stare at the door. I don't think he was even aware that I was standing next to him, but my lungs were burning in my chest. Every cell in my body was screaming at my brain to get out.

'Please.' I pulled on his arm. 'If you go in there you'll die. I'd never forgive myself. Please. Please, just get out.'

He took a step closer to the door and reached a hand towards the handle.

'Trevor, if you open that door we'll both die.'

'So run.'

'No.' I tightened my grip on his arm, then buried my face in his coat as I coughed violently, my lungs burning each time I sucked in the thick, black air. Trevor tried to shake me off but I clung on, my voice growing hoarser and weaker each time I spoke. 'I'm not going anywhere.'

'I need to save her,' he said again and took a step towards the door, dragging me with him.

I screwed my eyes tightly shut and braced myself for the inferno but, instead of being knocked off my feet by the backdraught, I was hauled back into the lounge, in Trevor's arms. I screamed as he lifted me through the window and the rain hit my face but Trevor didn't drop me onto the patio and turn back. He stepped through the window with me. Seconds later there was a noise like a bomb going off and the lounge was engulfed by flames.

'Anna's right,' Melanie says now. 'You saved our lives. You both did.'

She kisses Katie on the head then gets up, squinting as she walks towards us. She extends her hand as she nears Trevor.

'Thank you doesn't seem enough,' she says as he pulls his hood up over his head, slides his hands under his armpits and tucks his chin into his chest. 'It's not enough. I'm in your debt. We both are.'

Melanie's hand drops limply to her side. Our eyes meet and she mouths *Thank you*, then walks back to her niece. Trevor rocks gently to and fro, his eyes closed. It's all too much for him; he's blocking us out.

Out of the corner of my eye I see Malcolm shuffling to his feet. I gesture at him to stay where he is but he ignores me. His head hangs low as he drags his bare feet through the wet grass.

'I won't hold out my hand,' he says gruffly as he stops in front of Trevor. 'Because you're a better man than me and I don't deserve your forgiveness but I . . . I want to say sorry. I . . . I have no words . . . no excuses, no explanation for why I did what I did but I am deeply, deeply sorry.'

Trevor continues to rock silently and Malcolm turns to go. He manages to hold it together all the way back to Melanie and Katie but when he sits back down on the grass he wraps his hands over his head and sobs.

Trevor mumbles something I can't make out so I lean closer. 'Sorry, I didn't hear that.'

He turns so sharply he makes me jump. His pupils are huge behind his misted glasses and his eyes dart everywhere but in my direction.

'David,' he says under his breath.

'What about David?'

'I saw him die.'

For a second, I have no idea what he's talking about but then

I remember. He went for a walk after breakfast, just before David's heart attack.

'You were outside, weren't you?' I say softly. 'You watched Christine giving him CPR.'

He makes a low groaning sound and screws his eyes tightly shut.

'I'll make sure you get help, Trevor. When we get back to the mainland.'

'Will you?'

'Sorry?'

He shoots me a swift sideways glance. 'Will you get help too?'

My throat tightens and I stare up at the sky, blinking away the tears that prick at my eyes. Now I'm the one who can't speak.

I expected there to be a discussion when I announced that I was going to attempt to drive the Land Rover across the island; that one of the men would insist on coming with me. Other than Joe wearily shaking his head, no one reacts. The fire and the Valium have taken the fight out of them. All they can do is sit and stare as the hotel burns.

Damp air fills my lungs and the wind whips my hair from my face as I run away from the hotel, my hoody clinging to my skin and my wet trainers slapping on the patio slabs. I skid and nearly go over on my ankle as something darts out from the bushes and zips across my path but I don't stop to check on the cat. Instead I continue to run across the driveway, my feet crunching on the gravel, each breath getting shorter and shallower with each step. I slow as I approach the Land Rover and double over, coughing up horrible black lumps of phlegm. When I force myself upright again, my right shoulder throbs so much that I almost throw up, but desperation forces me on and I open the driver's side door. My stomach sinks as I fit the keys in the ignition, start the engine and pull away. Joe and Malcolm were right about the petrol gauge: this car's running on fumes but if I can get it across the river I'll walk all the way to the other side of the island if I have to.

I check the rear-view mirror as the car rolls down the driveway. In the few short minutes since I left the others, fire has engulfed most of the hotel. Thick black smokes pours through the window frames, flames dancing where once there was glass. The further away I drive, the more my breathing slows and, when the hotel finally disappears from sight, I let out a long, slow sigh of relief. Christine started the fire, there's no doubt in my mind about that, and she took the front door key so we'd all burn to death. But where did she go? I half expected to find the Land Rover gone but, without the key, there was no way she could start it. Gordon's cottage then? Is she hiding in there, or in the grounds of the hotel? What was her plan – to watch the hotel burn, wait for help to arrive then stumble out of the bushes crying that she was the only survivor? If she has been hiding out she'll have seen us escape and me leave. Have I abandoned the others while they're still in danger? The thought makes my breath catch in my throat. No, there's no way she'd try something with them all grouped together and conscious. She'd continue the charade, make out she'd been for an early morning stroll or something. The thought should calm me but the uneasy feeling in my stomach doesn't fade. Something's been rankling at me since I got into the car, something that's not sitting right, but I can't put my finger on exactly what it is.

I lean back into my seat and, as the river draws closer, I check the fuel gauge again. It hasn't moved. I read somewhere that a car can run for between thirty and a hundred miles on an empty tank but I've got no idea whether that's true or not, or how far the car has already travelled. The river doesn't look as fearsome as it did yesterday but I'm still going to have to gun the car to get across it. I tentatively roll my shoulder back and forth. It aches but it's not unbearable. If I do end up in the water, the last thing I'll be thinking about is whether it hurts.

I move down a gear as I approach the river and then it hits me, the thing that's been bothering me. The driver's side door opened when I pulled on the handle. Joe hadn't locked it after our failed river crossing. Instinctively I glance up at the rear-view mirror.

And Christine stares back.

She stares at me wordlessly, her cold blue eyes glittering in the mirror. I am frozen by fear. With the windscreen in front of me, Christine in the back seat and the seat belt strapping me in place there is nowhere I can run to, nowhere to hide. It's just me, Christine and this car. It's the only weapon I've got.

'Hello, Anna, I'm so glad you—' Christine begins but her sentence turns into a scream as I yank the steering wheel round to the left and the tyres slip on the muddy track. I keep my foot on the accelerator and lean my weight into the steering wheel, swinging the car round in a complete U-turn.

I twist round in my seat as I power the Land Rover back up the hill and away from the river. Christine hasn't got her seat belt on. She's clinging on to the door handle with one hand and reaching into the pocket of her hoody with the other.

'Take your hand out of your pocket.' I floor the accelerator, forcing us both to sit back in our seats.

'I don't know what you—'

'TAKE YOUR HAND OUT OF YOUR POCKET.'

'I'm not doing—'

'It was you. You followed me, leaving me messages telling me to sleep.'

'I don't know what you're talking about.'

The green-brown of the fields flash past in a blur and the hotel looms on the horizon like a fiery beacon.

'Why did you come after me?'

'I didn't come after anyone.' She bounces up and down in her seat as I turn off the track and power the car along the grass and past the cottage. 'Anna, please!' she screeches. 'You're going to kill us both.'

'Isn't that what you want? You burned the hotel down.'

'It wasn't me. I swear. I woke up and – Anna, please. Slow down.'

The car rumbles and bounces along the grass and I change gear from third to fourth. Five hundred metres until the edge of the cliff and the blue-grey sea that stretches into the sky. My heart is thundering in my chest and my palms are damp but my mind is clear.

'Why did you want to kill me, Christine? Because of Freddy? Did Steve tell you to come after me?'

'No!' she screams. 'I don't know who that is. Anna, you've got this all wrong.'

'You wanted to punish me, didn't you?'

Three hundred metres. Frightened gulls launch themselves into the air and wheel around on the air streams, crying silently, their voices eclipsed by the roar of the engine.

'How dare I live when everyone else died? Is that what you thought?'

Christine doesn't reply; she's found her own weapon, the syringe she's just pulled out of her pocket.

I laugh – a strange, manic sound I don't recognise, an explosion of anger and exhilaration. I was right. She was behind it all. She tried to kill me and she's not going to stop until I'm dead. But I'm not afraid any more. I am completely disconnected from my feelings. The sun has edged its way over the horizon, striping the sky with red, gold and pink. It's beautiful. The most beautiful sunrise I've ever seen.

'You wanted to punish me,' I say as the white-haired woman in the back seat stares at me, eyes narrowed. 'But I did that all by myself.'

I look back at the light, dancing on the sea, the sky striped like a scarf and the warm orange glow of the sun. I can't imagine never seeing that again. Or feeling the wind on my face and salt on my lips. I can't imagine being dead.

One hundred metres.

Christine clings to the headrest of the front passenger seat as she gets to her feet, the syringe held aloft in her right hand. She lunges at me, aiming for my neck. 'Don't be scared, Anna.'

'I'm not,' I say as I bend away from her and slam on the brakes.

Chapter 52

Christine

I thought I was done, that there were no more souls to save, that I could retire after a lifetime of nursing and caring and close the door on other people's pain, guilt and regret. And then the car crash happened.

I knew it was serious when I was asked to leave Critical Care to help out in A&E for a while; not an unusual request in the current short-staffed climate and I was happy to step in. What I didn't expect was for it to be so terribly distressing.

When you work at a hospital there's always a possibility you might come across a patient you know, but no nurse, no grandmother, wants to see the battered, broken body of her grandchild wheeled into A&E. I didn't recognise Mohammed at first, his face was so bloodied and swollen, but when I looked at his chart my blood ran cold. I've never cried at work, not in forty-six years, but I couldn't bear to look at him and I ran to the toilet and cried bitter tears. When the door squeaked, signalling that

I was no longer alone, I dabbed at my cheeks and regained my composure, forcing myself to smile brightly at a junior nurse as she washed her hands. Later, when Carol and Ali came to visit Mohammed I was the picture of professionalism again. I stood at the end of the bed, smiling and nodding as my daughter held her son's hand and sobbed loudly, seemingly oblivious to the pain in his eyes. Ali patted Carol's back, looking everywhere but at his son's broken legs.

Shortly afterwards I had to return to Critical Care and it was there that I learned from Becca Porter, a competent if naive young nurse, that the young woman in bed two had been driving the car that had crippled my grandson and killed two others. My chest swelled with pity for Anna Willis. Asleep since her operation, she had no idea of her colleagues' fates. How would she feel, I wondered, when she woke up and discovered the truth? Devastated, that's how. Broken. Guilty. Haunted. She'd blame herself for what had happened for the rest of her life. There was no way I could let another human being suffer like that. Sadly I wasn't able to do more than nick her skin with the injection before I was interrupted by her boyfriend and I didn't get the chance again.

After Mohammed was transferred to Neuro Intensive Care I sat with him as often as I was able, listening as he poured out his soul. It was distressing, seeing him in so much anguish, and I felt impotent rage at my inability to diminish it. But then something unexpected happened. When I talked to my grandson about the accident and asked him if he'd like to see Anna he said no. He didn't want to see her, he wanted her dead.

It was a sign. I had been wondering how I'd spend my retirement and now I had a purpose. Everyone else I'd helped was either comatose or unconscious but Anna Willis was very much awake. A new challenge but one that I relished. I would be her guiding light.

Something miraculous happens to a woman after she passes the menopause and abandons hair dye and embraces her natural colour and middle-aged spread. Without admiring or curious eyes cast in her direction, her grey hair and lined skin help her blend into her contemporaries and she disappears. Poof! The invisible woman. No cape or superpowers required. I found it disconcerting initially. Not because I missed the admiring glances of men – I'd never been an attractive young woman; handsome, maybe; striking, if you were being kind – but because I felt as though I'd been relegated to a different class, a less worthy one where I was barged in front of in queues, ignored by shopkeepers and patronised by telemarketers. I was still a nurse, a professional, but I was being shoved out of the way by society because of the simple fact that I'd aged. After Mohammed's accident, I put a lid on my sadness and embraced my invisibility. I followed Anna without once being seen. I mingled with the mourners at the funeral, hid in plain sight in the crowd outside the courthouse and wandered through the supermarket with a basket over my arm and an innocuous expression on my face. No one gave a second look to the white-haired woman wandering through the streets of North London at five o'clock in the morning as I delivered my third message to Anna by tucking it under the windscreen wiper of her car. I thought my messages would bring her comfort. That I wouldn't have to help her to sleep and she'd make the decision to rid herself of her guilt and pain by ending her own life. But no, she struggled on, looking more pinched and pained each time I saw her. It hurt my heart, knowing I'd failed her.

It took me a little while to realise that Anna had moved out from the flat she shared with her boyfriend (he, the interrupter) and I'll admit I felt a fleeting stab of panic when I realised I had no idea where she might be, but then dear Becca Porter supplied me with Anna's next of kin details, as well as her home address, and I made a phone call.

Anna's mother was wary when I rang to ask how her daughter was doing. I didn't give my name. I'm not that foolish. But her uncertainty turned to gratitude when I explained that I was a nurse who'd looked after her daughter at the hospital and that it was a courtesy call to check that she wasn't suffering any side effects from her medication. Imagine my surprise when she told me that not only was Anna fully recovered, but she'd also moved to the Isle of Rum to take a job at the island's only hotel.

Rum. I'd always had a soft spot for Scotland, not least because my late husband and I took a wonderful coach trip up to the lochs to celebrate our thirtieth wedding anniversary many years ago. When my local travel agent told me there was a walking tour in Rum at the beginning of June, I couldn't whip my credit card out of my purse fast enough. But deary me, what a troubled bunch my travelling companions were. I could sense the tension in their tight smiles and rigid postures the moment I set foot on the coach. I sat next to a wan, bespectacled man who tensed as I took my seat and looked studiously out of the window, avoiding all attempts at conversation for the first three hours of the journey. Only once did he move and then it was to pop two pills out of a blister pack he retrieved from his bag. Valium. I knew then that he had mental health issues but I didn't judge. I never do. It wasn't until I offered him a flapjack from the batch I'd cooked that he spoke a word and then it was a curt 'no thanks'. But as I've said before, I am nothing if not tenacious and I continued to needle away at him, looking for a way in. It wasn't until he spotted a goshawk, hovering over woodland, and his posture changed that I found it. An ornithologist. Not only that but a survivalist too. Not an unusual preoccupation for a former military man, especially not one so troubled by all that he'd seen.

Perhaps I was feeling overconfident, maybe even a little reckless, but why kill one bird with a stone when you can kill two?

Shortly after we'd arrived at the hotel I borrowed the spare master key from reception and removed the Valium from Trevor's rucksack. I'm not anti-medication, I am a nurse after all, but Trevor was using that drug to numb himself to all he had experienced. I knew that removing his crutch could help him to discover a much swifter, more permanent end to his pain. Especially with the cliffs being so close.

I was quite fond of Trevor until he ruined our friendship by rubbernecking David's passing. Death is such a private event and when I aid someone's sleep it's an intimate moment, not a public affair. I had to give David CPR, or at least look like I was while the others were in the room, but I knew he didn't want me to bring him back. It was his time. His soul knew that even if his body didn't, but I ignored the twitches and jerks of his arms and legs as I gently covered his mouth with my hand, pinched his nostrils closed and sang him a sweet lullaby, willing him to let go and sleep. It was the same lullaby my father asked me to sing to my mother after he found me, smiling, at the top of the stairs.

Trevor ran when I saw him at the window, as well he might.

I wasn't sure how much he'd seen but I couldn't take the chance he'd tell the others about it so, when he returned to the hotel, I took him to one side while the others were all running around like sheep. I told him that I'd overheard his conversation about something being stolen from his room and that I was sure Anna had been lying. He opened up to me then, telling me he'd been self-medicating his PTSD and, without his Valium, he was beginning to suffer terrible flashbacks. He'd had one while I was tending to David, he said, and thought I was killing him. He was visibly upset – his eyes darting wildly around and his hands shaking – so I offered him my bottle of whisky, knowing he'd use it to anaesthetise his discomfort. Later, when he smashed up the kitchen, I voted for him to remain incarcerated in the utility room. It's wonderful how things work out.

The second time I made use of the key it was to leave Anna the syringe full of insulin. The sound of footsteps on the stairs startled me and I fled to David's room and hid behind the door. If I'd known it was only sweet Katie sleepwalking, I wouldn't have panicked. Sadly, in my haste to hide, I left the key in Anna's bedroom door.

After that everything that could go wrong did. Anna didn't die when she fell down the stairs and I had to resort to desperate measures – feigning terror as we crossed the river – to ensure no one left the hotel.

The fire was all down to my mother. She didn't possess me or whisper in my ear, I'm not mentally ill. But she came to me in a dream, screaming about her lost family, and when I woke the memory lingered long enough for me to realise that she was sending me a message. Anna's not the only one who's in trouble, Christine, they all are. All you need is some crushed Valium, a hot drink and a lighter and they'll close their eyes and drift off to sleep.

Chapter 53

Anna

'Christine, Christine, can you hear me?' A drop of blood appears on her cheek, a scarlet stain on her pale, lined skin. She's lying on her side, several feet in front of the car, one arm outstretched as though grasping for the cliff edge, the other curled under her body. There is blood in her white hair, on her throat and across her chest where her sweatshirt is torn. Shards of glass from the shattered windscreen glint on her parted lips, the lids of her closed eyes and on her hiking boots. The hiking boots she wouldn't have on if she hadn't started the fire.

'Christine? Can you open your eyes?'

Another drop appears on her cheek, then another and another. I press the flat of my hand to her skin but blood drops onto that too. I blink as sweat drips into my eyes and swipe my hand across my face but it's not sweat on my fingers, it's blood. When I slammed on the brake my seat belt snapped tightly against my chest but not quickly enough to stop my head smacking against the steering wheel. I wipe my hand on my jeans and reach for Christine's wrist. As my fingers make contact with her skin her eyelids flicker and she groans.

'You can hear me, can't you?' I press my fingers into her pulse. It's weak but it's there.

Her right eyelid opens and her eye rolls in my direction. Her voice is little more than a whisper, carried away by the wind.

'What was that?' I lean over her, lowering my ear to her lips.

'Let me go. Let me sleep.'

'Why me, Christine? Just tell me that.'

She closes her eyes and sighs softly.

'How many people have you killed?'

She doesn't reply but her chest continues to rise and fall and her pulse twitches beneath my fingertips.

'I found your book. I read the notices . . . all those people. You killed them, didn't you?'

She makes a strange grunting sound in the base of her throat, half sigh, half laugh. 'I was merciful. I saved them from torment and pain.'

'By murdering them?'

Lying a metre or so from her outstretched hand is the syringe she was about to plunge into my neck. I crawl across the grass and pick it up. 'What's in the syringe, Christine?'

Her lips move and I force myself to draw close again. 'Insulin.' She takes a shuddering breath, her eyes still closed. 'Use it. Help me to sleep.'

My brain screams 'No!' but my grip tightens on the syringe.

'Do it,' she breathes.

Blood or saliva rumbles in her throat and she coughs, wincing and groaning with every intake of breath. A movement back up at the hotel catches my eye. Joe is running slowly through the rain towards us, his head dipped against the wind.

Christine's eyes flicker open and her watery blue eyes look up into mine. 'Do it for David.'

'What did you do to him?'

'I put him out of his misery.'

'You don't get to decide that!' I jab the needle into her hand and move my thumb over the plunger. 'You don't get to decide who lives and who dies.'

'Go on, Anna.' She smiles softly. 'Do it.'

I shake my head.

'We're more similar than you think.'

'No, we're not.'

'We're both killers,' she breathes, 'you've done it before. You can do it again.'

The rage I've been pushing down since I saw her in the back of the Land Rover courses through my body and I hurl the syringe away and scream into the wind. 'I DIDN'T KILL ANYONE. IT WAS AN ACCIDENT. IT WASN'T MY FAULT!'

'Anna, Anna.' Joe wraps his arms around my shoulders and pulls me back against his chest. I twist and I squirm and I fight and I scream at him to get off me, then all the anger and rage and frustration drains out of me and I slump against him, my chin tipped up to the sky.

'It wasn't my fault. It wasn't my fault.'

Joe says nothing; he keeps his arms tightly locked around me until I stop crying and go limp, then he smooths the hair from my face. 'We're getting out of here, Anna. Trevor did take the satellite phone from the cottage. He just gave it to Katie. We've radioed for help.'

Chapter 54

Anna

Thursday 2nd August

My phone bleeps with new WhatsApp messages as I climb the steps and emerge from the train station, blinking into the late afternoon sunshine.

The first one is from Melanie:

Good to hear from you, Anna. I'm fine, Malcolm less so since I mentioned divorce, but I'm still worried about Katie. She won't talk about what happened at the hotel and no amount of cajoling will get her to open up or talk to her school counsellor. Still trying to get a carer in for her mum but it's just SO . . . SLOW. Hope you're bearing up okay. M x.

After the helicopter ferried us back to the mainland we were all transferred to Belford Hospital in Fort William to be checked over. For most of us the main issue was smoke inhalation but I was told I'd have to have stitches in my forehead and an X-ray, plus scans to check on my arm and shoulder. I held it together for hours and hours, then sobbed like a baby when Mum and Dad turned up to take me home.

The second WhatsApp message is from Alex:

It was good to see you last night. I'm here for you, whenever you need me. Promise. x

I was shocked by how awful he looked when he walked into the pub near Paddington. His trousers were hanging off his hips, he had days' worth of stubble and dark shadows under his eyes. When he spotted me in the corner of the pub he stopped walking and stared as though he'd seen a ghost, then came rushing over. For a second I thought he was going to give me a hug but then he stopped abruptly and garbled a long, complicated apology about how sorry he was for going on Tinder while we were together and dating my nurse after I left and how he was a terrible human being for getting frustrated with me after my accident and a complete arsehole for not taking the sleep messages seriously, and how he wouldn't be surprised if I never spoke to him again but he was sorry and he had to let me know how much or he'd never be able to sleep. He was so contrite and yet so utterly OTT that I actually laughed. He looked so horrified that I told him to sit down and chill out while I got him a pint. By the time I got back, he'd managed to pull himself together and I'd processed what he'd just told me. We had a proper chat then, about what had gone wrong in our relationship and how, fundamentally, we hadn't been right for each other. Alex is not a bad person. Self-obsessed and selfish, yes, but his heart's in the right place. Mostly.

The third message is from Fiona:

I handed in my notice at work. I've decided to apply to be cabin crew. It's something I've always wanted to do and I want to see the world (though maybe not Rum for a while). No surprise that Michael didn't bother getting in touch when I got home – I thought he might give a shit after seeing all the stuff on the news – but I'm over him now. Onwards and upwards (hopefully literally). Fi xx

The final message is from Joe. It's a photograph of a sparkling turquoise sea, still and calm, tickling the sand of a clean white beach. In the bright blue sky, in scrawly fingertip handwriting, he's written, *FINALLY FREE.* A week after we left Rum he sent me a message saying he was going to Rhodes to get away from the press attention madness and clear his head. He was sorry, he said, for not believing me about Christine and he was really struggling with guilt. I rang him then and we talked for hours – about the fire, the hotel, my accident and his brother's death. By the end of the conversation we were both crying. We're going to meet up for a drink when he gets back from Rhodes, as friends for now. I don't think either of us is ready for anything heavier yet.

My phone bleeps again as the double doors of the rehab centre open:

Are you here yet? Just wanted to check that you're still coming.

There is already someone sitting beside Mohammed's bed as I draw closer, a woman slightly older than me with long dark hair pulled back in a ponytail, skinny jeans and an off-the-shoulder top.

'Anna,' Mohammed says, lifting a hand. 'This is Ellie, my girlfriend.'

'Oh.' I draw back. 'I'm sorry, I can come back—'

'No, it's fine.' She flashes me a smile and pushes her chair back from the bed. 'I was just going. I know Mo wanted to talk to you alone. I'm sorry, by the way, about everything you've been through.'

I return her smile. 'Thank you.'

As she walks away, the nerves I felt when I first received

Mohammed's text return. He nodded at me when he spotted me walking towards the bed but his lips were pressed together in a tight line. Now his eyes follow Ellie until she disappears from sight.

'I wouldn't let her see me for a long time after the accident.'

'Really?'

'Yeah, I wasn't in a good place . . .' He gives a small shake of his head and looks away, towards the window and the shaft of sunlight that illuminates the floor.

'We don't have to talk about this if you don't want to.'

'No,' he looks back at me, 'I'm done with bottling up my feelings. I . . . um . . . after the accident I told Ellie to stay away. I didn't want her to see me like this – I couldn't bear the pity on her face.' His gaze drifts towards his legs, long, straight and still beneath the tight pull of the sheets. 'It took me a while to come to terms with what had happened and to accept that I can't do the things I used to do. I still haven't, if I'm honest. Not completely. I'm still hopeful that I'll be able to walk again, eventually.'

'That's a possibility?'

'A small one. No one's getting my hopes up but I've got some sensation in my right leg.'

'That sounds hopeful.'

'Yeah. I certainly don't feel as bleak as I did, that's for sure, and it helps having Ellie around again. She's got enough determination for both of us. The whole time I refused to see her she stayed in contact with my mum, getting updates on how I was doing. Then when the stuff about Gran came out . . .' His lips tighten as he glances away. When he looks back at me the expression in his eyes has changed. He looks angry and upset. 'When the news about Gran came out Ellie refused to stay away any longer. She told Mum that she was going to come and see me whether I liked it or not and . . . um . . . I was glad she did because that, that stuff about Gran, that hurt more than the accident ever did.'

'Sorry.' He swipes at the tears that spill from his eyes. 'I've got no right to be upset, not after what you've been through.'

'You've got every right.'

'She went after you because of me.'

'She wasn't well, Mo.'

'That's not what they say. They think she's evil.' He grabs the newspaper from his bedside table and throws it down on the bed. There's a photograph of Christine in her nurse's uniform on the front, her chin tipped down, looking questioningly up at the photographer from behind her glasses. Above the photo the headline blares: *Angel of Mercy Death Toll Rises.*

'They're saying she killed over twenty people during the course of her career, maybe more, injecting them with insulin overdoses.' He snatches up the paper and turns to page three. 'Look at these, look at all these faces, all these people she killed. They're even going to exhume Freddy and Peter to see if she killed them too. For fuck's sake!' Bitter tears fill his eyes but he shakes them away. 'When Mum went to visit her in hospital she asked her why she'd done it. Do you know what she said?'

I shake my head.

'That those in torment deserve the right to sleep. How the hell did she know they were in torment? Half of the people she killed were in intensive care. They were unconscious or comatose. SHE DIDN'T KNOW FUCK ALL!'

A man in the corridor, passing the door, raises his eyebrows as Mo's voice rings around the room.

'Sorry.' He drops his voice. 'I shouldn't lose my shit like that. But I just . . . I can't . . . I've been over and over it and I can't make sense of it. I can't understand why she'd do something like that.'

'It said in the paper that her dad was a doctor.'

'And that he'd give her mum injections to calm her down, maybe even killed her on purpose. Yeah, I know. But how do you go from that to becoming . . .' He shakes his head. 'They're calling her a serial killer, for God's sake, comparing her to Shipman.'

'I'm so sorry, Mo.'

He slumps back against the bed and runs his hands over his face. 'I used to look up to her, you know, for how restrained she was, how calm and unemotional.' He laughs dryly. 'When she came to visit me I was glad it was her because I knew she was the one person who wouldn't make me feel shitter than I already did.'

'How could you have known who she really was? To you she was just your gran.'

And to me she was a stranger, one of seven who'd turned up at the door of the Bay View Hotel with rucksacks on their backs and excited expressions on their faces. I didn't know who they were, what secrets they were hiding or what kept them awake at night. They were our guests and I labelled them in my head according to what I saw – the married couple, the niece, the older woman, the single man, the single woman and the one who made me feel uncomfortable. Trevor was the only one whose pain leaked out, who couldn't pretend to be 'normal', who had no pretence. He wore his anguish and his torment on the outside while we struggled to keep ours pushed deep inside where it flickered and burned.

'You all right?' Mohammed asks, jolting me out of the hotel and back into my hard plastic chair. 'You look a bit . . . I dunno . . .'

'Yeah, I'm fine.' I force a smile.

Trevor's not the only one who's getting help. I've only seen my counsellor a handful of times since I returned to my mum and stepdad's house but the weight is slowly lifting from my shoulders and last night I fell asleep before midnight for the first time in a long time. And I slept all through the night with no dreams and no night terrors.

'You know it's not your fault.' Mo gestures towards his legs. 'This. The others. None of it was your fault, Anna. I hate myself for going there, I really do.'

'You were angry and in pain.'

'No.' He shakes his head. 'Don't make excuses for me. How I felt, what I said, it was wrong. And I'm sorry. I'm really, really fucking sorry.'

'It's okay.' I reach for his hand and squeeze it. 'Mo, it's okay. It's over. It's done. What matters now is us, learning from this, putting it behind us and getting on with our lives.'

'Is it?' He returns my squeeze. 'Is it all over?'

'Yes.' As I smile at him there is a warmth and lightness in my chest that hasn't been there for a very long time. I think it's called hope.

Chapter 55

Katie

Katie Ward creeps along the hall, stepping lightly, cringing at each tiny creak and groan of the wooden floorboards. Her mum was in a bad way when she got back from school. She'd had a terrible headache all day and vomited all over herself. She'd managed to pull off her top and change into something clean she'd swiped off the radiator but, with no energy to get up the stairs to the bathroom or into the kitchen, the smell of sick still clung to her skin and the pale pink lounge carpet. Since Katie arrived home two hours ago she's cleared up vomit, fetched and administered medication, bathed her mum and read to her and now, finally, she's asleep in her chair. But for how long?

Katie quickens her pace as she reaches the end of the corridor and swipes her school bag from the hook by the door, then crouches to scoop up the post. She sorts through it, tossing the junk mail back onto the mat. Three letters: one for her mum from social services and one that looks like a bank statement.

And – Katie raises her eyebrows in surprise – one for her. She deliberates between her school bag and the letter. Two of her mates are going to Alfie Bauer's party and she wants to check her phone so she can at least Snapchat her friends about what they're wearing. She was invited too but there wasn't any point asking if she could go. She looks back at the envelope. She never gets mail, particularly not mail with her name and address written by hand. It's too intriguing.

She slips into the kitchen and drops her bag onto the table, then rips open the envelope. Inside are a thin black book and a large, lined piece of paper. Along the top of the letter it says, 'When writing to Members of Parliament, please give your previous home address in order to avoid delays in your case being taken up by the MP.' Katie frowns. What the hell's that about? Whatever it is, it's been sent to her by mistake. Her eyes flit down the page:

Number: A6837CC
Name: Christine Cuttle
Wing: D-B107

What? She's got no idea what all the numbers and letters mean but she recognises the name. It's the old woman who was at the hotel with them. Something went wrong with the car when she and Anna were going to get help and she flew through the windscreen because she wasn't wearing her seat belt. That was what Auntie Mel said anyway. Auntie Mel's said a lot of things, most of them complete bullshit, like how she's going to get a carer in so Katie won't have to spend every weekend with her mum and she can actually get to go into town with her mates once in a while.

Anyway, Katie knows the truth about Christine Cuttle because she's been on the news. Every time she turns on the TV for her mum, there she is on the screen with her white woolly hair and her glasses and her tight little mouth. The Killer Nurse, that's what they've been calling her at school. Some of the Year 7s who still play tag (but pretend they don't) have made up a new game where whoever is 'it' has to try to poke everyone else with a biro and kill them. It pisses Katie off whenever she sees them doing that. Christine was really nice to her when they were on the Isle of Rum. She'd make her hot chocolate and bring her extra blankets and talk to her, really talk to her, not down at her like some of the other adults. She can't imagine Christine killing anyone. She's old. Old people aren't scary. They're weak and doddery and a bit boring, always going on about what life was like in their day.

Her eyes flick to the start of the letter and she begins to read:

Dear Katie
I hope this letter finds you well. I've spent a lot of time thinking about you and your predicament and how tough it must be, looking after your ailing mother when you're so very young and full of life and ideas and excitement. I wanted to let you know how very much I enjoyed our little chats during our very eventful holiday on Rum and I'm so glad you gave me your address so we could keep in touch once it ended. You are a very bright, insightful and charming young woman. You are also marvellous at keeping secrets (as demonstrated by your ability to keep your chats with Trevor to yourself). That not only shows a very caring nature, but also that you are able to keep your own counsel. I don't know if you've thought about what you might do for a career but I think you'd make a marvellous nurse. You certainly have all the qualities one might need. You have probably heard lots of horrible stories about me in the media but what they all fail to mention is the fact that

what I did was inspired by love, not hatred. I only ever wanted to end people's suffering, dear Katie. There is little a woman of my age and a woman of yours have in common but we are bonded by the fact that both of our mothers are (or in my case were) very ill indeed. No one likes to see the mother they love suffer, not me and certainly not a lovely, kind, caring girl like you. I would very much like to talk to you on the telephone about the struggle you are going through and ways in which you might ease your mother's pain. I think a friendship such as ours (and I do hope you don't mind an old lady considering you a friend) could bring us both a lot of comfort.

With best wishes and fondest thoughts,
Christine Cuttle (Mrs)

P.S. I am enclosing a book of poetry about sleep. It's such a special book – I always carry a spare.

Katie stares at the letter, trying and failing to make sense of it. The old lady was nice, sure, but she's not sure she wants to be friends with her, not the sort of friends that have long phone conversations anyway. She's hardly got time to talk to her own friends as it is. She crumples the letter up and throws it, and the book of poetry, into the bin, then snatches up her bag. She digs through it until she finds her phone, then keys in her password. Her face lights up as she clicks on the Snapchat icon and sees the photo her friends have sent her of them with their arms around each other's shoulders, massive grins on their faces and the words WE LOVE YOU in a neon font scrawled across the top. As she continues to stare at the photo, her smile slips and a hard stone forms in her belly. She should be there, with them, going to what everyone in her year is calling 'the party of the year'. She clicks out of Snapchat and walks out of the kitchen.

She might just go up to her room, try on a few outfits and take some selfies. It's not the same as going out but she can pretend.

'Katie!' her mum calls from the living room. 'Katie, love. I'm really sorry but I've been sick again.'

Katie stands stock-still, then she turns, walks back into the kitchen and fishes Christine's letter and the book of poetry out of the bin.

'Shall I bring you your medicine, Mum?' she calls as she shoves them into her pocket. 'It'll help you to sleep.'

Acknowledgements

Huge thanks to Phoebe Morgan, who stepped in when my editor, Helen Huthwaite, went on maternity leave and did an absolutely brilliant job; not just with the structural and line edits for this book, but also for supporting me every step of the way and patiently answering every question and query I threw her way. You are a star, Phoebe. Thank you too to the rest of team Avon who work their socks off to produce, sell, market and publicise my books, particularly Henry Steadman, Sabah Khan, Elke Desanghere, Dominic Rigby, Anna Derkacz, Molly Walker-Sharp, Rachel Faulkner-Willcocks, Oliver Malcolm and Kate Elton.

I couldn't do this job without the support of my superstar agent, Madeleine Milburn, and her stellar team: Giles Milburn, Hayley Steed and Alice Sutherland-Hawes. Thank you for spreading the word internationally and for ensuring that as many people as possible get to read my novels. Thanks also to all of my foreign publishers for believing in me and my books.

I would also like to thank everyone who gave me invaluable advice when it came to researching this book: Sharon and Steve Birch who answered my questions about how the coroner's office works, Stuart Gibbon for his police procedural expertise, my go-to pharmacist, Andrew Parsons, Trudi Clarke who is a Ranger on Rum and very patiently answered every single question I threw at her, Sam Carrington for talking to me about prison routines, Angela Clarke for sharing her experience of shoulder dislocation and putting it back in (ouch!), and Torie Collinge, Hazel Amanda and Sarah Chequer for their nursing know-how. If I've missed anyone I am truly sorry.

On a much sadder note, I couldn't write these acknowledgements without mentioning my friend Heidi Moore. Heidi was one of my best friends at school and we spent a huge proportion of our thirties together, drinking, chatting, travelling and having fun. She was a force of nature – kind, energetic, fun, generous, clever, silly and caring, and she was my biggest champion, especially when it came to my writing. To the outside world she seemed to have it all – friends, success, happiness and financial security – but she spent most of her life battling Borderline Personality Disorder and only her very closest friends knew about the demons that haunted her whenever she was alone. I was about two months into the writing of this book when Heidi took her own life. To say I was, and still am, devastated is an understatement. I thought long and hard about whether or not it was appropriate to dedicate this novel – a book about death and suicide – to my very dearest friend but the truth is my grief at losing her is trapped within the pages. I explained to Heidi's family why I wanted to dedicate this book to her – how I want her to live on in every copy – and they gave me their blessing.

I miss you, Heidi. I always will.

It's been a tough year, in more ways than one, and it was made easier thanks to the love and support of my family and friends. A big thank you to my mum and dad – Reg and Jenny Taylor – and my brother and sister, David and Rebecca Taylor. Thanks also to Sami Eaton and Frazer and Oliver, Sophie and

Rose Taylor, Loubag Foley, Ana Hall (I got it right this time, Ana!), James Loach, Angela Hall, Steve and Guin Hall and Great Nan Joyce Hall. The biggest hugs to Chris and Seth who are my whole world. None of this would mean anything without you two. Thank you to my friends Rowan Coleman, Julie Cohen, Kate Harrison, Tamsyn Murray and Miranda Dickinson for keeping me propped up with wise words and, more often than not, gin. Kisses to the Bristol SWANS, the Knowle Wine/Book Club (particularly Joe Rotheram), the Ellerslie Girls, the very naughty Crime lot (you know who you are), the Story A Fortnight alumni, the 17 Rothbury Terrace reprobates, the Brighton gang and my ex-kickboxing buddies, Laura Barclay and Amanda Haslett.

Finally, a big thank you to you, the readers. Whether you've never read a book of mine before and you liked the look of this one, or you've bought every book I've ever had published – thank you! This is my dream job and I hope I'm writing books for a very long time to come.

To keep in touch with me on social media follow me on:

Facebook: http://www.facebook.com/CallyTaylorAuthor

Twitter: http://www.twitter.com/CallyTaylor

Instagram: http://www.instagram.com/CLTaylorAuthor

And if you'd like to receive quarterly updates with all of my book news then do join the free C.L. Taylor Book Club. You'll receive THE LODGER for free, just for signing up:

http://www.callytaylor.co.uk/CLTaylorBookClub.html

Reading Group questions

1. One of the central themes in *Sleep* is guilt. How far does this influence the characters and do you think all the guilt Anna feels is deserved?

2. The book is set on the remote Scottish isle of Rum. How big a part do you think the setting plays in the book? Would the storyline have been as impactful if it had been set somewhere else?

3. *Sleep* contains a lot of very complex, damaged characters. Who stood out to you as the most engaging character, and why?

4. What do you think the future holds for Anna and Joe?

5. Did you find the ending of the book satisfying?

6. To what extent did you empathise with Katie by the end?

7. To what extent did you find Anna a relatable character?

8. Melanie and Malcolm have a difficult relationship. Do you think they are right to think about divorce by the end of the novel?

9. Do you think there's a relationship between sleep and mental health?

10. Would Christine still have been obsessed with sleep and death if her father hadn't been a doctor?